D1325041

MAELSTROM

MAELSTROM

a mystery by

Michael J. Bird
based on the BBC-TV serial

BRITISH BROADCASTING CORPORATION

Published by the British Broadcasting Corporation
35 Marylebone High Street London W1M 4AA

ISBN 0 563 20367 6

Typeset by Input Typesetting, London
and printed by Cox & Wyman Ltd, Reading

Chapter One

'But why, Oliver, for God's sake?'

Catherine was trying very hard to control her anger but it was proving to be increasingly difficult.

Oliver Bridewell poured her a large vodka, added a little tonic water to it, and then splashed in some ice cubes.

'Our billings are down more than twenty per cent. We're looking for savings all round. It's as simple as that,' he said with a sigh.

'So I'm fired!'

'Conditions have made you redundant. That's not quite the same thing.'

Cator and Bridewell's offices were on the tenth to twelfth floors of a building that dominated the skyline of London's West End and, looking down through the tinted glass of one of the many windows in the Executive Suite, Catherine could see the evening crush of traffic and pedestrians moving back and forth along the street below, ceaselessly and silently.

Reflected in the window was the large French Impressionist painting hanging above the red leather seating and low, marble-topped coffee table of the conference area behind her.

The painting was Oliver Bridewell's latest Sotheby acquisition. It had become a standard opening gambit of his to tell highly impressed visitors that he had only bid for it because, being exactly the same length as the settee beneath it, it fitted in so well. Then, once the uncertain laughter had died away and with a throw away smile, he would hasten to assure them that he was only joking of course.

'What's the difference?' Catherine demanded as, a glass in each hand, Bridewell approached her at the window.

He handed her the vodka and tonic and, with a nod, indicated the envelope she was holding. 'That cheque you've got there for a year's salary. And the kind of reference you'll get. That's the difference,' he purred. 'Cheers!' He raised his glass and sipped Glenfiddich.

Catherine studied him over the rim of her glass.

On her nineteenth birthday she had made two solemn vows to herself; the first was that she would never have an affair with a married man and the second that when any other affair she had was over she would make a clean break of it. In the seven years since then, though, she had broken both promises. And both of them with Oliver Bridewell.

The affair had started about a year after she joined the Agency. She was reluctant but infatuated, he was persuasive and promised imminent divorce. It had ended in ultimatums and excuses eighteen months ago and then faded away, with brief and very temporary remissions, until it had finally lapsed into cool disregard within a continuing professional association.

After all, Catherine had reasoned, just because I'm no longer sleeping with him hasn't made my job any less interesting. And the last thing she was going to do was to make it easier for him by resigning. Like hell she was! And now, to be grudgingly fair to him, she doubted if the real reason for this interview was so that he could dispose of a redundant mistress.

'It's still the elbow, isn't it?' she snapped.

Bridewell put a hand on her arm and she neatly side-stepped away from him. He smiled sympathetically.

'I'm sorry, Cathy. Really I am,' he said and then gave a helpless shrug. 'But you're not the only one we're having to do this to. Not that that's any consolation of course.'

'No, you're right. It isn't,' confirmed Catherine.

'And when things pick up again, well if you're available and you want to come back here. . . .'

'Thanks.' Catherine made no attempt to hide the bitterness in her voice. 'And meanwhile?'

'There are other agencies. And you're a bloody good account executive.'

She wasn't going to let him off the hook that easily. 'Yes I am,' she agreed. 'But if Cator and Bridewell are feeling the pinch I doubt if anyone else has got anything worthwhile on offer.'

'Not straight off perhaps. But in two or three months maybe. And you can afford to wait around a bit for the right kind of opening, can't you?' Bridewell suggested, gazing down into the street. 'But if I were you,' he went on, 'first off I think I'd take a holiday.'

Catherine laughed humourlessly. 'I've just started one, haven't I?' she reminded him.

Bridewell continued to stare down at the restless scene below him. 'You know what I mean,' he said patiently. 'Get away for a while.'

Too right, thought Catherine, mentally discounting both Venice and Crete because of the time they had spent there together. 'Well maybe I will,' she said. 'But more immediately I've got a better idea.'

'Oh, what's that?' Bridewell asked in a tone which had her wishing that he cared one way or the other and hating herself for doing so. He turned to her with a questioning smile.

'To get well and truly smashed!'

And to prove that she meant it Catherine drained her glass.

Later that same April evening as she leaned forward across a corner table in the Bistro Balzac she announced, in a slightly slurred voice, 'Of course I could always start up on my own I suppose.'

Frances Seward looked doubtful. 'Bad timing just now, wouldn't you say?'

Catherine gave her a knowing look and wagged a finger at her. 'That's where you're wrong. Not if you kept it small and specialised. Like in the medical field maybe. I've built up some very good contacts in that line.'

Her friend wasn't convinced but nevertheless she raised her glass in encouragement. 'So there you are then. A whole new bright future for you. Durrell Advertising. Congratulations!'

Catherine lifted her glass and drank from it. 'Thanks.'

Frances gazed across at Catherine and smiled. Poor bitch, she thought. Still, just the same, she'd not done badly out of it. With what she must have been earning a year's salary has to have been a tidy sum. And at twenty-six, redundancy was hardly the end of the world, was it?

Remembering the times, though, throughout their friendship when Catherine had provided her with a shoulder to cry on Frances decided that the least she could do now was to be loyally outraged and steadfastly sympathetic. And their aperitifs and the two bottles of Mâcon which they had already got through were making her feel even more than usually charitable towards Catherine.

'That's a tacky thing that bastard's done to you! You know that? Really tacky,' she said, stumbling over the words a little.

'It's nothing personal.'

'Did he say that?'

'No. Well not in so many words anyway.'

'So would you like to bet?'

'Why wait this long for God's sake? If he was that anxious to get rid of me he could have fired me a year ago.'

'That's true I suppose,' Frances admitted ungraciously.

'No,' Catherine continued. 'Like he said, there's a lot of it about just now. A victim of monetarism, that's me.' She giggled and raised her glass again. 'To monetarism!'

'If you say so.' Frances lifted her glass. 'And maybe Bridewell's done you a favour. I mean if you really are thinking of starting up your own agency.'

'Definitely. Only there's a problem,' Catherine confided.

'More than one I'd say.'

'You're right. Several. But one big one in particular. I just don't have enough money to get something like that off the ground.'

Frances frowned. 'But you can get all sorts of grants these days, can't you?'

Catherine shook her head sadly. 'Only if you're into making electronic egg-cups for export or some such. Or if you can show that you're going to take on a dozen unemployed lefthand-thread gismo-makers or whatever.' She giggled again. 'Preferably black.'

She picked up the wine bottle and seemed surprised that it was empty. 'Shall we have another?' she asked.

'Why not?' said Frances.

'That's a good idea,' Catherine agreed enthusiastically and, holding up the bottle, she waved to one of the waiters.

It was three weeks later that she received the letter from Lambert, Stoddard and Price and by that time, discouraged by the regrets she had received from every bank she had tried, she had almost given up the idea of Durrell Advertising.

'Your father's name was Richard Stephen Durrell and you were born in Oslo on 16th November 1958 to Kirsten Durrell née Enger.'

Ralph Stoddard recited the facts while studying a file which was lying open on his desk in front of him and then looked up enquiringly.

Catherine nodded. 'Yes, that's right,' she said.

She had had difficulty in finding the solicitors tucked away as they were down a narrow side street in the City. And when she had found them she had not been very impressed. But at the same time one possibility she'd suspected had been immediately discounted. Whatever this was about, she had decided, looking up at the grim, grey building with its air of decay and bank of well-polished nameplates alongside the entrance, it's not a joke and that's for sure. I doubt if anyone working here has much of a sense of humour.

But once inside she had been pleasantly surprised to discover that not only were the offices of Lambert, Stoddard and Price welcoming and brightly decorated but that, at sixty-plus and despite his greying hair and formal suit and approach, Ralph Stoddard was clearly a man who enjoyed a good laugh from time to time.

'Both your parents are deceased,' Stoddard went on, checking against the file. 'Your father died in 1962 and your mother in 1980.'

He looked up at Catherine again. What a very attractive young woman she is, he reflected. Almost beautiful but not quite. Extremely attractive though. And nobody's fool. I wonder if . . . Possibly. But anyway that's no business of mine, is it?

He smiled sympathetically.

Catherine nodded and took a birth certificate and two death certificates out of her handbag and handed them to him. 'I brought all the certificates with me as you asked.'

'Ah, yes. Thank you, Miss Durrell.' The solicitor unfolded the certificates and examined the entries.

There was no doubt whatever in Catherine's mind now. It certainly wasn't a joke. In which case . . .

'Someone's left me something in their will,' she said with a growing feeling of cautious excitement. 'Is that why I'm here?'

Stoddard smiled again. 'Indeed they have,' he said.

'What is it? A set of spoons?'

Stoddard gave her a good-natured but faintly reproving look and Catherine's frivolous smile faded.

'Rather more than that. In fact it's a very substantial bequest,' he informed her. 'For many years we have handled the legal business in this country of a group of Norwegian companies called Jordahl Industries. Three months ago Mr Hjalmar Jordahl, the chairman and managing director of the group, died.' He took a letter from the

10

file and held it up. 'And shortly after his death we received this letter from his lawyer in Alesund. . . .'

'Where?' interrupted Catherine, frowning.

'Alesund.'

'Where's that?'

'Oh I'm sorry.' Stoddard was clearly somewhat confused. 'I assumed that . . .' He smiled warmly once more. 'It's the town on the west coast of Norway where Mr Jordahl lived and where most of his business interests are based. And according to this letter among the other beneficiaries in Mr Jordahl's will is a Catherine Elizabeth Durrell whose last known address was . . .' he glanced at the letter, '16 High Bank Road, Guildford.'

'That was my mother's address,' Catherine said and looking totally perplexed. 'I left there ages ago.'

Stoddard nodded. 'So I understand. But with that information it wasn't too difficult to trace you.' He replaced the letter in the file.

'Well that address clinches it, I suppose. But I still don't . . .' Catherine frowned deeply. 'And it's a substantial bequest you say?'

'Well in my opinion, certainly,' Stoddard replied. 'And I'm sure you'll agree when I tell you that Mr Jordahl has left you a boatyard which he owned and some property consisting of two houses and outbuildings standing in, in all, fifteen hectares of land. That's about sixty acres.'

Catherine gasped and stared at him, stunned. 'You're not serious!' she blurted.

Stoddard laughed. 'Very serious I assure you, Miss Durrell. My warmest congratulations. You'll have to go to Alesund to finally establish your claim on the estate,' he explained. 'But that'll only be a formality. And meanwhile if you have any questions . . .' His voice trailed off in expectation.

Catherine regarded him blankly. 'Just one,' she said. 'Why did this Hajlmar Jordahl mention me in his will at all? I've never heard of him.'

11

Chapter Two

There was a lot of activity on the quayside when the taxi pulled up alongside the *Kong Olav*.

Catherine got out and the driver unloaded her luggage and set it down on the ground beside her. And that surprised her. One of the things she had quickly learned about Norway was that no one carried your luggage for you, not even for a tip. At least certainly not in Bergen.

And it wasn't like it was back home either, where the porters at air terminals or railway stations simply pretend you're not there until the crinkling of a banknote wakes them from their trance-like meditation and they reluctantly relieve you of your burden. In Norway it was clearly not part of anyone's job willingly or unwillingly to perform such a service, even in a four-star hotel. Catherine had concluded that this had to be the result of the years of Socialism that most of Scandinavia seemed to have enjoyed during which, as so often happens, the gracious art of fetching and carrying had become mistaken for inequality. Either that or that double hernias were endemic among the male population in that part of Europe.

The taxi pulled away and Catherine looked around her.

The *Kong Olav* was one of the older vessels of the Hurtigruten line and Catherine was pleased about that. With nothing better to do she had come down to the quay the night before and watched the sailing of one of the latest additions to the Coastal Express fleet and, to her, it hadn't looked like a ship at all; more like an angular and slightly top-heavy roll-on, roll-off car ferry and it lacked any character whatever. It didn't in any way resemble the kind of ship which she had imagined would regularly make the eleven-day trip from Bergen to Kirkenes – way above the Arctic Circle – and back.

But the *Kong Olav* was exactly as she had pictured it would be, and just like the ships she had drawn in crayons as a child; a sturdy weather-beaten coaster of about 2,500 tons with its funnel amidships, proper portholes along the length of its black hull and, around its white superstructure, lots of open deck space behind rails capped with scuffed oak. And all the cargo and the vehicles the ship carried had to be hoisted up and swung on board by a crane on the fore-deck and then either expertly lowered into the hold or secured forward of or alongside the hatch covers. I may not be going far but at least I'm travelling on the genuine article, Catherine congratulated herself.

She had taken the SAS flight to Bergen the previous day and she could have gone straight on to her final destination but when she had made her booking she had decided against that. Instead she had allowed herself a day and a half in the city to look around and get the feel of Norway.

And in the thirty-six hours since the Douglas DC8 had touched down at Flesland airport she had seen just about all there was to see. She had strolled around the open-air flower and fish market, gaped in horror at the price of everything in the shops and been bored out of her mind by the almost incessant tri-lingual commentary of a woman guide on a coach trip to Edvard Grieg's house. She had taken the funicular to the top of Mount Floyen, looked around the Hanseatic Museum and had an excellent dinner in a charming restaurant in one of the reconstructed medieval wooden buildings in the Bryggen. And she had also had her first experience of the seemingly endless daylight of a Norwegian summer. Even now, as she stood on the quay at half past ten at night, there was still enough light to read by. And she had been told that later in June and further north, she would find that there was hardly any darkness at all and that almost as soon as the sun had set it would start to rise again.

She picked up her suitcase and overnight bag and joined the end of the slow-moving queue of passengers on the gangway. The majority of them were Norwegians on their way home to towns and villages further up the coast or setting out on business trips. A few of them, middle-aged or elderly Germans and Americans for the most part, were clearly embarking at the start of what, judging from their frailty and the snatches of trans-Atlantic conversation Catherine heard around her, they expected to be a leisurely and restful round-trip cruise.

Halfway up the gangway Catherine looked back. Cargo was still being stacked on the quay in readiness for loading and a flow of cars and taxis disgorged yet more people clutching tickets. Freeing themselves from the embraces of those who had come to see them off, they joined the tail of the orderly column waiting to board the ship.

Glancing to her left Catherine saw that, beyond the broad, traffic-filled road fringing the docks, the mountains to the west of the city were now black silhouettes against the pink to crimson glow of the sun setting reluctantly behind them.

She had enjoyed her stop-over in Bergen but she realised that her reason for breaking her journey there had not really been because she had had any great desire to see the town.

As the date of her departure from London had raced up on her she had felt an increasing apprehension about her visit to Alesund. Unable to account for it, she had finally dismissed it as a foolish and illogical by-product of her nervousness at the thought of travelling all that way to claim an inheritance left to her by a total stranger. But just the same she had looked for and welcomed any excuse for delay *en route*.

And that was also why she had chosen to take the slow coastal steamer trip rather than complete her journey by air in less than forty minutes. But even so Alesund was now only about thirteen hours away, and much as she would have liked to have postponed getting there even longer she couldn't because Ralph Stoddard had written to Hjalmar Jordahl's lawyer and told him exactly when and how she was arriving. So she was expected. And despite the way she felt there was certainly no turning back now.

There was a throng of people in the hall on A deck and, sliding her luggage along in front of her with her foot, Catherine slowly edged forward to the window of the ticket office and surrendered her ticket.

'Cabin 74,' the Purser said with a smile, slipping the key across the counter to her. He pointed. 'Through there, down the stairs and on the left.'

'Thank you.' Catherine half-turned to move away but then looked back at him. 'What time do we arrive in Alesund tomorrow?' she asked.

The Purser was about to reply when the telephone on the far side of the office rang. He sighed deeply and, signalling to her to wait, moved away from the window and answered the call.

'Excuse me.'

Startled, Catherine spun round.

Standing behind her was a man she judged to be in his late fifties or early sixties, with a friendly, open face and gentle, good-natured eyes. He was carrying a battered but stout leather case which looked very much like a medical bag and, tucked under his other arm, was a bundle of magazines and a paperback book. He studied Catherine closely and, instinctively on guard at his approach, she returned his gaze with cool distance.

The man smiled. 'All being well,' he said, 'we will be in Alesund at about a quarter past twelve.' His English was almost perfect and only his accent labelled him as a Norwegian.

'Oh, thank you,' replied Catherine, reassured and returning his smile by way of an apology for her initial response.

She reached for her suitcases and, as she did so, reacted to the faint hint of uncertainty in the man's voice. Straightening up she looked at him again. 'All being well?' she questioned, frowning slightly.

The man chuckled.

'I do not think that you need have any fear,' he told her. 'The weather forecast is good. But of course one can never tell. The forecasts are not always reliable.'

'Oh I see,' said Catherine. 'I thought perhaps you meant we might not sail on time for some reason.'

The man feigned shock. 'Oh no! That is unheard of!' he assured her in a playfully hurt tone. 'The coastal steamers are never late leaving Bergen. They depart every night at eleven o'clock precisely!' He smiled again. 'That is one of the modern legends of Norway.'

Catherine grinned. 'Oh well, that's okay then. So long as this ship lives up to it. I'm not all that worried about the weather.'

'You are a good sailor?'

Catherine nodded. 'Well, up until now anyway,' she said with another smile. 'Goodnight.'

'Goodnight.'

Deep in thought the man watched her move away and then he turned to the window and handed his ticket to the Purser who had returned to the counter.

Cabin 74 was at the far end of a long and dimly lit corridor with doors off either side of it. Putting her suitcases down once more, Catherine unlocked the door and pushed it open. It was as she was reaching for her cases again that she was suddenly aware that she was being watched.

She glanced down the corridor and reacted with a start. About halfway along it, at a point where it connected at a right angle with another, shorter passage, a woman was standing staring at her.

She was partly hidden by shadows but despite that, and the fact that she was some distance away, Catherine could make out that she was young – probably not more than twenty-five at most – and strikingly beautiful.

But what held Catherine momentarily transfixed was the

look on the woman's face. Although half-hidden, there was no question whatever that her expression was one of unveiled, almost malevolent, hostility. Nor could there be any doubt that the malevolence and hostility were directed exclusively at her.

Discomforted and somewhat unnerved by the woman's unrelenting gaze, Catherine turned away and busied herself with her luggage. Just before she stepped into the cabin, though, and cross with herself for the way she had reacted, she looked down the corridor once more; this time defiantly.

But now it was empty again. The woman had gone; as silently and as strangely as she had first appeared.

Catherine frowned. The woman must have stepped into one of the cabins or turned down the other passageway, she decided. And with that thought she closed the door of cabin 74 behind her and surprised herself by locking it again immediately.

Later, when she had unpacked her overnight bag, she went up on deck and looked for the woman among the other passengers lining the rails but there was no sign of her. Nor was she in any of the lounges that Catherine inspected on her way back to her cabin, having watched the final preparations for departure and then seen Bergen, its streets and buildings at last ribboned and pinpointed with lights, fall away astern of the *Kong Olav*.

Clearly the woman had turned in before the ship sailed. That would account for my not having found her anywhere, Catherine concluded as she got into her bunk and switched out the light on the table beside it.

But there was no accounting for the look on her face and the memory of the naked hatred in it haunted Catherine. For some reason she couldn't explain, it perturbed her and prevented her from settling. At last, though, rocked by the gentle motion of the ship and to a lullaby of the murmured throb of the engine, she fell asleep.

When she woke the next morning the sun was shining

and the sea was like an endless pane of beaded glass through which the *Kong Olav* was making good speed. The stranger in the corridor, now seemingly part of a bad dream, was almost forgotten.

And an hour later, when Catherine entered the crowded dining saloon and, looking round, couldn't spot her at any of the tables, she dismissed her from her mind entirely.

Chapter Three

'Please! Won't you join me?'

Catherine glanced at the table and recognised the speaker as the man she had chatted with outside the ticket office the night before. He'd half risen from his seat and, with a smile, was indicating the empty chair across from him.

Catherine hesitated briefly and shot another look around the saloon. The breakfast rush was at its height and there were few spare seats at any of the other tables so she seemed to have little alternative anyway. And from their brief conversation he had seemed pleasant enough.

She smiled back at him. 'Thank you,' she said, taking the seat and setting the glass of orange juice and the roll and butter and jam which she had selected from the buffet table down in front of her.

The man settled himself back into his chair. 'Did you sleep well?' he asked.

'Yes, very well thanks. When I finally got to sleep that is.'

'You are making the round trip, are you?' the man enquired conversationally.

'No, I'm only going as far as Alesund.'

Studying her, the man's eyes flickered and took on a look of even greater interest. He nodded as though confirming something which he had already half suspected.

'Ah! Is that so? Well we should arrive on time I think. We make a brief stop at Torvik around 10.30 and from there Alesund is only a short distance away.'

A waitress approached the table with a silver pot in

each hand. 'Tea or coffee please,' she asked, looking at Catherine and smiling shyly.

Catherine nodded and moved her cup to the edge of the table. 'Coffee, thank you.'

The waitress filled her cup and then refilled the man's and moved on.

'Originally I was going to fly up,' Catherine volunteered, buttering her roll. 'But when I was booking my ticket the travel agent told me about the coastal steamer service and that sounded like a much more interesting way to make the journey.'

'And are you enjoying it?'

'Yes, very much. But then I love the sea and ships.'

Her companion nodded in agreement. 'For me,' he said, 'unless I am in a great hurry which, fortunately, is seldom the case, this is the only way to travel in this part of Norway.'

Catherine picked up her cup of coffee. 'And are you going far?'

The man shook his head and smiled. 'Like you, only to Alesund.'

'Oh really!' exclaimed Catherine. 'Is that where you live?'

'Yes, I'm happy to say.'

'What's it like?'

Again the man studied her closely. 'You have not been there before?'

'No, never.'

'It is only a small town. But it is very beautiful.' He laughed. 'But then of course I am prejudiced. Oh, forgive me!' He put out his right hand to her. 'My name is Albrigtsen. Dr Albrigtsen.'

Catherine shook hands. 'And I'm Catherine Durrell,' she told him.

Her companion nodded knowingly. 'Yes,' he admitted. 'Well, to be honest, having been told that you were expected today, from the beginning, when you said you were leaving the ship in Alesund, I thought then that that was possibly who you might be.'

Taken aback, Catherine frowned and gave him a puzzled look. 'I'm sorry I don't understand,' she said.

Anxious to put her at her ease, Albrigtsen smiled. 'But you will, I think, when I tell you that I have been doctor to the Jordahl family for many years. And that I am also a close friend who enjoys their confidence.'

'Oh I see,' said Catherine, marvelling at the coincidence but at the same time welcoming it.

'And since I also received a bequest,' the doctor continued, 'I was present when Hjalmar Jordahl's will was read.'

'Well then I'm very glad to have met you like this, Doctor,' Catherine assured him. 'Because perhaps you can explain why a complete stranger, someone I've never heard of or laid eyes on, should have left *me* anything. Let alone . . .'

'Hjalmar Jordahl was unknown to you!' interrupted Albrigtsen, surprised and confused.

'Totally,' Catherine said. 'Until two weeks ago.'

'But your parents then,' Albrigtsen probed. 'They must surely have . . .'

'They're both dead,' Catherine interjected.

'Oh forgive me please!'

Catherine dismissed his apology with a gesture. 'But anyway,' she went on, 'I'm positive that neither of them knew Jordahl either. I don't really remember my father. But my mother only died three years ago. And she never mentioned anyone of that name. Not even in a passing reference. And yet she was the only possible connection because she was Norwegian.'

Albrigtsen seized on this instantly. 'Ah! From what part of Norway was she?'

'Oslo.'

'And what was her name before she married?'

'Enger. Kirsten Enger.'

The doctor turned the name over in his mind and then,

disappointed, shook his head. 'Well as far as I know the Jordahls have no blood ties with anyone called Enger,' he said.

'Or any other kind of ties. Not with these Engers at least. I checked. I telephoned my grandparents in Minnesota.'

Her companion gave her a questioning look.

'My grandfather was a chemist in a brewery in Oslo,' Catherine explained. 'But then he was offered a job in America. So he and my grandmother emigrated there a year or so before I was born. And they're as mystified as I am. Because the name Jordahl means nothing whatever to them.'

'Perhaps some other branch of your family?' suggested Albrigtsen.

Catherine shook her head. 'They're the only relatives I've got, the ones in the States.'

Albrigtsen stared at her, lost in thought. Then he tried again. 'Mr Jordahl was very active in the Resistance during the war. Perhaps he met your father at that time and, afterwards, felt indebted to him for some reason. And your father having died he wished to repay his debt to him through you. Is that possible?'

Again Catherine shook her head. 'That's a nice romantic thought,' she said. 'But there's no mileage in it I'm afraid. My father wasn't old enough to fight. He was still at school during the war.'

The doctor picked up his cup and drank from it, all the while regarding Catherine intently.

'Then there can be no question about it,' he said as he lowered his cup again. 'Clearly the legacy was meant for you. In your own right.'

'But why?' implored Catherine. 'I mean you just don't leave a boatyard and a house with sixty acres to someone you've never met or had anything to do with.'

'But it cannot be that you were a complete stranger to him,' insisted Albrigtsen. 'He gave your address in his will.'

'That was my parents' address.'

'Even so. That in itself proves that there has to have

been a link of some kind.' Albrigtsen gazed out of the window. 'When did your father and mother marry?' he asked casually.

'1955,' Catherine told him and then looked puzzled. 'Why?'

Albrigtsen turned his head to her again. 'And your mother had been living in Oslo up until then, had she?'

'Yes. That's where they got married. And that's where I was born.'

'And when was that?'

'Three years later. November 1958.'

Realising now how Albrigtsen's mind was working, Catherine fixed him with a weary look. 'Oh, now I see what you're getting at,' she said. 'Yes, I have to admit that possibility crossed my mind too. But I don't believe it. And if you'd ever met my mother you'd know why. She just wasn't like that. What's more she adored my father.'

Albrigtsen nodded and smiled apologetically. 'Of course. Again forgive me. That, I am certain, was an unworthy thought.'

'Just the same,' Catherine retorted with more than a hint of scorn in her voice, 'I wouldn't mind betting that it's a thought that's in the mind of a good few people right now.'

Albrigtsen shrugged. 'If only there was a more obvious explanation,' he said. 'But then Hjalmar Jordahl was never a man for the obvious.'

Then he tactfully changed the subject and, throughout the rest of the meal, they talked of many things but mostly about Norway.

Breakfast finished, Albrigtsen suggested a stroll round the deck. Catherine welcomed the idea. Side by side they promenaded the length of the ship, weaving their way through the knots of amateur photographers crowding the rail and around obstructions of loaded deck-chairs.

'Tell me about Jordahl,' Catherine asked, as they walked.

'He was a good man,' replied Albrigtsen. 'But a very

private person. Even I, who was his friend, could not say that I really knew him. And after his wife died, well then he seemed to draw back even more from those around him.' He sighed deeply. 'But then her death was a terrible blow to him.'

'Did they have any children?'

'Yes. Two daughters. Ingrid and Anna Marie. Anna Marie is the eldest by two years. She'll be twenty-five this year.'

'Hjalmar Jordahl can't have been very old when he died then,' Catherine said. Then she frowned. 'But you said he was in the Resistance.'

Albrigtsen nodded. 'He was in his middle sixties. He married quite late in life.'

'Oh I see.'

They paused by the rail and Albrigtsen put his elbows on it and leaned forward. 'There are moments,' he said, 'when I still find it difficult to accept that he has gone, you know. But then he was a remarkable man. And a strong one. In every way. He seemed indestructible.'

'What was it?' enquired Catherine. 'A heart attack?'

'No, nothing like that. Hjalmar had a heart rate that a man half his age would have envied. And the constitution of a bull elephant in the prime of life. I can't remember him once being ill.' Albrigtsen smiled. 'He was the best kind of patient.'

'What happened then?'

Albrigtsen stared out across the water at the rugged coastline only two hundred yards away. 'It was an accident. He took his boat out on the fjord alone when he really ought not to have done. There was a storm blowing up. He got into difficulties and was washed overboard and drowned.' He sighed again and straightened up. 'He is greatly missed. And not just by his family and friends. By the whole town.'

They walked on.

'Are his daughters married?' asked Catherine.

The doctor nodded. 'Ingrid is,' he said.

Catherine frowned. Up until then the possibility that there might be Jordahl children hadn't occurred to her.

Seeing the concerned look on her face, Albrigtsen smiled quietly. 'You feel that you are robbing them of their inheritance. Is that what's troubling you?'

'Well I am. Part of it anyway.'

Albrigtsen laughed. He stopped walking and turned to her.

For a moment they were separated by a boisterous party of Germans hurrying along the deck. When they had passed, the doctor drew Catherine into the shelter of one of the lifeboats. 'It is a very small part I assure you,' he said gently. 'And they will not miss it. When he was twenty-six Hjalmar Jordahl had nothing. He was the only son of a poor family and he worked for one of the local factories processing dried fish. By the time he was forty, though, he owned that factory. Half of Alesund too. And that was just the beginning. Today the dozen companies that are Jordahl Industries have a turnover each year of many millions of kroner. And, between them, Anna Marie, Ingrid and her husband, Lars, now own Jordahl Industries.' He smiled encouragingly and then went on. 'So you see, my dear, you're robbing no one.'

When the ship made its first port of call at the village of Torvik, Catherine, now alone, watched from the deck as a handful of passengers disembarked and the cargo was swung ashore. Albrigtsen had told her that the coastal steamer service was the lifeline of the towns and villages along the west coast of Norway, particularly further north, and now, seeing the excitement which the visit of the ship had caused among the local people, most of whom seemed to have gathered on the quay to welcome the *Kong Olav*, she could well believe it.

When the ship, with a farewell blast on its siren, set sail again Catherine returned to her cabin and re-packed her overnight bag. Back on deck again, she settled herself into a deck-chair and dozed. She was still hanging pleasantly between wakefulness and sleep when she became conscious of someone standing alongside her. She opened her eyes and looked up. It was Albrigtsen.

'Journey's end,' he said. 'We have arrived.'

Catherine got to her feet and crossed to the rail with him. He pointed. 'That's Alesund,' he told her.

The ship, dodging between a cluster of small islands, was approaching the town fast and, staring out from the deck, Catherine could see that Albrigtsen had not exaggerated when he had described Alesund as beautiful.

It lay before her, a kaleidoscope of grey-roofed buildings, white and pastel green and red and yellow, spilling out from the fringe of the mainland and across three narrow off-shore islands, each apparently linked to the other. Dominating the town and providing a magnificent background to it was a tree-clad mountain and behind that, and to one side, were range upon range of higher, starker peaks, still covered in snow.

As the *Kong Olav* drew nearer to the town and Catherine began to make out figures waiting on the dockside, the trepidation which she'd been feeling all morning was quite suddenly and unaccountably replaced by a stab of very real fear.

Chapter Four

The last thing Catherine had expected was that there would be anyone waiting to meet her when the *Kong Olav* docked. Least of all any members of the Jordahl family. But as Albrigtsen, carrying her luggage for her, led the way down the gangway and across the quay to where a couple were standing alongside a large Volvo she realised who they must be.

The woman was in her early twenties, slim, very attractive and dressed in a fashionable summer outfit which Catherine doubted had been bought in Alesund; the man, some six or seven years older, was well-built and athletic looking, but with an interesting rather than a handsome face.

The couple greeted Albrigtsen warmly and exchanged a few words in Norwegian but, throughtout their conversation, Catherine was aware that the woman seldom looked away from her and that when she did it was only very briefly.

She was also very conscious of the air of tension and anxiety generated by the woman, which was enhanced by her forced and hesitant smile and her nervous, fluttering gestures. It was as though she were gripped by a feeling of panic which she was only just, and with considerable effort, succeeding in holding in check.

Albrigtsen switched to English. 'This is who you are waiting for I think,' he said. 'Catherine Durrell. Catherine and I became friends on the trip.' He turned to Catherine. 'Let me introduce you. This is Ingrid. And this is her husband Lars Nilsen.'

Ingrid smiled weakly and shook hands. 'Hello,' she said almost in a whisper and with her eyes lowered. 'Welcome to Alesund.'

'Thank you.' Catherine was feeling very uncomfortable at having been trapped by this surprise reception.

Lars Nilsen shook hands with her. 'We are very pleased to meet you,' he said sincerely.

Catherine shot a look at Albrigtsen. 'What are they doing here?' she wanted to ask him and it was Ingrid who came up with the answer. 'The solicitors in London wrote to Bjarne Langva and told him when you were coming and, naturally, he informed us,' she explained.

'Mr Langva is our lawyer,' added Lars.

Catherine nodded. Ralph Stoddard had given her Langva's address and telephone number before she left London and she had intended to call him as soon as she was settled. And if he had been there to greet her, well that she could have understood. But Ingrid and Lars Nilsen! And, outwardly at least, genuinely if diffidently pleased to see her! She had allowed for the possibility of a stiffly formal and somewhat embarrassing meeting with the other Jordahl heirs during her visit, but this she had never imagined.

And then to her even greater surprise Lars picked up her luggage. 'Can we give you a lift, Arne?' he enquired of Albrigtsen, moving to the boot of the Volvo and opening it.

The doctor shook his head. 'No thank you. It is not necessary. My car is at the surgery and the walk there will do me good.' He smiled at Catherine. 'Well goodbye. I hope we meet again.'

Catherine took his hand gratefully. 'So do I,' she said. 'Goodbye. And thank you for your company.'

Albrigtsen kissed Ingrid on the cheek and then, with a nod to Lars, he walked away and was soon out of sight among the crowd on the quay.

Lars closed the boot of the car. 'Well, shall we go then?' he suggested with a smile.

Catherine hesitated, and seeing her obvious bewilderment Ingrid interjected quickly, 'You will stay with us I hope?'

Her husband laughed. 'Of course she will. Where else?'

'For the time being at least.' Ingrid urged flatly but with very real concern. 'We were counting on it.'

'That's very good of you,' Catherine floundered. 'But I really wasn't . . .'

Ingrid didn't let her finish. 'Unless of course you would prefer an hotel,' she said anxiously, now even more clearly holding a tight inward grip on herself.

'No, it's not that,' Catherine faltered, 'It's just that . . .' She smiled. 'Well I don't want to impose.'

'Believe me, you are not,' Ingrid informed her gravely. 'It is our pleasure.'

'After all,' said Lars with another laugh and coming to her support, 'in a way you are part of the family, aren't you?'

Catherine saw the frown on Ingrid's face and the warning look which she gave him.

Lars blushed. 'Well you know what I mean,' he said, hurrying to cover up his gaffe. 'We have a sort of bond, don't we? And from what Bjarne Langva has told us about you we feel that we know you already. So you are not a complete stranger as far as we're concerned.'

Catherine smiled to put him at his ease. 'Well, if you're sure.'

'We would be disappointed if you didn't,' murmured Ingrid and she gestured toward the car. 'So, please.'

They got into the Volvo and it glided away from the quay with Lars driving, Ingrid sitting beside him and Catherine grandly isolated in the back. Looking out of her window she took a childlike pleasure in the buildings and the acitivity around them as they passed through the town centre.

Further along the waterfront a fleet of a dozen or more fishing boats were tied up against the sea wall and the crews were selling freshly boiled shrimps and gleaming, recently caught fish to a crowd of eager buyers. Close to where the fishing boats were moored a line of cars, vans and lorries slowly followed a stream of foot passengers onto a ferry which swallowed them all through the gaping jaws of its raised bow.

The shops, some old, some very modern, looked worthwhile investigating and it seemed to Catherine that there was a bank of one kind or another on just about every street corner. Everywhere people were going about their business in a purposeful but leisurely and comfortably relaxed way. And that has to be an improvement on London, thought Catherine, remembering the grey-faced and unsmiling crowds in the West End; hordes of men and women rushing to get nowhere fast and with no time for one another.

A cruise ship flying the Russian flag was alongside the quay on the other side of the town from where the *Kong Olav* had berthed. From that point on, the main road ran parallel to a fjord which appeared to stretch for miles and which, on the far side, was bounded by one of the mountain ranges that almost encircled Alesund.

Catherine turned from the window and saw that Lars Nilsen was studying her in the rearview mirror. He smiled sheepishly and turned his attention back to the road ahead. 'You find it interesting?' he asked.

'Fascinating,' Catherine replied. 'And not at all what I expected. But then Norway's full of surprises for me. Like I'm very surprised at how many Norwegians speak such excellent English.'

'We learn it in school from when we are very young,' Lars explained. 'So it is a second language for us. And if you are in business it is very important to speak it well.'

'You have not been to this country before?' Ingrid asked quietly and without looking at her.

'No,' said Catherine. 'Never.' And then hastily corrected herself. 'Well, not since I was a very small child anyway.'

She gazed out of her window again and so she did not

see that her reply prompted a surreptitious exchange of glances between the couple in the front seats.

The Nilsens' house was four or five miles out of town, well off the main road, and set in a large garden with a wide, tree-fringed lawn that ran down to the edge of the fjord.

As soon as they arrived Ingrid showed Catherine to her bedroom and Lars followed them up the stairs with the suitcases. Catherine looked around admiringly. 'What a beautiful room!'

'I am pleased that you like it,' said Ingrid. 'I hope you will be comfortable.'

'I don't think there's any doubt about that.'

Lars put the cases down on the bed. 'May we call you Catherine?' he asked.

'Of course.'

'Good!' He smiled. 'Well then, Catherine, I will see you later.' He turned to Ingrid. 'I must go back to the office for a while,' he told her.

Just for an instant Ingrid's face was that of a frightened child. But then she nodded and Lars kissed her on the cheek. 'But you will not be home late though, will you?' she said fretfully, half pleading.

Her husband put a hand on her arm and squeezed it comfortingly. 'By four at the latest,' he said lightly. Then, looking at Catherine, he said, 'Please feel at home here.'

'You are very kind,' said Catherine. She smiled at Ingrid. 'Both of you.'

Lars left the room, closing the door behind him. Ingrid watched him leave and then gave Catherine a half-smile as though apologising for her foolishness a moment earlier. 'I will leave you to unpack,' she said. 'And you would perhaps like to take a shower.' She indicated the partly open door of the *en-suite* bathroom. 'Anyway, come down when you are ready.'

She crossed to the doorway where she paused and looked back. 'Are you hungry?' she asked.

'Not desperately,' Catherine said truthfully.

'Then I will prepare something light for us for now because you will eat well tonight I think.'

Catherine nodded in agreement. 'That sounds great.'

Ingrid stepped out into the hall and closed the door again and for a few moments Catherine stood staring thoughtfully after her.

There's one very neurotic lady, she decided. Either that or it's my being here that's got her so uptight. But if that's the case why invite me to stay with them? She shrugged. Could be I'm misjudging her, though. Maybe she's just nervous at meeting me for the first time and it'll pass. Heaven knows I've been twitched up enough about coming to Alesund, she conceded. Still am, if it comes to that. And on the surface she seems friendly enough. They both do. Surprisingly so. And I couldn't really decline the invitation, could I? Not without offending them. And I wouldn't want to do that. My being in the will has probably caused enough offence already. Though you'd never guess it from the way they're acting. And spending a couple of days or so with them, well that's no great hardship. Anyway, who knows, perhaps they can explain why Jordahl did what he did. Maybe there *is* a link of some kind and I just don't know about it.

She walked over to the bed and, opening her overnight bag, took her things out of it. Among them was a small, leather diptych-style photograph frame. She opened it. On one side was a photograph of her mother taken when she was eighteen and in her last year at school in Oslo. And, from a matching oval in the other half of the frame, the picture of Kirsten Durrell now aged fifty-one smiled up at her.

Since her mother's death Catherine had never left home for any length of time without taking the diptych with her. She stared at the later picture and smiled back. My God, she mused, how beautiful you were. Right up to the end. And at eighteen you must have turned all the men on. And I really wouldn't blame you if . . . She shook her head. But no, you just didn't do that kind of thing, did you? There was only one man in your life. And even after he died and you were still only – what were you, thirty-three was it? Yes, thirty-three – well I very much doubt if even then you ... She laughed. I certainly don't recall having had any transient uncles when I was a kid anyway. So there's no way you could've ever been Hjalmar Jordahl's mistress, and that's for sure.

She kissed the photograph and stood the diptych on the table beside the bed.

A little later, as she was still emptying her suitcases, she heard a car approaching the house and then pull up in the drive. Crossing over to the wardrobe, she glanced out of the window in time to see a woman get out of a Ford Sierra and hurry to the front door. From that angle it was not possible to tell much about her, except that, like Ingrid, she was fair-haired and was casually but elegantly dressed.

Her luggage unpacked, Catherine had a shower, put on a blouse and skirt and went downstairs. In the front hall at the foot of the stairs was a door which Catherine felt sure opened into the kitchen, judging from the rattling of plates coming from behind it. Beyond, and on a lower level than the hallway, was a large sitting room with two doors off it. A window at the far end took up almost the entire wall area; half of it could be slid open to give access to a patio and the garden behind it.

Catherine stepped down into the room and strolled over to the window. The sitting room was tastefully and expensively decorated. The furniture, imaginatively designed and unmistakably Scandinavian in style, was expertly made and clearly comfortable and luxurious.

Standing at the vast window Catherine looked out into the garden and saw that where the gently sloping lawn met the fjord there was a stone jetty. Tied up to it was a powerful motor cruiser.

A boat like that would set you back a fortune in England, she thought. God knows what it must have cost here! But then of course the same applied to the Nilsens' car and the house and the furnishings in it, and she had to remind herself that these were not just wealthy people she was among. As Dr Albrigtsen had been at pains to explain to her, between them they had a controlling interest in companies turning over millions each year.

Close to the window there was a baby grand piano on top of which stood a photograph in a silver frame. Curious, Catherine crossed to it and picked it up.

It was a studio portrait of a handsome, broad-shouldered, rugged-looking man whose age it was difficult to pin down. He could have been anywhere between fifty and sixty when the photograph was taken but, however old he was, he wore his years easily and with defiance.

You have to be Hjalmar Jordahl, Catherine decided. Well how do you do, Hjalmar! Meet Catherine Durrell. Or have we met before somewhere? If so I'm afraid I don't remember you. And if we had've done I'm sure I wouldn't have forgotten such a strong face. Or the kind of forceful personality you obviously had. So, Mr Jordahl, what's the answer to this mystery you've got me tangled up in, eh?

Bemused and shaking her head, she put the photograph back down on the piano and started a slow tour round the room, wondering if she should stay where she was or go and look for Ingrid.

There were several paintings in the room and one of them, hanging above a very attractive, antique wood-burning stove, immediately caught her eye. She walked over to it and stood gazing up at it.

It was of a group of fishermen sitting mending their nets on the quayside of a small fishing village.

In style and texture it had the feel of a late Goya, although it was plainly not the work of the Spanish master. The uniquely Nordic background and the unmistakable northern European features of the men, together with the fact that it had clearly been painted fairly recently, confirmed that. Nevertheless, to Catherine's mind, it had in it more than a hint of the same savage cruelty and contempt which sprang from the dark despair which tortured Goya in his later years.

And the more she studied the picture the more worrying and disquieting it became, alarming even. Although, if asked, she would not have been able to explain precisely why it had that effect on her. But as far as she was concerned, there was no question about it; it had a very strange and disturbing quality. And one which, if the painting had been given to her back in England, she would have found it impossible to live with.

'Hello, Catherine!'

Startled, Catherine swung round.

The woman she had seen arrive earlier was standing at the top of the step up into the hall and Catherine wondered how long she had been watching her.

She bore a striking resemblance to Ingrid, the same colouring, the same regular features and vibrant complexion, the same trim figure. But she was an inch or so taller and her eyes were more deep set and betrayed a quiet confidence and depth of intelligence which Ingrid patently lacked.

'I'm Anna Marie Jordahl,' the woman said with a genuine smile.

Instantly Catherine warmed to her. 'Hello.'

Anna Marie stepped down into the room and crossed to her. 'Do you like it?' she enquired, looking at the painting.

Catherine hesitated. And then she said, evasively, 'It's very well done. Who painted it?'

'Ingrid.'

'Really!' Catherine exclaimed, greatly surprised. She studied the picture again. 'Is she a professional artist?'

'No, just an amateur. But a good one I think.'

'Yes, extremely good.' Catherine gazed around the room. 'Is there any more of her work here?'

Anna Marie shook her head. 'Sadly no. Two years ago my sister suddenly decided that none of her work had any merit. And no one could convince her otherwise. So she burned all of her canvases.'

'Oh, how could she!' demanded Catherine, appalled by the thought of such wanton destruction of talent.

'That one only survived because I threatened never to speak to her again if she didn't keep it. Which was a good thing because now she has given up painting. Would you like a drink?'

'Thank you.'

'Sherry? Vodka? Gin? Whisky?'

'A vodka and tonic please.'

As Anna Marie walked over to a drinks cabinet and opened it, Catherine, again feeling awkward and very much out of place, slowly returned to the window and took refuge in the scenery. 'What a lovely garden!' she ventured, for want of anything better to say. 'And what a stunning view! All those different shades of green on the other side of the water. It's strange but somehow, back in Britain, you never think of Norway without seeing it covered in snow.'

Anna Marie looked up from pouring their drinks. 'But you know better than that surely,' she said. 'I understand that you were born here. In Oslo.'

'Yes, but only just. And I don't remember it at all,' replied Catherine.

Aimlessly she strolled over to the piano and glanced at the photograph of Jordahl. Anna Marie joined her with the drinks. 'That's my father,' she explained, her eyes on Catherine.

'Yes, I guessed it was. He was a handsome man, wasn't he?'

'Yes,' Anna Marie acknowledged flatly. She handed her her drink.

'Thanks.' Catherine sipped the vodka and tonic and then, looking at Anna Marie and unable to continue with the polite charade they seemed to be playing, burst out, 'Oh God! What the hell am I doing here? I've no right to be. And I can't imagine why you're all being so pleasant. Resentment I could've understood. Outright hostility even. But this!'

Anna Marie studied her closely. 'Why should we have any feeling of resentment?' she asked soothingly.

'Oh come on now! A stranger inherits part of your father's estate. Someone you've never even heard of. If the positions were reversed I think I'd resent that. And I can't give you any explanation as to why I was in his will. You see . . .'

'Yes I know,' Anna Marie told her, interrupting. 'I met Dr Albrigtsen in town and he told me. It's a complete mystery to you. Well it's a mystery to us too.'

'You have no idea why he did it?' Catherine said, disappointed, and searching Anna Marie's face.

Anna Marie shook her head. 'We have not been able to trace any family connection.'

'There is none. I'm sure of that.'

'For some other reason then,' Anna Marie said. She shrugged. 'And one which we will probably never know. But that is what my father wanted. And as far as my sister and I and Lars are concerned that is the end of the matter.' She studied Catherine again. 'And while it is true that you have arrived here as a stranger,' she smiled, 'it is our hope, believe me, that when you leave it will be as a friend.'

Relieved and grateful, Catherine smiled back at her. 'Thank you.'

Anna Marie looked away from her and moved over to the window. 'What are your plans?' she asked.

'I'm not really sure. But to be honest just now I'm looking for capital and, well, selling the boatyard seems like it might be a good way to raise some.'

Anna Marie nodded. 'And the property? What are you going to do with that?'

'I don't know. But Alesund's a fair distance from London. A bit too far away to have a weekend cottage here.'

Anna Marie laughed. 'Well, whatever you decide,' she said, 'I hope that, once the formalities are completed, you will stay on for a while.'

Catherine turned as Ingrid came into the room through

one of the doors behind her, allowing her a momentary glimpse of the dining room beyond it.

'Lunch is ready,' Ingrid announced quietly as she approached them. 'But it is only a cold table so there is no hurry. Whenever you feel like it.' She looked at her sister. 'Lars is going to barbecue some steaks for us tonight so I thought we would just have something simple for now,' she explained, half apologetically.

'Good idea,' said Anna Marie and then, holding up her glass, she asked, 'Do you want one of these?'

'What is it?' enquired Ingrid uncertainly.

'Vodka and tonic.'

Ingrid nodded. 'Yes, thank you.'

Anna Marie moved away and across to the drinks cabinet.

There was a difficult silence. 'Do you have any children?' Catherine asked Ingrid in an attempt to fill the gap.

Ingrid frowned and looked down at the floor. 'No,' she said sharply. Then, as if regretting her abruptness, she lifted her head and gave Catherine a faint, embarrassed smile. 'Lars and I decided to wait for a while before starting a family. First we wish to enjoy just being together. And there is plenty of time.'

'Of course,' agreed Catherine. She tried again. 'I was admiring your painting earlier,' she told her.

At this Ingrid frowned even more deeply and looked away from her again. 'It's not very good I'm afraid,' she said dismissively.

'I think it's remarkably good,' Catherine assured her. 'And very powerful. But your sister tells me that you've given it up.'

Ingrid nodded. 'It no longer interests me,' she said, uncomfortably. And from her expression Catherine was left in no doubt that was as far as that conversation was going to go.

Anna Marie rejoined them and handed Ingrid her drink. 'Thank you,' she said and then, shyly, she raised her glass to Catherine. 'Cheers!'

'Cheers!' acknowledged Catherine.

'Good luck,' added Anna Marie with a smile, joining her sister in the toast.

Catherine smiled back and sipped her drink. And, as she did so, she glanced once more across the room at Ingrid's painting.

And to her astonishment, and quite involuntarily, she shuddered.

Chapter Five

Later that first day, Catherine was reclining comfortably in a chair on the patio, lazily watching Lars barbecuing their steaks, when Anna Marie, who was sitting alongside her, announced that the next morning she would drive her out to see the two houses that now belonged to her.

'That's very nice of you,' Catherine said. And then she added quickly, 'But only if you can spare the time.'

'Oh I think they can manage without me at work for a few hours,' Anna Marie assured her.

The news that Anna Marie had a job came as a great surprise to Catherine. From what she'd been told by Albrigtsen and from the evidence around her as to Lars' and Ingrid's lifestyle, it was obvious that no Jordahl *needed* to work for their living. Or not in the way that she had always had to anyway. 'What do you do?' she enquired, intrigued.

'I design furniture,' Anna Marie said. She smiled. 'You're sitting in one of my chairs.'

Catherine had coveted the unusual and futuristically shaped easy chair, one of a set of four on the patio, from the moment she'd seen it. And the longer she had sat in it the more pleased with it she'd become. 'You designed this!' she exclaimed, greatly impressed.

Anna Marie nodded. 'And most of the other furniture in the house as well.'

'Really! Congratulations!'

'Thank you. You like the modern, Scandinavian style then, do you?'

'Very much. And I'm very taken with that suite in the sitting room. Is that your work?'

'Yes.'

'Well, it's great!' Catherine enthused. 'But this chair though! I've never seen anything like it anywhere before. And it's incredibly relaxing. It's almost as though you were suspended in mid-air. Who do you design for?'

'Since my father died, for myself,' Anna Marie told her. 'The factory is mine now.'

Carrying a bowl of salad, Ingrid emerged from the sitting room through the sliding glass panel in the vast window behind them. She set the bowl down onto the table which, earlier, Anna Marie had laid for dinner, and then walked over and joined them.

'I hope this is all right for you,' she said diffidently, directing her enquiry at Catherine. 'Anna Marie thought that we should take you to a restaurant but I felt that, well having just arrived, you would prefer . . .' She broke off and gave a half-apologetic shrug.

'And you were absolutely right,' Catherine said, smiling. 'This is much better than going anywhere. I mean, what could be better on a beautiful summer's night like this than having a meal out here?'

This had the desired effect on Ingrid but nevertheless she clearly felt that Catherine deserved some compensation. 'Tomorrow night we have invited a few of our friends here to meet you. You will like them I'm sure. And it will give you a chance to get to know some people.'

'Oh, how nice,' Catherine murmured politely. Inwardly, though, the prospect appalled her. And the following morning when Anna Marie called for her, even after a good night's sleep, she was still dreading the idea.

From the easy way in which Anna Marie conducted herself in the Nilsen house Catherine had assumed that she lived with Lars and Ingrid and she'd been surprised when, at around eleven o'clock the previous night, she had said that she must go home.

Now, though, as she drove Catherine along the side of

the fjord in her Sierra, Anna Marie revealed in the course of their conversation that home for her was a penthouse apartment above the Jordahl Industries building in the centre of Alesund.

'I also have a little summer house on Brusdalsvatnet. That's the freshwater lake we'll be passing shortly,' she said. 'It is a beautiful spot but not, I have to admit, as beautiful as Jordahlsholmen.' Then, in response to the questioning look on Catherine's face, she continued, 'That's what the place my father left you is called, Jordahlsholmen. Jordahl's island.'

'It's on an island!' said Catherine.

'Part of the property is. It's sort of in two halves. You'll see. First, though, I thought that, as it's not far out of our way, you would probably like to have a look around the boatyard. I have already telephoned Olav Tunheim who is the General Manager there and he is expecting us. Is that all right with you?'

'Fine,' agreed Catherine.

The boatyard turned out to be much bigger and far busier than Catherine had imagined it would be. In her mind she had seen it as being something very much like the rather tumbledown and haphazard yards which serviced the boats on the Blackwater and around Hayling Island; both sailing areas which she knew well. But once past the sign at the entrance which read, 'Jordahl Batbyggeri AS', what she saw was vastly different; a large, modern complex set on the edge of another wide fjord which, in several long buildings, manufactured rather than built sleek and expensive fibreglass motor cruisers. And she knew then where the craft which was moored at the end of Nilsen's garden had come from.

If she needed any confirmation that this was no backwater operation it came from Anna Marie when, as they walked across to the administration building, she said, casually, 'This has become a very profitable business in the last few years, you know.'

Once inside the building they were ushered immediately into Olav Tunheim's office. He was a somewhat surly-looking man of medium build and, Catherine guessed, around forty-five years old. He greeted her politely enough but with a noticeable coolness and lack of enthusiasm. And there was no change in his attitude until towards the end of the conducted tour on which he insisted on taking her.

Watching the final touches being put to the various processes that went into turning out the Jordahl boats, Catherine sighed and then said ruefully, 'It's such a shame. But it seems that just about every boat's made of plastic these days.'

Tunheim gave her a faintly disparaging look. 'Fibreglass is by far the best material,' he said pompously. 'Light, strong, resilient. And it demands so little maintenance.'

'I'm sure you're right,' agreed Catherine. 'But it's just not the same as wood, is it?'

The general manager shrugged. 'Perhaps not. But the cost of a wooden boat today, it is ridiculous. So there is little demand for them. There was a time when wooden boats were built here and we still have the means and the skills to do it but,' he shook his head, 'that is a thing of the past.' And then, suddenly remembering that he was talking to the new owner, he hastily added and with a hint of anxiety in his voice, 'Unless of course you decide . . .'

'No,' Catherine assured him quickly. 'I love sailing and I wouldn't have a fibreglass boat if you gave me one. But building them, out of whatever – well that isn't my line of business.'

At that Tunheim gave her a sidelong and interested glance and, later, as they were walking back to his office where Anna Marie was waiting, he paused and turned to her and said, 'If you are thinking of disposing of the boatyard, Miss Durrell, would you perhaps do me a great favour?'

Catherine nodded. 'If I can. What is it?'

'Well,' he explained, 'I would very much like to buy it

myself. But although I have some money it is not enough and so I would need to raise a loan from my bank in order to do that.'

'What kind of money would be involved then?' Catherine asked, studying him thoughtfully.

Tunheim looked at her, surprised and confused. 'Why a great deal surely,' he stammered.

And it was then, for the first time, that Catherine realised that with her inheritance she was now a very wealthy woman, rich even. She smiled delightedly. 'Yes, I suppose so.'

'I am very serious about this, believe me. And I am quite sure that there will be no problem for me in raising the necessary funds,' Tunheim went on. 'But it may take two or three weeks before the bank finally approves my application. Would you be prepared to wait that long to consider my offer?'

Catherine met his earnest gaze, her head full of new and exciting possibilities, and smiled again. 'Yes, of course, Mr Tunheim,' she replied generously. 'I'm in no great hurry to dispose of the yard. And I like it here.'

They shook hands.

About an hour later they left the boatyard. As she drove back in the general direction of Alesund, Anna Marie swung the Sierra onto a side-road and then, three or four miles along it, turned down a narrow track that led to the shore of the fjord which had been on their right for some distance.

'This is it,' Anna Marie announced as she steered the car along the uneven track. 'This is Jordahlsholmen!'

Catherine stared ahead excitedly though there was little to see except for the carpet of wild flowers on the open grassland on either side of them and the thick copse of trees towards which they were heading. But then, as they passed through the screen of trees and emerged on the far side of them, she saw the house and the island, and she gasped.

Anna Marie had said it was a beautiful place and it was.

The main house stood almost on the edge of the fjord and was surrounded by an extensive garden which was a mass of colour and dotted with clumps of silver birch and fir trees. In front of the house the gravelled drive which began at the gateway to the property dropped gently down to a boathouse and wooden jetty.

But, as stunning as its surroundings were, it was the house itself which held Catherine's attention as Anna Marie parked her car in the drive and they both got out.

It was old, probably more than a hundred years old Catherine suspected, and its walls were clad with timber painted a subtle shade of green and overhung by a roof of rust-red tiles. There were six large, white-framed windows on the fjord side of the building and a smaller one almost at ground level which Catherine assumed was there to let some light into a cellar. Running along the front of the house was a verandah, its roof and supports thatched and entwined with honeysuckle and clematis. In its centre was a porch and, beyond that, a stout front door.

Anna Marie had been watching Catherine's reaction closely. 'Do you like it?' she enquired unnecessarily.

'Oh, it's lovely!' Catherine swung round and looked across at the tree-clad island behind them.

It was almost exactly opposite the house and about a hundred yards away across a channel of water that glittered and shimmered in the sunlight. Catherine could make out a shingle beach and another jetty. And, on higher ground above them, a second and smaller wooden-sheathed house. 'And the island belongs to me, too, you say?'

Anna Marie nodded. 'The island and both houses.' She pointed in the direction of the track they had driven down. 'And all that land beyond the garden and on either side. This was once a farm,' she said. 'Many years ago though. But, as you can see, it is still very isolated. I don't think there's another house closer than a mile away.'

Catherine slowly turned in a full circle, taking in the

45

whole scene again. 'What a stunning place to live!' she murmured, almost overcome by it all.

Anna Marie pointed to the boathouse. 'It was from there that my father sailed his boat on the day that he was drowned,' she said dully.

Catherine frowned and shot a look at her. But Anna Marie's eyes were on the boathouse and she continued to stare at it for several seconds. Then, taking a bunch of keys from her shoulder bag, she led the way over to the house and, stepping into the porch, unlocked the front door. Beyond it was a square hall with a flight of stairs at the far end and a door on either side. Anna Marie pushed one of them open and Catherine followed her into the sitting room. It was fully furnished with fine antique, traditional furniture in Norwegian farmhouse style. Against one wall was a late Victorian rolltop desk and, positioned around the large, open fireplace, was a moquette upholstered sofa and two high-backed armchairs.

Catherine gazed about her, enchanted. She found the furniture a little too heavy for her taste but it suited the room very well and contributed greatly to the general atmosphere of ordered calm and peace. 'What a splendid room!' she said, her eyes going to the portrait which was hanging above the fireplace and which dominated everything around it.

She reacted with a start.

It was a full-length oil painting of a girl in her late teens or early twenties, wearing a white dress and holding a posy of flowers. She was outstandingly beautiful and the artist had brilliantly captured the impression of innocence and vulnerability – and the strange quality of distance – in his subject.

Catherine moved to the fireplace and studied the picture closely. There was something familiar about the subject and she could have sworn that she had seen her before somewhere; or someone very much like her, and recently. But try as she would she couldn't place her. And then she realised what the answer had to be. The girl had an unmistakable and striking resemblance to Anna Marie and Ingrid.

'That's my mother,' Anna Marie said, coming alongside her and staring up at the portrait. 'My father commissioned it the year they were married.'

Catherine gave her a puzzled look and her companion read her mind. 'She was more than twenty years younger than he was,' she said. 'And only thirty when she died. Just a week after my tenth birthday.'

Catherine acknowledged the explanation with a smile. 'Well now I know where you and Ingrid get your looks from,' she said. 'Both of you are so like her.'

'In some ways perhaps,' agreed Anna Marie noncommittally, her eyes still fixed on the portrait. 'Her name was Freya.'

Catherine shook her head sadly. 'How tragic that she should have died so young. And how unjust.'

'It was her choice,' Anna Marie said in a flat, matter-of-fact voice. And, seeing the bewildered look on Catherine's face, she went on in much the same tone, 'Didn't Dr Albrigtsen tell you? She committed suicide.'

With a visible effort, she shook off old and painful memories and moved briskly over to the desk and opened the top of it. 'My father's personal papers have been removed of course,' she said. 'But before they were, out of curiosity, I looked through them to see if I could find any references to you or your parents.' She shook her head. 'There was none. No clues at all. Nothing that might have explained why . . .' She broke off and stared thoughtfully at the empty pigeonholes. Then, closing the desk again, she turned to Catherine and held out the bunch of keys she was holding. 'But now this house and everything in it is yours.'

'Not your mother's portrait though,' Catherine protested uncomfortably. 'You'll want to have that surely.'

'No.' Anna Marie was adamant. 'It was my father's and it belongs in this house. And Ingrid and I do not need a painting to remind us of her.'

'I feel guilty enough as it is,' Catherine confessed, taking the keys from her. 'But now . . . Well I didn't realise that this was your family home.'

'Please!' said Anna Marie. 'Don't feel that way. There is no reason for you to.' She glanced around the room. 'This house was never my home. Nor Ingrid's.' With that she crossed to another door and opened it. 'The kitchen's through here.'

Catherine had fully expected that after Anna Marie had shown her round the house they would visit the island so, when she had locked the front door behind them, she moved out of the porch and gazed across the water. 'Does the other house have electricity?' she asked.

Anna Marie nodded. 'Yes. But there is no telephone. Over there you're almost completely cut off from the outside world.'

Catherine examined the bunch of keys which Anna Marie had given her. 'Which is the key for it?'

'That one I think,' Anna Marie replied uneasily and pointing.

'And how do we get across there?'

'There's a dinghy with an outboard motor in the boathouse.'

'Great!' exclaimed Catherine, looking over at the island again. And then, glancing at Anna Marie, she saw that she too was gazing in the same direction and that there was an expression of dismay on her face. 'Are you all right?' she enquired anxiously.

Anna Marie nodded. 'Yes. Perfectly all right,' she said shortly.

Catherine was not entirely convinced. 'Are you sure?'

Anna Marie gave her a weak smile. 'Yes, I'm fine. Really I am. It's just that . . . Well, if you'll forgive me I won't come to the island with you.' Again she stared out over the water and her face clouded once more. 'That was my mother's house,' she said. 'Hers alone. It was a place where she could be entirely on her own whenever she wanted to be. And she was living there when she . . .' She baulked at finishing the sentence and then went on, 'I haven't been there since. No one in the family has. Not even my father. But you go ahead. I'll wait for you here.'

Catherine regarded her sympathetically. 'No, I wouldn't dream of it,' she said.

Anna Marie smiled weakly again. 'I'm sorry.'

'Don't be silly!' Catherine told her. 'I understand.' She put an arm comfortingly around Anna Marie's shoulders. 'Come on, let's go.' And side by side they walked over to the car.

The party at the Nilsens that night was not anything like the ordeal which Catherine had expected it to be. In fact she very quickly found herself enjoying it. With few exceptions most of Lars' and Ingrid's friends were contemporaries of hers and even those who were much older turned out to be interesting, relaxing and, in conversation anyway, uninquisitive company. The food was excellent, the background music on the stereo player was her kind of music and Lars was very quick to refill empty glasses.

Catherine was particularly delighted to find that both Albrigtsen and his wife had been invited. Liv Albrigtsen was a slim, handsome woman four or five years younger than her husband with greying hair, a great enthusiasm for living and an infectious laugh.

'Well at least you must stay until 23rd June,' she told Catherine as she and Albrigtsen stood chatting to her.

'Oh, what happens then?' enquired Catherine.

'It's Midsummer Eve,' explained Albrigtsen. 'And that's a big celebration here in Norway.'

'The festivities go on all night,' his wife said. 'You mustn't miss that. People take their boats out on the fjord or have a picnic down by the water. There are bonfires everywhere and fireworks. Everyone sings and dances. . . .'

'And a good many round it all off with a very nasty hangover,' Albrigtsen said, interrupting her flow.

Catherine laughed and then stepped to one side to allow

Ingrid and a newcomer, a well-dressed, alert-looking man of around fifty, into the group.

'Ah!' said Albrigtsen. 'Here is someone you were bound to meet sooner or later. Good evening, Bjarne.'

The stranger shook hands with him and then kissed Liv Albrigtsen on the cheek. 'Hello, Bjarne,' she greeted him. 'How are you?'

The man raised his eyes despairingly. 'So much work,' he complained, 'I cannot tell you. That's why I'm late.'

'Catherine, this is Bjarne Langva,' said Ingrid. 'We told you, I think, that Bjarne is the family lawyer.' She smiled awkwardly. 'But then you knew that already, didn't you?'

Catherine nodded. 'Yes.' She shook hands with the lawyer. 'I'm sorry, I really ought to have contacted you as soon as I arrived, Mr Langva, I meant to but . . .'

Langva smiled and held up a hand to silence her. 'I'm glad you didn't,' he said, his eyes fixed on her face and clearly appraising her. 'I haven't had a minute to spare these last two days. But I'm delighted to meet you, Miss Durrell. And perhaps if you could come to my office tomorrow morning at, say, ten o'clock we can settle everything then. Would that be convenient?'

'Yes, that'll be fine,' said Catherine.

Some time later, when Catherine and Albrigtsen, who had just returned with another drink for her, were standing alone in a corner of the room the doctor said, 'I hear you went out to Jordahlsholmen today.'

'Yes.'

'And what did you think of your property?' he asked.

'It's a glorious spot and the farmhouse is lovely.'

'Did you go across to the island?' Albrigtsen enquired casually.

'No.' Catherine wondered if she should say why she hadn't but then decided not to. 'By the time we got there it was a bit late for that.'

Albrigtsen nodded understandingly and looked relieved, Catherine thought. 'What a beautiful woman Freya Jordahl was,' she remarked.

The doctor gave her a puzzled look but then the realisation came to him. 'Ah yes, of course! The portrait.' He nodded again. 'Extremely beautiful.'

'And how sad. For her to die the way she did I mean.' Albrigtsen frowned questioningly.

'Anna Marie said she killed herself,' Catherine told him.

'Yes,' he confirmed uncomfortably.

'That must have been a terrible time,' Catherine probed gently. 'Particularly for her and Ingrid.'

'They were both quite young.' Albrigtsen would plainly have preferred to talk about something else. Just the same Catherine persisted.

'Exactly,' she said. 'It can't have been easy for anyone to cope with something like that. Children especially, though.'

'It was a great shock for everyone.' Albrigtsen sipped his whisky and then he asked, 'What else did Anna Marie tell you?'

'Nothing. Just that her mother committed suicide. Why did she do it?'

Albrigtsen shrugged. 'She left no note,' he said. 'But she had not been well for many months. So, who knows, a fit of depression perhaps. And as far as Hjalmar Jordahl was concerned that question was largely irrelevant. He had lost her and knowing why she did what she did would have done nothing to ease the pain with which he lived from then on. And now he, too, has gone.' He held Catherine in a steady gaze. 'So "let the dead bury their dead",' he smiled sadly. 'That is best. Don't you agree?'

Catherine studied him. Was that an entreaty, she wondered. Or a warning?

She slept fitfully that night, plagued by a nightmare she couldn't shake off in which she was being chased across a limitless desert by someone or something. And when finally she forced herself to look back at her pursuer she found herself standing in the sitting room at Jordahlsholmen, staring at Freya Jordahl's portrait.

With a frightened whimper she woke and sat up in the bed. And she knew then that it wasn't just a likeness to Anna Marie and Ingrid which she'd recognised in the painting. What she had seen, and what had startled her, was the fact that Freya Jordahl was the twin of the woman she had glimpsed in the corridor of the *Kong Olav*.

Chapter Six

As arranged, Catherine was at Bjarne Langva's office promptly at ten o'clock. It took more than an hour to complete all the legal formalities. She had to produce her mother's and father's birth and death certificates, her own birth certificate and passport and a copy of the sworn affidavit which she had made in London. She was then asked to swear another declaration on oath and sign several documents. And all the time Langva kept up a subtle interrogation about possible connections between her family and Jordahl, asking questions which Catherine had been hoping the lawyer himself might be able to answer.

Finally however, when Langva saw there was nothing to learn from the Englishwoman, he brought the proceedings to a close by suggesting that, rather than handing over the deeds to the land and property at Jordahlsholmen and the document transferring ownership of the boatyard there and then, he should hold them in safekeeping for her, at least for the time being.

Catherine agreed and then told him of her plan to sell the boatyard, and of Olav Tunheim's interest in buying it from her.

'Tunheim will have no difficulty in raising a loan,' Langva told her. 'He is very well thought of locally and it is a sound investment. But he is also a very sharp businessman so you will need to be wary about accepting his first offer. Always remembering that there will undoubtedly be others who will be interested in the sale. And if you would like me to act for you in this matter, either with Tunheim or whoever puts in a better bid, I would be happy to do so.'

'I'd be grateful,' Catherine said. 'Thank you.' And with that she shook hands with the lawyer and left.

Back out on the street, she went into the first newsagents she came across, and bought a street plan of the town and a map of the Alesund district. From the map she worked out the route to Jordahlsholmen and with the aid of the street plan she found her way to the local Avis office where she hired a Ford Fiesta. And an hour later, after an enjoyable drive and still marvelling at the glorious Norwegian summer weather, she turned onto the track which led to the farmhouse.

Closing the front door behind her, she walked into the sitting room and stood for a while looking up at Freya Jordahl's portrait.

Well, whoever the woman on the boat was, she can't have been you and that's for sure, she mused. But the likeness was uncanny. No question about that.

Turning from the fireplace she walked over to the kitchen door. The only room Anna Marie hadn't shown her the day before was the cellar; she'd merely indicated the way down to it and by inference had dismissed it as unimportant. Now, crossing the kitchen, Catherine lifted the trapdoor, switched on the light and descended the open-tread stairs.

The cellar was much as she had anticipated. It had a musty smell and, on its own, the one small window could never have been expected to let in enough light to see by, even on a bright sunny day such as today. It was stacked with wooden and cardboard boxes, battered suitcases and bric-à-brac of all kinds. There was even an ancient upright piano in one corner.

Catherine edged her way through the boxes, discarded pieces of furniture and old garden tools, pausing every now and then to gingerly lift the corner of a heap of neatly folded curtains or rummage through a basket of odds and ends. She was about to leave when she spotted, standing in a row on top of a packing case in the gloom beneath the stairs, several attractively bound books.

Ducking into the narrow space, she pulled out one of them and opened it. She couldn't read the Norwegian text, but from the illustrations it was obviously part of a set of encyclopaedias published in the early nineteen hundreds. The pictures were fascinating and others, showing the fashions and the transport of the period, made Catherine smile. She closed the book to replace it and, in so doing, some of the books at the end of the row toppled over. Two of them fell onto the floor, and it was as she was retrieving them that she saw the canvases tucked between the packing case and the wall.

There were six of them.

Curious, Catherine put the encyclopaedias to one side and reached for the pictures. Taking them over to the light, she laid the paintings down on top of an old cabin trunk and examined them one by one.

They were all done in oils and the first thing that struck her was that the artist's style was reminiscent of that used by Ingrid in her painting of the fishermen. The subjects, all local, were not in themselves very interesting but the treatment of them was startling. While the top picture had only a hint of the macabre in some of its features, the remainder were increasingly demented and grotesque until, staring in sickened disbelief at the last of the canvases, Catherine was in no doubt whatever that what she was confronted with had to be the product of a sick and tortured mind.

Greatly disturbed, she put the paintings back where she had found them and went upstairs. And, as she left the house and walked down to the jetty, she found that they were still vivid in her memory.

The door of the boathouse was not locked and there were two boats moored inside it; one a dinghy with an outboard motor mounted on its transom, as Anna Marie had said, the other a clinker-built sailing dory, some fifteen feet long with its mast unstepped and lying across its thwarts.

Catherine climbed down into the dinghy and checked the fuel tank of the outboard. It was almost full. She primed the carburettor and pulled hard on the starting rope. At her second attempt the motor coughed, spluttered and then fired, and she steered the boat out into the fjord and headed for the island.

It took only a minute or so to make the crossing. A few yards off from the beach, Catherine cut the outboard and let the dinghy gently ground itself on the shingle alongside the jetty. Stepping ashore she hauled the boat further up the beach and turned and looked at the house.

It was much smaller than the farmhouse but, as far as she could tell, about the same age and, like it, its wooden walls were painted, but in a warm yellow. It too had a red-tiled roof and white-framed windows but there were only four of them in front, two up and two down, and there was no verandah or porch.

Catherine mounted the four stone steps up from the shingle and opened the front door. It led directly into a sitting room which was attractively decorated and furnished in a very feminine style. The colour scheme of the paintwork and the design of the wallpaper and curtains were all in predominantly pastel shades; the delicate furniture was made of rosewood and the pictures on the walls were of flowers and birds.

And the room had a lived-in feel to it.

There was a book lying open on a table beside one of the armchairs, a small grandmother clock was ticking away quietly and, to Catherine's astonishment, she saw that it was showing the right time. There were fresh flowers in one of the vases and several magazines were spread out untidily across one end of a low coffee table.

It was almost as though the occupant had just stepped out for a while and would be back at any moment.

So strong was this impression that Catherine hesitated

just inside the doorway and wondered if she had perhaps entered the wrong house.

That isn't possible, though, she decided. This has to be Freya's house; the house which, according to Anna Marie, no one had visited for more than thirteen years.

Bewildered but intrigued, Catherine moved further into the room and started on a tour of inspection, stopping frequently to examine an ornament, look at a picture or admire a piece of furniture. She ran her finger along a shelf and checked. There was hardly a trace of dust anywhere. Absently she picked up the book lying on the table beside the armchair and, to her surprise, found it was an English edition of *Alice in Wonderland*.

I know how she felt now, she thought, carefully replacing the book.

The magazines on the coffee table were a selection of French, British and Scandinavian fashion and up-market *Homes and Gardens* type monthlies. She picked one of them up. It was dated December 1969.

Standing on another table near to the fireplace was an outdated-looking portable record player, the lid of which was raised. Catherine crossed to it and, finding an old shellac record on the turntable, switched the player on tentatively. To her further surprise it worked, the turntable began to spin. Curious, she placed the pick-up arm on the record. It was a crackling rendition of a waltz, haunting and romantic, one which Catherine felt sure must have been recorded before the Second World War.

Humming softly with the music she listened to the record for a while and then, after lifting the stylus, switched off the motor and, frowning, moved to the foot of the banistered staircase which ran down steeply to the front door.

There were four heavy, panelled pine doors leading off the landing above. Three of them had brass doorknobs and finger plates and their original locks but the fourth, at the end of a short corridor on Catherine's right as she came up the stairs, was fitted with a steel lever handle and a modern mortice lock.

Catherine opened the door nearest to her and peered into a bathroom. Moving down the corridor she found that the door at the end was locked and that none of the keys in the bunch which Anna Marie had given her fitted in the keyhole. Disappointed and annoyed, she retraced her steps and tried the third door. It opened at a turn of the knob, and Catherine stood in the doorway and gaped at what she saw.

It had obviously been Freya Jordahl's bedroom, and here there was an even stronger impression that the house was still occupied. A sheer black nightdress was laid out across the bedspread of a made-up double bed, a freshly laundered bath towel was draped over the back of a chair, and a pair of casually abandoned slippers were lying on the floor nearby.

Catherine walked over to the dressing table directly opposite her. There was an array of expensive make-up and exclusive perfumes on it, and an amber necklace, two or three bracelets, a string of pearls and other trinkets littered the top. The centre drawer overflowed with dainty and filmy underwear and when Catherine opened the wardrobe she found that it was filled with dresses, trouser suits and other clothes; all of which would have been highly fashionable in England fifteen or twenty years before.

Feeling even more like a trespasser now, Catherine almost tiptoed back across the room and out onto the landing.

The fourth room was in close to total darkness when she opened the door and stepped into it and only a narrow chink of sunlight led her over to the thickly curtained window. Drawing back the curtains, she turned towards the room. A sharp intake of breath and a look of stunned amazement betrayed her astonishment.

The room was furnished like a nursery. There were baby dolls everywhere. Dolls covered the bed and the bedside table. There were dolls huddled together on a chest of drawers and sitting in groups or singly on chairs. There were dolls ranged along the mantelpiece, clustered in gatherings on the floor and perched in rows along the top of the wardrobe. European dolls, African and Indian dolls, Chinese dolls, antique and modern dolls. Dozens and dozens of them, all fully dressed; a regiment of silent, motionless, scarlet-lipped, bow-mouthed, sightless and staring infants.

Recovering from her initial shock, Catherine walked over to the chest of drawers and picked up one of the dolls. Its mouth fell open. 'Mama,' it said.

Putting it down again, Catherine checked each of the drawers in the chest and found that they contained nothing but dolls' and baby clothes.

Her mind was still in a turmoil when, ten minutes later, she locked the front door of the house again and headed back to the beach. And on the return journey to the mainland she tried desperately to make some sense both of the paintings she'd stumbled across and of what she'd just discovered. But she couldn't.

And then, as she neared the shore, all else was forgotten when she saw that there was a battered Fiat 127 parked in the drive outside the boathouse. She altered course slightly, cut the outboard and steered the dinghy alongside the jetty. Stepping ashore she secured its painter to a mooring ring and then, cautiously, she approached the door of the boathouse and quietly eased it open.

A man was crouching in the sailing dory and closely inspecting the port side of it. He looked up and saw Catherine watching him and, startled, barked something at her in Norwegian.

'Who are you?' Catherine challenged him indignantly. 'What are you doing here?'

The man climbed out of the boat and stood looking at her.

He was about thirty, fair-haired and good looking with a strong, determined set to his chin, a resolute mouth and cynical, questioning eyes. Unconcerned, he smiled. 'Ah!' he said. 'You must be the Englishwoman, Catherine Durrell.'

'Yes I am. And you're trespassing,' Catherine snapped, alert and on her guard.

'Possibly,' the man acknowledged. 'I didn't know you'd already moved in.'

'I haven't. But that's beside the point. You're on my property.'

The stranger moved slowly down the landing stage toward her. 'My name is Bjornson,' he told her. 'Anders Bjornson. I'm a journalist with the local newspaper, *Sunnmorsposten*.' He took a press card out of his pocket and showed it to her.

Catherine glanced at the card. It seemed to confirm that he was telling the truth. 'How did you know who I am?' she asked.

Anders Bjornson regarded her, amused by her naïveté. 'Everyone in the district knows you have arrived I think. And why you have come.' He moved past her and out of the boathouse. Catherine followed him.

'I'm sorry,' he said, turning to her again. 'If I had known you were here I would have asked for permission.'

'My car's parked outside the house,' Catherine reminded him.

Anders shrugged. 'Could've been anyone's. And I've said I'm sorry.' He made a move towards his car.

'What were you looking for in there?' Catherine demanded.

The journalist paused and turned to her once more. He considered her thoughtfully for a while and then he said, 'I'm following up a theory of mine.'

Catherine studied him. 'Oh! And what theory's that?'

Anders held her gaze levelly. 'I don't believe Hjalmar Jordahl's death was an accident,' he said quietly. 'I think he was murdered.'

Chapter Seven

'Do you have any evidence to go with this theory of yours?'

Taken aback by what Anders Bjornson had said, Catherine found it difficult to accept. Dr Albrigtsen had not suggested, even in a veiled way, that there had been anything suspicious about Hjalmar Jordahl's death. Neither had Anna Marie nor Lars nor Ingrid. And nobody at the party had even as much as hinted that it had been anything more than an accident.

In any case, at that moment, she had enough mysteries to contend with as it was. True or not, it didn't really concern her. Nevertheless she was curious to hear more and, after a revelation like that, there was no way she was going to let Anders drive off without another word. So she had invited him into the house and now stood facing him across the sitting room.

'No. Not yet,' Anders admitted.

'So what's it based on?'

'The fact that, whatever else he was, Jordahl wasn't a fool.'

Catherine gave him a questioning look.

'What have you been told about his death?' Anders asked.

'Just that he went out sailing and got caught in a storm and was drowned.'

The journalist nodded. 'And that doesn't make any sense.'

'It sounds perfectly reasonable to me.'

'The storm that day,' Anders told her. 'It wasn't sudden and unexpected you know. It had been forecast. And it had been blowing up the night before. So Jordahl can't have been caught unawares. It has to be that he cast off from here with the weather already against him.'

'So?'

'He just wasn't that stupid. Not to go out on the fjord alone in a boat that size with a force-nine gale building. He was a very experienced sailor and he'd never have taken such a risk. Not without a very good reason anyway.'

'Perhaps he had a reason.'

'Such as?'

Catherine shrugged. 'I don't know. That question must have been raised at the time though.'

'Only it wasn't. Not seriously.'

'Why didn't you bring it up?'

'I wasn't here,' Anders explained. 'The day Jordahl died I flew to Strasbourg to research a series of articles on Common Market fishing policy. By the time I got back a fortnight later the inquest was over. I mentioned my doubts to a couple of people, though, including a friend of mine in the police, but they weren't impressed. They were quite happy to accept that it was an accident and that he was out there for pleasure.'

'Well that's possible, isn't it? Despite the storm. To test himself maybe. Okay, so it was foolhardy but people do crazy things like that.'

'Not Hjalmar Jordahl,' Anders said adamantly.

Catherine studied him searchingly. 'You knew him well?' she asked.

Anders shook his head. 'No one did. That wasn't possible,' he said.

He turned away from her and moved slowly round the room. Catherine watched him. 'He didn't let you get close enough for that,' Anders went on. 'But I knew him better than most people around here did I think.'

'How come?'

'A couple of years ago I did a piece on him for the paper. A sort of business profile. And he liked it. Enough to invite me out here for a meal. It was then that I got the idea of writing a book about him. He was an important man in this country but he'd always been a bit of a mystery so it would have sold well.'

'Would have? He didn't go for it then, eh?'

Anders glanced at her and gave her a wry smile. 'No, he wasn't interested. And he made it very clear that as far as his private life was concerned that's the way it was going to stay. Instead he suggested I had a try at writing a history of Jordahl Industries. Just so that it would be on record somewhere. And he said that if no one else would, he'd publish the book. So after that we met fairly regularly.'

His wandering had brought him much closer to Catherine and now he stood facing her once more. 'And when someone tells you in detail exactly how they worked their way up from having nothing to becoming a millionaire, well you learn a lot more about them than just how clever they were at making money,' he said.

'My impression is that he wasn't a very happy man.'

'Certainly not in his later years,' Anders agreed. He looked across at the portrait of Freya. 'And even less after she died.'

'Maybe there you have it then,' Catherine suggested. 'Not murder but not an accident either.'

'Suicide!' Anders shook his head. 'You don't understand,' he said. 'Hjalmar Jordahl never admitted defeat. In anything. And for him misery would have been just another challenge.'

Catherine moved over to the fireplace and looked up at the portrait. 'Did you ever meet her?' she asked.

'No. I vaguely remember seeing her in town a couple of times,' Anders replied. 'But then I was only sixteen when she died. And my family was right outside the kind of circle she moved in.'

Catherine turned to him. 'Well I'm afraid you're a long way off convincing me that there's anything in your theory, Mr Bjornson,' she said.

Anders shrugged. 'I'm not trying to convince you. Why should I? You're only visiting as I understand it.'

'Then why did you tell me about it?'

Anders crossed to her. 'You asked me what I was doing in the boathouse. And I couldn't think of a convincing enough lie,' he said disarmingly.

Catherine smiled. 'I wouldn't have thought you were that slow-witted.'

Anders held her look. 'Only when confronted by a beautiful woman,' he teased, returning her smile.

Wondering why this disconcerted her as much as it did, Catherine averted her eyes and, to the journalist's obvious amusement, moved away from him a little.

'Is it true that you'd never heard of Jordahl until just recently?' he asked. Catherine frowned and shot him a look. 'That's the story that's circulating,' he told her.

'My God! The local gossips picked that up incredibly quickly.'

'It's been going the rounds for a week or more.'

'Really!' Catherine exclaimed. 'That long? So who started it on its way I wonder.'

'My guess would be someone in lawyer Langva's office.'

Catherine sighed and shrugged resignedly. 'Well now I know how Maggie Thatcher feels about Cabinet leaks,' she muttered.

'Well? Is it true?'

'Yes. A month ago I was totally unaware of his existence.'

'So why did he leave you this place and the boatyard at Skorgenes?'

'Good question. But I can't help you with the answer because I honestly don't know why,' Catherine said. And then she added bitterly, 'But no doubt the members of the Alesund Ladies Guild or whatever have got it all worked out.'

'The favourite explanation is that he has to have been your father.'

Catherine stiffened. 'Of course. But he wasn't,' she said coldly.

Anders studied her again closely. 'Are you sure?' he asked quietly.

'Quite sure,' Catherine said, holding his gaze unflinchingly.

'Not that it matters,' Anders said.

'Only to me perhaps.'

Anders frowned. 'Yes of course. It might. I'm sorry.' He glanced at his watch. 'I must get back to the office.' He moved over to the door and Catherine followed him.

In the doorway Anders paused and looked at her. 'That's the second time I've had to apologise to you in less than half an hour,' he said with a grin. 'How about that for a bad start, eh?'

'Well I shouldn't let it worry you,' Catherine told him tartly. 'I very much doubt if Fate ever intended this to be a lasting relationship.'

She stood just outside the porch and watched him get into his car.

Anders turned the Fiat and drove up towards her and, as he drew level, rolled down his window. 'By the way, I'd be grateful if you didn't say anything to anyone about my theory,' he said.

'Why?' asked Catherine. 'Do you really think you have a chance of proving it?'

'No probably not,' he conceded. 'But I'll go on digging when and where I can. And it wouldn't help if what I was up to was common knowledge.'

Catherine shrugged. She could see no point in repeating what he'd said to the Nilsens or Anna Marie, anyway. There was nothing to be gained by her doing so; by anyone. 'Okay,' she said.

'Thanks.' Anders settled back behind the steering wheel. But then, as though suddenly inspired, he leaned out of the window once more. 'About my theory,' he said. 'There's something more to back it up. I was out here with Jordahl the night before he was drowned. Going over some old company records. And he could hardly move his right arm. Seems he'd pulled a muscle in his shoulder earlier in the day. It was causing him quite a bit of pain. Of course it could have cleared up by the following morning but I doubt it. So, with only one arm working properly, would you have gone out sailing in bad weather? Now that's something to think about, isn't it?'

And with that he let out the clutch, gave a wave and drove off.

There was no one at home when Catherine got back to the Nilsen house and let herself in with the key which Ingrid had given her before she left that morning. But going out onto the patio, she saw the Nilsens' motor cruiser approaching the jetty at the end of the garden and went down to meet it.

By the time she got there Ingrid was already in the bow of the boat, gathering up the mooring line.

'Hi,' called Catherine.

'Hi.' Ingrid's response was diffident and guarded.

'Here, I'll take that,' Catherine said, reaching out for the rope.

Ingrid threw it to her and while Catherine secured it she moved to the stern line. Stepping ashore with it, she looped it around a bollard.

'Just the day for a trip on the fjord,' Catherine said with a smile.

'I've only been into town,' Ingrid replied bleakly. 'When there is much traffic it is quicker by boat from here.'

Well, if you went in to do some shopping, thought Catherine, you didn't find anything you liked because you've come back empty handed. 'Pleasanter too, I'd say,' she said.

'Yes,' Ingrid agreed flatly. And then she enquired anxiously, 'Did you go to Jordahlsholmen again?'

'Yes. I've just got back.'

'And this time did you also visit the island?'

Catherine nodded. 'Just briefly.'

Side by side they walked slowly up toward the house. This has to be as good a time as any Catherine decided. 'Tell me something,' she said. 'According to Anna Marie no one's been to the island since your mother died but . . .'

Ingrid pulled up sharply. 'Yes. That's right,' she said. 'No one has, except the woman who cleans it.'

Catherine silently cursed herself for not having thought of that possibility. 'Of course,' she exclaimed. 'How stupid of me. I should have realised. Does she go across regularly?'

'Not every week I think. But often enough.'

Catherine laughed. 'Well that's that mystery solved then,' she said. And then she frowned. 'Only that still doesn't explain . . .' She broke off.

Ingrid looked at her blankly. 'Explain what?' she asked.

Catherine studied her. Perhaps she doesn't know how things are out there, she speculated. If what she says is right and she hasn't visited the island since Freya's suicide, then she almost certainly doesn't. Anna Marie either. And saying anything might just upset them. She shook her head. 'Nothing,' she said. 'It isn't important.' They walked on.

'The same woman still looks after the farmhouse too,' Ingrid told her. 'She is a good worker I understand. But perhaps you will want to make other arrangements from now on.'

'Oh, I don't think so,' Catherine said dismissively. 'Not if she's happy to go on doing it.'

They climbed up the steps onto the patio and once inside the sitting room Catherine glanced at the picture above the wood stove. Frowning, she crossed over to the painting for a closer look. 'Is it true you destroyed all your other pictures?' she asked casually, turning to Ingrid. 'Anna Marie said you made a bonfire of them.'

'Yes that's right. I did,' Ingrid said stiffly. 'Some time ago.'

'All of them?'

Uncomfortable, Ingrid nodded.

'That was a bit drastic, wasn't it?'

'I had the right!' Ingrid said, scowling and beginning to flare up. 'They were mine.'

Catherine smiled placatingly. 'Of course. Seems a pity though.'

Embarrassed, Ingrid reddened. 'No. I do not think so,' she stammered. 'They were not good. I found them . . . unacceptable.' And then, quickly changing the subject, she enquired, 'Would you like something to drink?'

'Well, a cup of tea would be nice,' Catherine replied. 'But only if you're having one.'

Ingrid nodded. 'I will bring it out onto the patio,' she said.

And when, a little while later, she reappeared carrying a tray with the tea things on it she seemed deeply preoccupied. She said nothing as she poured the tea, though, but as Catherine raised her cup to her lips and took a sip from it, she suddenly burst out, 'Catherine, will you sell Jordahlsholmen to me?'

Surprised by both the question and the urgency in it, Catherine lowered her cup. 'Well I don't know,' she said, nonplussed. 'I haven't really thought . . .'

'The property is of no use to you, is it?' Ingrid pleaded. 'And I will give you a very good price. More than it is worth even.'

'Oh no, I couldn't take . . .'

Ingrid ignored the protest. 'It's very important to me that it stays in the family,' she blurted. 'Of course, if you were going to live there, even for a little time each year, that would be all right. But since you're not . . .' She looked at Catherine beseechingly.

'Well that's unlikely, I admit,' Catherine said.

'So it could pass into the hands of strangers. And I would not want that,' Ingrid said desperately. 'It must not happen. So I want you to know that I will buy it from you for whatever you ask.'

She swung round in alarm at the sound of Lars' voice behind them. 'Hello! Anyone at home?' he called as, slipping his keys into his pocket, he advanced through the sitting room.

Ingrid put a hand on Catherine's arm. 'Think about it,' she whispered imploringly. 'And we will talk again. But say nothing to Lars about this. Or to Anna Marie. They would only think I was being foolish. Please!' she begged. 'Promise me.'

Mystified and bewildered, Catherine nodded. 'Okay. Sure,' she whispered back. 'I won't say a word.'

'Thank you,' Ingrid breathed.

'Ah! Tea!' Lars exclaimed as he walked out onto the patio. He smiled at Ingrid. 'You must have read my mind,' he said and, putting his arms around her, he kissed her on the mouth.

Ingrid froze. With a murmured protest in Norwegian, she twisted herself out of his embrace. She glanced guiltily at Catherine and then gave Lars a fleeting smile and took his hand and held on to it.

Lars smiled back at her encouragingly. 'Did you have a good day?' he asked Catherine.

'Well, an unusual one,' she said. 'And very interesting.'

'Good,' beamed Lars. 'So what did you finally decide with your sister about tonight?' he asked Ingrid.

There had been talk after the party about the three of them dining out that night with Anna Marie at her favourite restaurant but the arrangements had been left very fluid. 'She will be with us at seven o'clock,' Ingrid said. 'And then we will go on to the Keiser Wilhelm from here.'

'Fine,' said Lars. 'You will like the Keiser Wilhelm, I think,' he told Catherine, 'the food is excellent there.' And then, smiling at Ingrid, he went on, 'And it will be good for you to have an evening away from home.' He glanced at Catherine again. 'Persuading Ingrid to go out anywhere is not easy, believe me,' he joked.

Ingrid hung her head and Catherine noticed that her grip on Lars' hand tightened. 'Well you should take that as a compliment,' Catherine said smiling. 'Obviously she has everything she needs to make her happy right here.'

Seizing on this gratefully, Ingrid looked up. 'Yes, that's right,' she said fervently. 'You see! Catherine understands.' She turned to her. 'You do, don't you?' she pleaded.

Catherine nodded sympathetically. 'Of course,' she said, wishing that she did.

That night, as she was struggling with a zip at the back of her dress, there was a gentle tap on her bedroom door. It was Ingrid. 'Oh let me help you,' she said, standing in the doorway. She crossed quickly to the dressing table and drew up the fastener for her.

'Thanks,' said Catherine. 'I always have trouble with this dress.'

'So how do you manage when you are on your own?' Ingrid asked gravely.

'Happily,' Catherine told her, 'on the other occasions I've worn it I haven't been on my own.' She smiled. 'Getting in or out of it.'

'Oh, I see,' Ingrid said primly and blushing.

Catherine laughed. 'You're not shocked, are you?'

'Of course not,' Ingrid floundered. 'Someone as attractive as you are — I mean, I didn't imagine for a moment that . . .'

Catherine let her off the hook. 'Was there something you wanted?' she asked gently.

Ingrid shook her head. 'I only came to tell you that Anna Marie has just telephoned,' she said. 'She had a meeting that went on much longer than she thought it would so she will be late I'm afraid. But at least that means we do not have to hurry to get ready.'

'Right. But I'm almost there now though.' Catherine picked up a comb and ran it through her hair.

Ingrid made for the door. As she did so she saw the diptych standing on the bedside table and, going over to it, she picked it up and gazed at the photographs.

'That's my mother,' Catherine said, watching her in the

dressing-table mirror. 'She was still at school when the one on the left was taken.'

'She was beautiful,' Ingrid murmured admiringly, her eyes still on the photographs. 'Were you very close, the two of you?'

Catherine turned to her. 'Yes we were. More so because my father died when I was so young. And that's all we had then, each other.'

Replacing the diptych on the table, Ingrid sighed wistfully. 'It was different for me,' she said. 'I hardly knew my mother.'

Catherine frowned. 'Oh, why was that?'

'I never got the chance to really. Nor did Anna Marie,' she said quietly and staring into space. 'Neither of us did. He kept her away from us, you see.'

She gave Catherine a sorrowful look and then moved out onto the landing and closed the door.

Perplexed and moved, Catherine gazed after her.

The Keiser Wilhelm was crowded and prospective customers were being turned away when Catherine, Anna Marie and the Nilsens got there and, with great deference, were shown to the table that had been reserved for them. And their entrance caused a whispered stir among the other diners.

Glancing up from her menu, Catherine saw that two middle-aged couples at a table a little way off from them were staring brazenly at her. The women were quite clearly talking about her, and it was obvious that many other people in the restaurant were equally, although not quite so blatantly, interested in her. Catherine smiled wryly.

'What is it?' asked Anna Marie, who was sitting opposite her.

'We seem to be attracting a lot of attention,' Catherine said.

'Oh, really!' exclaimed Anna Marie, amused. She turned in her chair and smiled and waved at the two women who, shamefaced, smiled and waved back and then hastily got on with their meal.

'Alesund is only a small community,' Ingrid said. 'And yours is a new face. There is bound to be curiosity about who and what you are.'

Catherine laughed. 'According to Bjornson everyone in town knows who I am. And I gather they've also worked out what I am. To their satisfaction anyway.'

Lars and Ingrid exchanged glances and Anna Marie gave Catherine a questioning look. 'Bjornson?' she queried.

'Anders Bjornson. He told me he works on the local newspaper.'

'Ah! That Bjornson!' Anna Marie nodded. 'Yes, he is with the *Sunnmorsposten*.' And then she asked casually, 'Where did you meet him?'

'At Jordahlsholmen.'

Anna Marie frowned. 'What was he doing there?'

Catherine hesitated and reached for her glass of water. 'Fishing,' she said, congratulating herself on the cleverness of her lie.

'I hope you reminded him that it's private property,' Lars said.

'Yes I did,' Catherine told him.

'Good.'

'So have you made any plans?' Anna Marie asked her.

Catherine shook her head. 'No, not really,' she said. 'Apart from selling the boatyard that is.'

'And what about Jordahlsholmen?'

Catherine was aware that Ingrid, who was seated next to her, was regarding her anxiously. She shrugged. 'I haven't got around to thinking about that yet,' she said.

Relieved, Ingrid relaxed a little.

'I understand that Olav Tunheim is interested in buying the boatyard,' said Lars.

'Yes, and I've promised to consider his offer first. But it's going to take a couple of weeks or so for him to come up with it.'

'Well, that's good,' said Anna Marie with a smile.

'Because while you're waiting to hear from him it will give us a chance to get to know you better. And for you to explore the area a little.' She laughed. 'Who can tell? You may even decide to live here.'

'No, I don't think so,' said Catherine, joining in her laughter. 'I'm not sorry to be staying on for a while though.' She turned to Ingrid. 'But I really can't go on imposing on your hospitality,' she said. 'So tomorrow I thought I'd move into the farmhouse.'

Ingrid paled and shot an incredulous look at her. 'No, you mustn't,' she gasped. 'Please!'

Catherine stared at her in surprise. Anna Marie and Lars were equally taken aback. 'Why not,' enquired Anna Marie with a faintly reproving look, 'if that is what Catherine would like to do? There is everything there she will need to make her comfortable.'

'Yes, of course. I know that,' Ingrid retorted, confused and attempting to cover up her concern. 'But it is not necessary. We are very happy to have her staying with us.' She appealed to Lars. 'Aren't we?'

'Of course,' he said.

'And Catherine knows that,' Anna Marie assured her gently. 'But, just the same, she would perhaps prefer to be on her own. And since the house belongs to her . . .' She smiled at Catherine. 'That's a good idea.'

'I wouldn't want you to think I'm ungrateful,' Catherine said, glancing in turn at the Nilsens. 'But I really do feel that it would be best all round.'

'Well, of course, if that's so,' Ingrid allowed grudgingly. 'It's just that . . .' She shrugged and reached for the water jug.

'And if it doesn't work out, or you get bored, well you know you're always welcome,' said Lars, retreating behind his menu.

'Well, that's decided then,' murmured Anna Marie. Then giving her menu a cursory look, she asked Catherine, 'What are you going to have? I can recommend the beef. That's always good here.'

But Catherine wasn't listening. She was reliving Ingrid's despairing reaction to her news and wondering why it had had such an unexpected and unsettling effect on her. If she never lived there, why does she feel so deeply about Jordahlsholmen she pondered. And why is she so anxious to buy it from me? And at any price!

She glanced at Ingrid. Staring down at the tablecloth, she had her hands clasped firmly together in her lap in a vain effort to stop them trembling.

Chapter Eight

When Catherine came down to breakfast the next morning Ingrid handed her a letter. 'This has just arrived,' she said.

Catherine looked at the envelope. Her name and the address were written in an unsteady hand and she was surprised to find that it had been posted locally.

'Coffee?' enquired Ingrid, watching her reaction to the letter closely.

'Yes, thanks,' Catherine said and, sitting at the table, she slit open the envelope.

'When will you be leaving us today?' Ingrid asked as she filled her cup.

'Some time this morning I thought. If that's okay.'

'I wish you would change your mind,' pleaded Ingrid, but without any of the depth of concern which she'd shown at the Keiser Wilhelm. 'You will be so alone at Jordahlsholmen.'

'No, I'll be fine. Honestly,' Catherine told her, relieved that Ingrid seemed reconciled to the idea now. 'And it's not that far away. So I can soon pop back here for a chat from time to time, can't I?'

She unfolded the single-page of the letter and read it.

'*Dear Miss Durrell*,' it ran. '*I would be pleased to see you at my home for tea this Friday. I shall expect you at four o'clock and you need only telephone me if this day and time are not convenient for you.*

Sincerely yours, Astrid Linderman.'

The embossed address at the top of the letter bore the name of a street on the outskirts of Alesund which

Catherine remembered seeing on the street plan she'd bought.

'Does the name Astrid Linderman mean anything to you?' she asked, looking up at Ingrid.

Ingrid nodded. 'Yes. She is our great-aunt. My mother's aunt.'

'She wasn't at the party the other night, was she?'

'No,' Ingrid said evasively. 'We see very little of her nowadays. She is quite old and she seldom leaves the house.'

'She wants me to have tea with her,' Catherine told her. And then, suddenly realising what day it was, she added, 'Today!'

Ingrid made a moue. 'She has obviously heard of your arrival and wishes to meet you. My father's will will have surprised her as much as it did us. Will you go?' she asked.

'Be a bit rude not to, wouldn't it?'

Ingrid shrugged. 'You could telephone her and say that you are very busy. Or I will do it for you if you like. I'm sure she would understand.'

'Oh no, I couldn't do that,' Catherine protested. 'Besides I'd like to meet her. And I've nothing else on.' She re-read the letter and then looked up again. 'She writes very good English.'

'She was a teacher once,' Ingrid said.

Catherine regarded her searchingly. 'You didn't tell me you had a great-aunt living here in Alesund.'

Ingrid reached for the butter. 'Didn't I?' she said flatly.

After breakfast Catherine went up to her room and put on a simple blue dress which she thought would be suitable for her meeting with Astrid Linderman later in the day. There seemed little point in going out to Jordahlsholmen only to come all the way back for her four o'clock appointment. Besides, she needed to cash some travellers cheques and she would have to buy some food to take with her to the farmhouse, so she had decided to spend the day in Alesund.

She packed her suitcases and put them in her car. Then she kissed Ingrid, thanked her again for everything, and, having assured her yet again that she would be fine on her own, drove into town.

It was as she was leaving the bank and putting the bundle of notes she'd just been given into her handbag that she literally ran into Anders Bjornson. Crossing to the exit without looking where she was going, she collided with him as he stepped out of a lift. Mumbling an apology she looked up. He was smiling at her. 'Hello,' he said.

'Oh, hello,' she responded guardedly, but at the same time unexpectedly glad to see him again.

'How are you today?' he asked.

'Only slightly less confused.'

Anders pulled a wry face. 'I didn't help with that theory of mine I'm afraid.'

Catherine shook her head. 'Even if you're right about that and, in spite of everything you said, I still don't think you are, it's really none of my concern, is it? Unless you suspect me of course.'

'No, you're the one person definitely in the clear,' Anders said with a smile.

'Are you on your way in or out?' Catherine enquired.

'Out. I'm going to have some coffee.' Anders hesitated, gauging his chances. 'Join me?' he asked.

Catherine studied him interestedly and debated in her mind whether or not to accept his invitation. She nodded. 'Yes. Okay. Thanks.' she said.

At Anders' suggestion they drove up to the Fjellstua, a small café on top of one of the mountains overlooking the town. While he went inside to get the coffee Catherine stood on the terrace and admired the panoramic view.

The whole of Alesund was spread out beneath her and, in the bright sunlight and crystal-clear air, it was a breath-taking sight. Way out beyond the harbour she could see the islands which she'd passed when she had arrived on the *Kong Olav*, and she felt that she had only to reach out a hand to touch them. As she gazed, she saw a plane taking off from the airport behind the hills on the largest of them.

And all around were range upon range of snow-tipped mountains stretching away into the distance. From one side of the terrace she could see almost to the end of the fjord along which she had driven that first day with Lars and Ingrid and, from the other, another vast expanse of water bordered by hills which she tried to name from her memory of the map she'd bought, but couldn't. She was studying the coastline of this fjord through a coin-in-the-slot telescope when Anders came out of the café carrying their coffee.

'What a fantastic view you get from here!' Catherine exclaimed as she joined him at a table and sat down.

Anders handed her a coffee and took the seat opposite her. 'You're impressed?'

'Very,' Catherine told him enthusiastically. 'It's stunning. Are you from Alesund?' she asked.

'Yes.'

'And are you planning on staying?'

Anders shrugged. 'Today, tomorrow, next week, next month. That long at least. I haven't made any plans beyond then though.' He grinned. 'For me, doing that's like looking through that telescope. The view's too narrow and you get the perspective all wrong. Are you a great planner?'

'Yes, I suppose I am,' Catherine admitted. 'But then I like to know where I'm going.'

'I'd rather just arrive hopefully, having enjoyed the trip,' said Anders.

'You're not ambitious then?'

'Yes, reasonably. But, like with planning, I think it's best to keep ambition to a timescale you're more likely to have some control over. Beyond that, well I'm all for surprises.' He leant back in his seat and glanced around the terrace.

Catherine picked up her cup and, sipping her coffee, studied him again. But when he looked back at her she lowered her eyes. 'I've been thinking about you,' he said.

'And about this will business. And I've decided that your family has to have had some connection with Hjalmar Jordahl. Way back in the past perhaps.'

Catherine shook her head. 'None whatever. I've been into that.'

'But that's the only possible explanation for his having put you in it. Other than that . . .'

Catherine put her cup down with a clatter. 'I'm his bastard child,' she said scathingly, without letting him finish.

Anders gave her a searching look. 'And you've discounted that possibility, you said.'

Catherine hesitated. If only I had, if only I could, she thought. But however forceful were the arguments that she had been able to put up against that being so, she had still not entirely convinced herself that it wasn't the answer. And since her arrival in Alesund she'd become even less certain. But she wasn't ready to admit that yet. 'Yes,' she said firmly. 'Totally.'

'So what's the answer then?'

'God knows!' said Catherine, wishing he'd drop the subject.

And as if he'd read her mind, Anders didn't pursue it any further. 'You're staying with the Nilsens I understand?'

'Yes. Well, at least I was until today,' Catherine said. 'I'm moving into the farmhouse this afternoon.'

Anders looked surprised. 'It won't bother you, living way out there?'

'No, not a bit. I shall enjoy it.'

'Well, I'd certainly want to take up residence if I were in your shoes,' Anders agreed. 'But then I'm not a great one for towns. And I'm even less keen on suburbs.' He sipped his coffee. 'Are you going to stay out there permanently?'

'No, I just want to play lady of the manor for a while. I've never owned sixty acres before. And I don't suppose I will for long.'

'You're going to sell everything?'

Catherine nodded. 'Probably. The boatyard's as good as sold and I've already got one potential buyer for Jordahlsholmen. But for the next two or three weeks I'm going to have it all to myself.'

Anders gave her a concerned look. 'Do you swim?' he asked.

'Just about. Why?'

'Well if you're not a good swimmer stay out of the channel between the farmhouse and the island,' he warned her. 'At times there's a very strong current running through there and if you got caught up in it you could be in serious trouble very quickly.'

'Thanks,' said Catherine gratefully. 'I'll remember that.'

'Yes, do. Please.'

Catherine drank some more of her coffee and then enquired, 'Have you ever been out to the island?'

'No, never.'

'That house on it.' And remembering it, Catherine shook her head in bewilderment. 'It's very strange. Eerie in a way,' she said.

'Oh! In what way?' Anders asked interestedly.

'Well, when you walk into it it's as though someone's still living there. My guess is that everything's been left exactly the way it was the day Freya Jordahl committed suicide.'

Anders nodded thoughtfully. 'I can believe it,' he said. 'Jordahl adored his wife. So maybe after what happened, for him, that house became a sort of shrine to her memory. To be left unchanged and undisturbed. Have you asked Anna Marie or Ingrid about it?'

'No. In different ways they both seem to have quite a hang-up about the place so I haven't liked to mention it.'

'So what are you going to do?'

Catherine shrugged. 'Leave it just as it is I suppose. And hand that problem on to whoever buys it.' And then she added, 'Unless Freya claims it back first of course.' Anders looked at her in astonishment and she laughed, 'I'm only joking,' she assured him. 'It's just that when I was coming up here from Bergen on the coastal steamer there was this woman on board. I only saw her briefly, standing at the end of the corridor staring at me. And the next time I saw her was when I first saw that portrait of Freya Jordahl in the farmhouse. The likeness was uncanny.'

'Oh, I see,' said Anders, laughing.

And then they talked of other things and the more they talked the more Catherine was surprised to find how much she was drawn to this man whom she had only met twenty-four hours earlier; and then rather inauspiciously. And whilst she welcomed his company her feelings confused her. Worried her a little, even. Although she couldn't imagine why.

When at last she glanced at her watch she was surprised to find that nearly two hours had passed since they had left the bank. 'Here, I've got to go!' she exclaimed, gathering up her handbag. 'I've got some shopping to do.' They stood up. 'Thanks for the coffee,' she said.

Anders smiled. 'I'm glad you ran into me,' he said.

'So am I,' she told him.

Side by side they walked across the terrace. At the entrance Anders paused and turned to her. 'Do you like sailing?' he asked.

'Very much,' said Catherine.

'Then will you come out with me some time?'

Catherine regarded him a little uncertainly. 'With just you or with you and that theory of yours?' she asked with a smile.

'Just me,' he promised.

The idea appealed to Catherine. And why not, she thought. 'Yes. Okay,' she said. 'When?'

'This Sunday? I could bring the boat down to Jordahls-holmen and pick you up there. We'll make a day of it.'

'That sounds as if it might be fun,' Catherine said. She nodded. 'Fine. Sunday then.' And then she added with a grin, 'But no mysteries. Right?'

Astrid Linderman's house stood well back from the road

in the middle of a garden that was hemmed with tall trees. It was solid looking and, compared with the houses on either side of it, old fashioned. A flight of stone steps set between two lace-curtained bay windows led up to a porch of stained glass. And, at either end of the roof, there were small towers with green-tiled spires.

Catherine parked her car in the drive, climbed the steps and rang the doorbell. After a while the front door opened and a squat, grey-haired, muscular-looking woman stepped into the porch, opened the outer door and gazed at her dourly.

Catherine gave her her name and the woman grunted in response, then led her down a gloomy passageway and into a drawing room where, without a word, she left her, closing the door again.

Catherine looked around the room. It was large. And it needed to be in order to accommodate all the weighty and heavily carved pieces of late nineteenth-century furniture it contained. The bay window overlooking the drive was enclosed within long velvet curtains and a pelmet of the same material, and on one side of the room open french windows gave onto the garden.

The most remarkable thing about the room, though, was the number of framed photographs in it. They were hanging in rows on the walls, crowded together on tables and lined up in ranks along a sideboard. Almost all of them were head and shoulder portraits of girls, none of whom looked older than eighteen or nineteen or much younger than eleven. And as Catherine moved fascinated among them she saw that the lower shelves of an ornate mahogany bookcase were filled with bulging photograph albums.

She was studying the rows of pictures on the wall alongside the bookcase when the door opened and the woman who'd admitted her wheeled Astrid Linderman into the room. The wheelchair, together with the old woman's general appearance, came as a shock to Catherine.

Her hair was white, her skin like pallid, veined parchment. While there was a positive, almost aggressive, set to her thin-lipped mouth and angular jaw, her face was gaunt and drawn, and her intelligent, piercing eyes, which were fixed on her visitor, had an unnatural brightness to them. Lying across her lap was an ebony walking stick with a silver handle.

With her eyes still on Catherine, Astrid jerked her head in dismissal and the servant withdrew, closing the door behind her.

Catherine gave her a faint, awkward smile. 'Hello,' she said.

'How old am I?' Astrid demanded in a surprisingly strong voice.

'I'm sorry,' Catherine stammered, confused and taken aback.

'How old am I?' repeated Astrid. 'And I want the truth. Not a polite lie. And I'll know if it is.' She sighed impatiently. 'Well, come on!'

Unnerved and embarrassed, Catherine shrugged. 'I'm not very good at guessing anyone's age I'm afraid, Miss Linderman,' she said.

Irritated, Astrid shook her head. 'No. Astrid, I think,' she said tetchily. 'You shall call me Astrid.'

'Oh, thank you,' Catherine murmured, chastened.

'Well?' Astrid persevered. 'Say what you see.'

Catherine ventured a guess. 'Seventy-six, seventy-seven?' she suggested tentatively.

Astrid let out a bitter, triumphant laugh. 'I knew it!' she cried. 'That fool Albrigtsen told me this morning that I was looking better. So much for doctors! I shall be seventy in four months.' She put out her right hand and smiled warmly. 'I'm so glad to meet you, my dear.'

Bemused but relieved and captivated, Catherine returned her smile and took her hand. 'I'm delighted to be here,' she said.

'And of course you don't like to ask what's wrong with me. You're far too polite for that. Well I'll tell you. It's arthritis. At its worst in my hips but now it's starting to get into my hands.' Astrid raised her other hand and Catherine saw in it the unmistakable signs of the crippling disease.

'I'm sorry,' she said sympathetically.

'So am I,' Astrid said, removing her good hand from Catherine's hold on it. 'Very sorry. It is extremely painful at times.' And then she asked brightly, 'Do you like this house?'

Again Catherine was taken off-guard and again she stammered. 'Yes, it's very nice.'

'And what do you think of this room?' Astrid's eyes were fixed on Catherine's face again.

Catherine looked around, desperately trying to come up with a reasonably honest description, one which wouldn't offend. Astrid didn't wait for her. 'It's hideous, isn't it?' she said scornfully. 'Most of this furniture belonged to my parents and it's worth a great deal of money I'm told.' She chuckled. 'That's the only reason I hold onto it. Not because it's valuable, you understand. Simply because I get a great deal of perverse pleasure out of refusing to sell it to all the greedy dealers who regularly call on me. And, in my condition, pleasure of any kind is in rather short supply, believe me.' She indicated a nearby armchair. 'Do sit down, please.' And once Catherine was seated she went on, 'It was Dr Albrigtsen who told me you were here in Alesund. Not that he needed to. I had already heard that you had arrived.' She smiled. 'You were looking at my photographs?'

Catherine nodded. 'Yes,' she said. 'You've got so many!'

Astrid gazed lovingly around the room at her collection. 'I have one of almost all the children I taught throughout my career. And certainly one of each of my girls when I was a head teacher. Stupid of me, isn't it?'

'Oh, I don't know. We're back to pleasure again, aren't we?' Catherine said quietly.

'Exactly!' Astrid exclaimed delightedly. She studied her closely and then smiled once more. 'Oh, I knew I'd like you.' Her smile faded. 'But I'm going to be a big disappointment to you, I'm afraid. Because you came here hoping to learn something from me, didn't you?'

Catherine nodded. 'Well, partly for that reason,' she said. She looked questioningly at her. 'You can't help me?'

Astrid gave her a regretful look and shook her head. 'Unfortunately I can tell you nothing more about your inheritance than you know already. When Hjalmar's will was read no one was more astonished than I was, I assure you. So, sadly, if information is all you came for . . .'

'I said it was partly the reason,' Catherine reminded her with a reproving look. 'You asked me to tea, remember?'

Astrid nodded enthusiastically. 'Good!' she said. 'Yes, indeed I did.'

There was a knock on the door and the servant entered and stood just inside the room. As Astrid glanced at her, the woman nodded. 'And it is ready,' Astrid announced. She braked the wheelchair, shifted herself forward in it and stretched out her clawed hand to Catherine. 'Give me your arm,' she demanded. 'I told Gerda we would have tea in the garden and I would like to walk to the table with you.'

Catherine helped her out of the chair and then supported her as, with the ebony stick in her other hand, Astrid shuffled painfully and stiffly toward the french windows and out into the garden. With Gerda pushing the wheelchair just behind them, they made their way slowly along a path that led to the rear of the house and over to where a table had been laid for tea in the shade of a silver birch.

Catherine settled Astrid into the wheelchair and sat down at the table facing her. Gerda poured tea for them and then, having double checked that everything she'd prepared for the meal was to hand, went back into the house again.

It was a warm afternoon and Catherine found it very pleasant sitting in the dappled shade beneath the tree. As they ate and drank, Astrid questioned her about her life in England but, in turn, revealed very little about Hjalmar Jordahl that Catherine hadn't learnt already.

'Tell me about Freya,' Catherine said at last.

Astrid frowned and stared down at her plate. Then, raising her head again, she smiled and said, 'I more or less adopted her you know.'

'Oh, really!' Catherine said, surprised.

Astrid nodded. 'My sister and her husband were killed when Trondheim was bombed in 1940,' she said. 'Freya was only a baby then. Just about a year old. So after the funeral I took her back to Oslo with me. And I looked after her from then on.' And, remembering, she stared distantly into space and then added wistfully, 'To the end.'

With an effort and a fleeting, apologetic smile she snapped out of her reverie and sipped her tea.

'That can't have been easy,' Catherine said quietly.

Astrid sighed. 'No. At times it wasn't. But she was a good child. She gave me hardly any trouble when she was growing up. And she did very well at school. I still have all her exercise books. And every one of her school reports.' Again she was momentarily lost in thought. 'She was an excellent student,' she said distantly. 'She really was.' And, putting her cup down again, she continued, 'And she was such a talented artist.'

Catherine looked at her quizzically.

'She painted,' Astrid said. 'That's what she was studying when she met Jordahl.'

'Oh, really?' exclaimed Catherine. 'So that's where her daughter gets it from. Her style too, perhaps?' Astrid regarded her blankly. 'Ingrid,' Catherine explained. 'She paints too, doesn't she?'

'Ah, yes,' Astrid said dully and clearly unimpressed. 'But Freya was really exceptionally gifted.'

So that's the answer then is it, Catherine thought. Those canvases I ound in the cellar are some of Freya's work. 'Do you have any of her pictures?' she asked.

Briefly Astrid looked flustered. She frowned and hesitated before replying. She shook her head. 'Sadly no,' she said. 'She did very little painting after she was married. And none of the pictures she did at art school ever satisfied her. So she gave them away.' She smiled. 'To people who didn't know any better according to her.' Catherine laughed politely. 'You have been to the island of course,' Astrid said, looking at her intently.

'Yes.'

'And into the house?'

Catherine nodded. 'Yes.'

'And were you surprised?'

'Very,' Catherine said. She frowned. Was this the explanation then? 'You know about that?' she asked.

'Of course,' Astrid told her. 'I was the one who laid everything out the way it is. Hjalmar asked me to. As a last favour to him. So before I left . . .'

'You were living there?' Catherine broke in.

Astrid nodded. 'With Freya.'

'And were you there when . . .?' Catherine left the question hanging in mid air.

'Yes,' Astrid said, wincing.

Catherine regarded her sympathetically. 'I'm sorry. That was thoughtless of me. I shouldn't have . . .'

'She had been ill, you know,' Astrid said, waving away her apology. 'For quite a long time.'

'So I gather.'

Astrid sighed deeply. 'Clever, artistic people,' she said. 'I do so envy them. But I pity them too. Life is often just too much for them, isn't it?'

Catherine studied her thoughtfully. 'And all those dolls. Were they Freya's?' she asked.

'Yes. She collected them.' Astrid smiled. 'Some of them are lovely, aren't they?' Again she seemed to drift away into the past. 'Not that they were any comfort to her though.'

Her eyelids drooped and slowly her chin sagged forward onto her chest. Catherine looked at her in alarm and was on the point of running into the house to find Gerda when, getting up from her chair and moving close to Astrid, she saw that she had merely fallen asleep.

Not wishing to disturb her but uncertain as to what she should do, Catherine resumed her seat.

Ten minutes or more passed with the only sounds those of Astrid's steady breathing and the drone of the bees plundering a nearby flowerbed. Then, as Catherine was deliberating whether or not she should leave a note and just tiptoe away, Astrid opened her eyes again and looked around, getting her bearings. She glanced across at Catherine and smiled wanly. 'Forgive me,' she said. 'But these days I snatch moments of sleep whenever the pain allows me to.'

'Of course. I understand,' Catherine assured her. 'In any case it's time I was going I think.'

Astrid nodded. 'Shall I wheel you back into the house?' Catherine asked.

'No. I'll stay here for a while,' Astrid said. 'Gerda will do that by and by.'

Catherine stood up. 'Thank you for inviting me. And for the tea.'

'I'm only sorry I couldn't help you,' sighed Astrid.

'Oh but you have. Quite a lot,' Catherine said, thinking about the canvases.

'How long are you staying in Alesund?' Astrid asked her.

'I'm not sure. But two or three weeks at least.'

'Good.' Astrid smiled. 'Then come and see me again if you have time.' And then she added. 'And should you need a friend while you are here, look on me as one.'

Catherine held her gaze. 'Yes, thank you.' she said. 'I will. Goodbye.'

She put out her hand. Astrid took it and held on to it. 'And do not trouble yourself greatly over Hjalmar Jordahl's motive,' she begged earnestly. 'Whatever his reason was for naming you in his will, accept that it was good enough. For him and for you.'

Catherine smiled wryly. 'I'm going to have to,' she said.

Astrid released her hand and watched her move away from the table and across the lawn. 'Do you know why

Hjalmar wanted Freya's house left the way it is?' she called after her.

Catherine stopped and looked back. 'As some kind of memorial I imagine.'

Astrid shook her head. 'It was because he could never really accept that she was dead,' she said. 'He loved her so much you see. And, poor man, he was quite sure that one day she would want to come back there.'

Catherine frowned and then, with a half-smile, turned and walked on. At the end of the path, though, she paused and looked back once more. Astrid Linderman was sitting hunched in her wheelchair lost in memories again.

When Catherine arrived at the farmhouse she unpacked the car and carried the box of groceries she'd bought into the kitchen. Then, going down into the cellar, she pulled the six canvases out from beside the packing case and examined them again.

There was no question that the artist's style was almost identical to that of Ingrid Nilsen. And the increasing frenzy and dementia in each of the paintings was even more apparent now.

Dr Albrigtsen had said that Freya had been ill for months before she killed herself. And this had been confirmed by Astrid who had also hinted that her illness had been some kind of mental disturbance. Catherine sighed and shook her head. 'You poor thing!' she murmured out loud. 'How sad. And how wretched you must have been.'

Leaving the canvases face down on top of the cabin trunk where she'd laid them, she retraced her steps and, going into the sitting room, gazed at Freya's portrait. She sighed again and then picked up her suitcases and took them upstairs.

It was close to midnight and as dark outside as it was going to get when Catherine finally went to bed. She had thoroughly explored the house and got everything organised more or less the way she wanted it to be. And she had greatly enjoyed the simple meal she had prepared for herself. Tomorrow, she promised herself, I'll try something more ambitious, and I must take a trip out and see what shops there are locally.

She undressed and turned back the duvet on the bed. Then, crossing to the bedroom window, she reached for the curtain and began to close it.

Glancing out into the summer night she froze with shock.

She had a clear view of the island and what she saw sent a sudden shiver down her spine. She felt the sweat breaking out on her forehead and she could hear her heart pounding.

There was a light on in the sitting room of Freya's house and a woman was standing at the top of the steps up from the beach. Even at that distance and in the twilight between sunset and sunrise there was no doubt whatever in Catherine's mind as to who she was. And if she had needed any confirmation the white dress the figure was wearing was enough. Catherine had seen it before. It was identical to the one in the portrait hanging downstairs in the sitting room.

The woman was Freya Jordahl. And she was staring across at the farmhouse.

Chapter Nine

As her initial shock and fear gave way to bewilderment and angry curiosity, Catherine swung round from the window and ran to the wardrobe. I don't believe in ghosts she reminded herself, hurriedly putting on a blouse and jeans and then slipping her feet into a pair of sneakers. 'Besides ghosts don't need electric light to see by,' she muttered.

She ran down the stairs two at a time and, deviating only to snatch up the bunch of keys which she'd left on top of the desk, raced out through the porch.

In the drive she paused and looked across at the island.

The woman had gone but the sitting-room light was still on and Catherine saw now that the front door of the house was half open.

Sprinting to the boathouse, she cast off the dinghy, jumped down into it and started the motor. The bow of the boat lifted as, once clear of the landing stage, she gave the outboard full throttle, both for speed and also to compensate for the powerful current that threatened to sweep the dinghy off course. Steering across it, Catherine recalled Anders Bjornson's warning.

It was when she was halfway across the channel that she heard the music and recognised the tune as the waltz which she had found on the old record player during her first visit. And, hearing it again, melancholic and evocative, getting louder and louder as she approached, she shuddered. 'Bloody nerve,' she growled, bolstering her resolve.

When she reached the island and scrambled ashore she looked around for another boat but couldn't see one anywhere. Securing the dinghy, she cautiously made for the house. Outside the front door she hesitated and looked up at the bedroom windows. They were all in darkness. Summoning up her reserves of determination and courage she pushed the door open further and stepped into the sitting room.

Her eyes widened and her mouth fell open in astonishment.

A child's tea service had been neatly set out on the coffee table. And sitting on the floor around it and packed onto the settee and into the armchairs which had been drawn up close to it were all the dolls from the room upstairs.

Catherine stared incredulously at the bizarre party, taking in every detail of it, and then she shot a worried glance up into the gloom at the top of the stairs.

The music from the record player was almost deafening now that she was inside the house. She moved quickly across the room and switched it off. In the welcome silence, broken only by the ticking of the grandmother clock, she listened for any sound of movement from either the kitchen or dining room or from the floor above. There was none.

She shouted and the sound of her own voice made her start. 'Who are you?' she demanded. 'What are you doing here?'

She listened again. Nothing, just the ticking of the clock.

Going to the foot of the stairs she peered up them. Then, switching on the light on the landing and encouraged by it, she climbed them warily.

At the head of the stairs she paused and looked around. The doors of all the upper rooms were closed. Resolutely she threw open the one to Freya's bedroom and, after reaching in and turning on the light, swung round the door frame into it. Her reaction was a mixture of frustration and relief when she found there was no one there. What's more nothing had been disturbed; the room was exactly the same as she had last seen it.

Moving back out onto the landing she realised that she

was trembling slightly and that her hands were clammy with sweat.

She called out again. 'Come on out! I know you're here somewhere.' And even as she said it she knew that she was making a complete and utter fool of herself. She had assumed that the woman was in the house but she could be anywhere on the island. She could have dodged in among the trees and even now be standing outside listening to Catherine's shouted challenges and laughing at her. Or when she had seen the dinghy approaching she might have run back to her own boat and be well clear of the island by now.

But that didn't make any sense either, Catherine decided. Not if the woman she'd seen *was* Freya Jordahl. Why should she hide? Why should she run? This is her house. But then it can't have been her, can it, she reasoned, her mind racing. Freya's dead. Her double then, she argued, remembering the woman on the coastal steamer. But wearing the same white dress that Freya had worn to have her portrait painted? That was too much of a coincidence. And it was Freya's music that had been playing and they're Freya's dolls downstairs, she told herself.

She moved down the corridor and tried the door at the end of it. It was still locked. Then, wondering why she'd left it until last, she went to the door of the second bedroom and, putting her ear up close to it, listened intently. Reassured, she opened it and flicked on the light.

There was no one in there either but, gazing around the room, Catherine saw that not all the dolls were at the tea party. One of the more modern ones, a girl with hair much the same colour as her own and, unlike the others, dressed in grown-up clothes, was sitting facing the wall on a stool in the far corner of the room as though in disgrace.

Puzzled, Catherine walked over to the doll and picked it up and, as she turned it towards her, she started violently when she saw the tears that were dribbling out of the corners of its eyes and running down its cheeks.

She stared in horror at the doll with its round, pink china face and staring blue eyes and its grotesque simulation of sorrow. When she tilted it backward a little it let out a tinny cry of despair.

Terrified, Catherine dropped the doll, stood transfixed for a moment and then, with a half sob, half scream, ran from the room, down the stairs and out of the house.

And she didn't stop running until she reached the beach.

Urgently she pushed the boat out into the water and, splashing through the shallows, climbed headlong into it. The outboard fired with her first pull on the starter and with a sigh of relief Catherine settled in the stern.

Fifty yards off from the island the motor faltered and died and the boat, now at the mercy of the current, immediately started to drift sideways.

Catherine frowned and swore silently. She thought she had turned the fuel on but obviously, in her panic, she couldn't have done. Swinging round over the transom she fumbled for the tap and to her alarm saw that the plastic fuel lead was no longer connected to the carburettor. When she checked the fuel tank she found that it was empty.

By now the dinghy was beginning to spin leisurely but ominously as it was carried down the channel. Puzzled and deeply worried, Catherine grabbed for the oars which were stowed under the thwarts. And as she slotted them into the rowlocks she saw the motor cruiser.

It was coming around from the far side of the island and moving fast. Catherine was surprised to see that it was showing no lights. What's more, with the canvas hood down over the aft cockpit, it was impossible to tell how many people were on board.

For a moment Catherine wondered if she should try to attract the attention of whoever was at the wheel of the cruiser but then decided there was no need for her to; she was in mid-channel so she hadn't far to go to the boat-house and even allowing for the pull of the current she reckoned that she could make it easily enough with the oars.

She straightened the boat and began to row, only to find that it was a lot harder than she had thought it was going to be. It was difficult enough keeping the dinghy on a level course. She had already been swept some distance down from the farmhouse and for every foot she gained so she moved further and further sideways.

Catherine glanced over at the motor cruiser again and, to her horror, saw that it had altered course and that it was now bearing down on her. She shipped the oars and waved her arms above her head. 'Hey! Hey!' she shouted. 'Watch it! Hey there!'

But this had no effect. Not only did the motorboat not change its heading but it accelerated and when Catherine, snatching up the oars again and pulling on them desperately, managed to manoeuvre the dinghy just clear of its path, its bow swung inexorably in on her.

Terrified, Catherine stood up and waved frantically. 'You bloody fool!' she yelled at the top of her voice. 'Get over! For God's sake! Get over!'

Mesmerised, she watched the cruiser closing on her. Seconds later it struck the dinghy amidships and, as it splintered and capsized under the impact, she was catapulted into the fjord.

Kicking her legs and thrashing her arms wildly she was buffeted down the length of the cruiser and only narrowly escaped being struck by its propeller. She opened her mouth to scream and it filled with water.

Twice she was dragged under in the cruiser's wake and, weighed down by her clothes, she was certain that she was going to drown. Coming up for the second time, though, coughing and gasping for air, she trod water furiously. Seeing an oar drifting past her, she lunged for it and grabbed it.

By now the cruiser was some distance away and swinging around behind the island again. Hanging onto the oar and just managing to keep her head above water, Catherine looked around but she could see no sign of the dinghy and she realised that, stove in on one side and waterlogged, it would have sunk almost immediately.

When she had told Anders that she could just about swim Catherine had not been minimising her ability. It was a fact. In a normal public swimming pool the most she could manage was a couple of lengths with a steady but not very powerful and inelegant breast stroke. And all things being equal she might, just might, be able to reach the shore. But with the current that was running, and trapped and helpless in the grip of it, she knew that she hadn't a chance of making it. All that she could do was to hang onto the oar and pray.

So, trapping it under her armpits and endeavouring to keep her face clear of the water, she stopped struggling and let the current carry her out of the channel and down the fjord.

An hour later, chilled to the bone by the icy, glacier-fed water in the deeper parts of the fjord, her body aching from a dozen bruises, her lungs half filled, and more tired than she had ever been, Catherine was close to passing out. Her arms seemed like lead weights, and she had no feeling in them. Several times her head had drooped forward over the oar into the water and only the frigid shock to her face had jerked her back from sleep.

She had been swept several miles down the fjord and the current, although not nearly so strong now, was still carrying her along. She had given up any hope that she would be spotted by a passing boat and picked up. There were no boats out that early in the day. The fjord was empty and, as far as she could see, there wasn't even any traffic on the road which ran beside it.

Close to giving up, she managed all the same to lift her head once more. What she saw through a haze of exhaustion gave her some heart and spurred her into making a final effort.

The dying current was taking her towards a narrow spit of land that ran into the fjord ahead and to her left. It would, in fact, bear her around the tip of it unless, once she was close enough, she could break free of the flow. Then, still supported by the oar, she might just be able to propel herself to the shore.

She waited until she was almost level with the promontory and then began to kick with her legs once more. At first they didn't respond. Wincing with the pain, she persevered, willing them into movement, and slowly she achieved sufficient power and rhythm to drive herself forward and out of the grip of the current. And with each kick she steadily narrowed the gap between her and safety.

Reaching the shallows of a small bay, she discarded the oar and tried to stand up but her legs wouldn't support her and she pitched forward into the water again. Sobbing with relief, and in even greater pain now as full circulation was restored to her limbs and body, she dragged herself up onto a narrow strip of sand.

Catherine lay there for what seemed a very long time but she refused to allow herself the luxury of the sleep that she felt in such desperate need of. At last, forcing herself first up onto her knees and then hauling herself upright, she staggered drunkenly up the heavily wooded slope and towards the road.

Once there, she stumbled across to a pile of fencing posts that had been left on the verge. Gratefully, she sank down onto it, sitting first, but then toppling sideways to stretch herself out full length along the posts. On the brink of sleep, she closed her eyes, only to open them again almost immediately as she heard a vehicle approaching.

She sat up and looked down the road. It was a pick-up truck. Tottering across the road she waved it down.

The driver, a middle-aged man wearing overalls and a light jacket, gazed at her from the cab in astonishment. Catherine opened the nearside door. 'Can you . . .?' she gasped weakly. 'Can you take me to . . .?' She retched and brought up some of the water she'd swallowed. The man continued to stare at her in total and now somewhat wary disbelief. She tried again. 'English. Do you speak English?'

she asked, but it was clear from his expression that he didn't. 'Jordahlsholmen,' she exhorted, enunciating the word carefully. 'Do you know Jordahlsholmen?'

The name registered with him and, recovering a little from his surprise and suspicion, he nodded and beckoned her into the cab.

Catherine slumped into the seat beside him as he said something to her in Norwegian. Seeing that she didn't understand, he made swimming movements with his arms. Catherine nodded. Slipping off his jacket the driver draped it over her, turned the heater on full blast and, shaking his head in amazement, put the truck into gear.

Her outer clothes were practically dry by the time they reached Jordahlsholmen. Too tired to speak she thanked the man with a smile and returned his jacket to him. Concerned, he watched her get down out of the cab and walk unsteadily into the house. And then, still confused and bewildered, he drove off.

In the sitting room Catherine opened the cupboard where she had stored the bottle of whisky she had bought on the flight from London and poured herself a stiff drink. Gulping some of it down she looked across at the portrait of Freya and frowned. Then she glanced at the clock on the wall. It was five past two. She tried to work out how long she must have been in the water. One hour? Two hours? Three hours? She gave up. Her mind just couldn't cope with any calculation, even one as simple as that.

Draining the rest of the whisky, she turned for the door. At that moment the telephone rang. She picked it up. 'Hello,' she said wearily. There was no response. 'Hello,' she repeated. The line went dead and then she heard the dialling tone. Irritated but too befuddled by exhaustion to attach any significance to the call, she slammed down the receiver and went upstairs. But before she did so she locked the front door.

She was already gingerly stripping off her blouse as she walked into the bedroom and seconds later she was naked, her discarded clothes lying in a heap on the floor. Wrapping herself in the duvet, she collapsed onto the bed. And instantly she was asleep.

'But it can't have been Freya Jordahl, can it?' Anders said patiently.

Catherine had been surprised to find when she had woken up that it was only nine-thirty and her first thought was that she must have slept the whole day away. But when, bleary-eyed and still aching from her bruises, she had looked out of the bedroom window she had realised from where the sun was that it was still morning.

Putting on her dressing gown, she had gone downstairs, desperately needing to talk about what had happened. But who with? Not Anna Marie or Ingrid. Telling either of them that she was half convinced that she had seen their mother on the island the night before was out of the question. At best she would upset them and at worst they would think she was out of her mind. She wasn't entirely sure how Anna Marie would take it, but she would be risking not only offending her but perhaps putting the friendship that was developing between them in jeopardy. And, in her nervous state, Ingrid would probably go to pieces. Besides Catherine didn't know either of them well enough to confide in them.

But she had to discuss it with someone. And it couldn't be with Dr Albrigtsen because he was too close to the family and that could amount to the same as telling them direct. Nor Astrid Linderman. She wasn't well. Besides it would be too much of an imposition and come as an even greater shock to her.

That left only one person for her to turn to; and he was the one that she most wanted to talk to anyway.

So she had rung the offices of *Sunnmorsposten*, only to be told that Anders Bjornson wasn't there. 'He is not working today,' the man on the other end of the line had told her. 'But you might perhaps get him at his apartment. Unless he has already gone to the country of course. He usually does on his weekends off.' And he had given her a number to try.

'I'll come immediately,' Anders had said briskly, once Catherine had given him a sketchy and rather incoherent account of all that had occurred.

And now he was with her, seated at the table in the sitting room and drinking the cup of coffee she had poured for him.

'Who else can it have been?' Catherine said. She pointed to the portrait. 'I mean with her looks she's pretty unmistakable, wouldn't you say? And she was wearing the same dress as she is there.'

'Or one very much like it perhaps,' Anders countered.

'The same,' Catherine insisted.

'You can't be sure of that. Not when she was that far off from you. It could have been just about anybody. Most likely some woman from a group who'd landed on the other side of the island for a midnight picnic or whatever.'

Reflectively Catherine put down her cup, stood up and moved over to the window and looked out.

'And that would account for the accident too,' Anders went on, joining her. 'If they'd pulled out shortly after you got over there and they'd been drinking . . .' He shrugged. 'Well, with some drunk at the wheel of a motor cruiser anything can happen. And does. Quite often.'

'It wasn't like that,' Catherine told him, gazing out of the window. 'I just didn't happen to be in the way of that boat. It changed course and came straight at me.'

Anders frowned. 'Are you saying it was deliberate? That someone tried to kill you!' he asked.

'Well it certainly looked that way.' Catherine shook her head and sighed. 'I don't know. Why should anyone want to?'

'Yes. Why? It's not likely, is it?' Gently Anders turned her to him. 'But if you even suspect that then you must report this to the police,' he said, studying her face. 'What type of cruiser was it?'

'I haven't a clue. It looked like so many you see around

100

here. Very much like the ones turned out by the Jordahl boatyard.'

'Well, it might well have been a Jordahl 29,' Anders said. 'They're very popular in these parts. A lot of people have one.'

Catherine nodded. 'And with only a vague description like that what hope would anyone have of tracking it down?' Restlessly she moved away from the window and across to the fireplace where she stood looking up at Freya's portrait again. 'So who opened up the house then, turned on the record player and organised that weird tea party?' she asked.

'The drunken trespassers off the cruiser. When they discovered that the house was empty. As their idea of a joke,' Anders replied, walking over to her.

'But how did they get in?'

'The door hadn't been forced?'

Catherine shook her head. 'No,' she said. And then, suddenly unsure, she added, 'At least I don't think so.'

'Let's take a look,' Anders suggested.

'We can't. The dinghy's at the bottom of the fjord.'

'There's the dory in the boathouse,' he said.

Catherine turned to him. 'I shouldn't have bothered you with this,' she said abjectly. 'It isn't fair. But there was no one else I could call. I'm sorry.'

'Nonsense!' Anders said, taking her hand. 'Only why didn't you do it the moment you got back here?'

'I was out on my feet. Mind you when the phone rang I sort of hoped . . .' Catherine broke off and, removing her hand from his, crossed to the table and busily gathered up the cups and saucers and put them on a tray.

'Who on earth was calling you at that time of the morning?' Anders asked, nonplussed.

'I don't know. Whoever it was just hung up.'

Anders frowned a little. 'Shall we go?' he said.

Having first removed the mast and the sail from the dory, Anders expertly rowed them over to the island.

To Catherine's surprise, as they approached the house, she saw that the front door was shut. Anders examined the door frame for any sign of a forced entry but there was none. Catherine shot him a look of vindication. 'They could have got in through a window,' he said defensively.

He tried the door. It was locked. Catherine frowned deeply. 'I didn't do that,' she said. 'I was in too much of a hurry.' She took the bunch of keys from her pocket, unlocked the door and led the way inside.

Just inside the sitting room she pulled up sharply. The dolls and the tea set had gone and the furniture had been put back the way it was the very first time she'd entered the house.

Anders looked at her questioningly. 'The dolls!' Catherine gasped. She pointed. 'They were there. Sitting around the coffee table. And the child's tea service has been removed too.' Bewildered, she glanced across at the record player and saw that it was now closed. She walked over to it and raised the top of it. 'And this was open when I left,' she stated.

She moved quickly across the room and, perplexed, Anders followed her up the stairs.

The dolls were all back in their original positions. 'What the hell's going on?' Catherine exclaimed angrily. Recognising the doll that had frightened her, she grabbed it up from the chest of drawers where it was sitting slightly apart from the others that were crowded onto the top of it. 'This was the only one up here last night,' she said. 'It was sitting on a stool in that corner with its face to the wall. Just like it was being punished. And it was lying on the floor when I ran out.'

Anders took the doll from her and while Catherine moved around the room he studied it.

Catherine opened a cupboard. 'There it is,' she cried triumphantly. 'That's the tea service.'

Replacing the doll, Anders crossed to her and glanced inside the cupboard. Then, turning from it, he gazed around the room. 'It must have taken a few years to build up a collection of this size,' he said.

Catherine closed the cupboard and, moving over to the chest of drawers, opened the top one. 'And look!' she said. 'And it's the same with the others. Every one of them's full of dolls' clothes.'

They went out onto the landing and Anders walked down the corridor to the door at the end. 'What's in here?' he asked, looking back at Catherine who was still standing outside the nursery.

'I don't know,' she said. 'The door's locked. And I haven't got a key for it. I meant to ask Anna Marie if there is one but I forgot.'

Deep in thought, Catherine showed Anders around the rest of the house. Then, as they were leaving and after she had locked the front door again, she faced him and said, 'You think I'm crazy, don't you? Or that I imagined it all.'

Anders shook his head. 'No,' he said.

'Then what's the answer?' Catherine pleaded. 'And don't try to tell me that a bunch of drunks bothered to come back and tidy up after themselves, because I couldn't accept that.'

They walked down toward the beach and Anders asked, 'Who else has a key to the house?'

'Only the cleaning woman as far as I know.'

Anders gave her a look and she could see what he was thinking. 'Well yes, I suppose it's possible that she's been across this morning,' she said. 'God knows how she got here though. But at least that might be the explanation for the way the place is now.'

'Where does she live?'

Catherine shrugged. 'I don't know.'

'Well she's bound to be local,' Anders said with a smile. 'We'll ask.'

Once back on the mainland a trip to the general stores and post office in the nearest village was enough to establish that the cleaning woman's name was Brigit Tovan and that she lived close by. She turned out to be a thin, timid-looking woman of around fifty and she was working in the garden alongside her husband when Anders parked his Fiat in the road that ran past their cottage. Mr Tovan was a thickset, bearded man with a truculent, almost aggressive air about him.

The couple paused in their work and exchanged looks as Catherine and Anders walked over to them. Mr Tovan regarded them suspiciously. Anders introduced himself and then spoke to Mrs Tovan in Norwegian.

'Do you speak English?' Catherine asked her with a warm and reassuring smile.

'A little,' Mrs Tovan said haltingly and after another glance at her husband. 'At school I learned some.'

'We were told in the village that you looked after the house on the island at Jordahlsholmen,' Anders said.

The woman nodded. 'Yes,' she admitted warily. 'The farmhouse too.'

'Well, this is Miss Durrell. I expect you've heard. She owns Jordahlsholmen now.'

Mr Tovan glared at Catherine hostilely. 'Yes, I have heard,' his wife said. And then with a worried frown she asked anxiously, 'Have I done something wrong?' She looked at Catherine. 'My work, it is not good?'

'Oh no, it's nothing like that, Mrs Tovan,' Catherine said smiling again. 'Your work's fine. And I'm very happy with the arrangement. All we want to know is when you were last on the island.'

Mrs Tovan was clearly relieved but nonetheless wary. 'Last week,' she said guardedly. 'On . . .' She groped for the word and looked at Anders for help. 'Torsdag?'

'Thursday,' Anders prompted.

The woman smiled her thanks limply. 'Yes. Thursday,' she said. 'I go there every two weeks. On Thursday.'

Catherine frowned. This was Saturday so it couldn't have been Mrs Tovan who tidied up the house that morning. In all probability she hadn't been to the island all that week. Mrs Tovan mistook her frown for disapproval.

'There is little to do,' she explained. And then, in an attempt to forestall any criticism, went on, 'And I touch nothing. As I was told. I only dust and sweep.' She paused, waiting to be challenged on this. When she wasn't she dropped the defensive note in her voice. 'But at the farmhouse. There I am two times a week. Mondays and Thursdays. That is not good? You want me to come on other days?'

'No, that's fine,' Catherine told her.

Anders looked at her and shrugged. 'Well, thank you for seeing us, Mrs Tovan,' he said.

'That is why you came? Just to ask me that?' Mrs Tovan exclaimed, mystified.

'Yes, that's all we wanted to know,' Anders said. 'Thanks.'

He made to walk away but Catherine put a hand on his arm and restrained him. 'How long have you been going to the island?' she asked Mrs Tovan.

'For three years only. When the woman who worked before for Hjalmar Jordahl moved away then I . . .' She looked at Anders for help again.

'Took over?' he suggested.

The woman nodded.

'And since you've been working there have you noticed anything strange about the house?' Catherine said, watching closely for any reaction. 'Apart from it being kept the way it is I mean.'

Mrs Tovan looked uncomfortable, almost as if she'd been caught in some guilty act. Again she shot a nervous look at her husband. He glowered. 'It is just a house,' he grunted surlily. 'A house that is not lived in. That is all. My wife does what she is paid to do. She is not a foolish gossip as some women are.'

Anders smiled appeasingly. 'No, of course not,' he said. 'I'm sure Miss Durrell didn't mean . . .'

But Tovan didn't let him finish. 'You have the answer to the question you came here with?' he demanded.

'Yes.'

'Good day then,' Tovan said uncompromisingly, terminating the interview. His wife lowered her head, ashamed and embarrassed.

Angered by the man's rudeness, Anders' eyes narrowed. But there was obviously no point in pursuing the subject any further. 'Good day,' he said. 'Thank you for your courtesy.' He nodded to Catherine and they walked back across the grass.

The woman gave Tovan a timorously reproachful look and when, with a contemptuous snort, he went back to his hoeing she ran after the couple and caught up with them at the gate. 'I'm sorry,' she blurted. 'My husband. He is . . .' She gave a helpless shrug.

'Please,' Anders said with a smile. 'It's all right.'

Mrs Tovan looked back over her shoulder and then in a low voice, almost a whisper, she said, 'Eivind does not understand such things. He will not speak about them. And he will not let me speak about them. Because, I think, he is afraid.' She looked at Catherine. 'But I will tell you. Many times in that house I have felt that I am not alone. There is no one in that place now. But some days when I go there I see that things have been moved and I have not moved them. And all the time I am looking behind me.' She glanced back apprehensively at her husband who was now staring across at them. 'That is all I can say,' she said fearfully. Then she hurried away from them and went into the house and Tovan followed her.

As they were getting into the Fiat Catherine gave Anders a jubilant look as if to say, 'What about that then?' Anders shrugged. 'And I don't know about you,' she said, 'but I don't believe in ghosts.'

Anders switched on the engine. 'So what are you suggesting?' he asked.

'Don't you see?' Catherine urged. 'Well, look, I've seen Freya Jordahl twice now. Once on the ship coming up here and again last night on the island.'

Anders sighed. 'Someone who looks like her perhaps.

But you can't be any more definite than that,' he said firmly.

'Okay. Maybe, just maybe, you're right,' Catherine allowed. 'But what if it was Freya I saw both times. If you don't go along with the haunted houses and ghosties and ghoulies bit either, then what's the explanation? There can only be one, can't there?'

Anders looked at her aghast. Catherine nodded. 'That she's still alive,' she said.

'Two visits from my doctor in as many days! And on Saturday! I must be dying,' Astrid Linderman exclaimed.

'Nonsense,' Albrigtsen said. 'I just happened to be passing so I thought I'd drop these in to you.' He took a bottle of tablets from his bag and handed them to her.

'More pills!' she muttered tetchily.

'They're new. I'd like you to try them. Take one four times a day.'

'So I'm a guinea pig now, am I?'

Albrigtsen smiled indulgently. 'Hardly. They've done all the field trials on them. And the results are very encouraging.' He closed his bag. 'How are you feeling?'

'No less wretched.'

'Well let's see how you get on with these,' Albrigtsen said, crossing to the french windows. 'Your garden's looking lovely,' he said cheerfully.

Astrid grunted. 'I sometimes wonder why I bother to pay anyone to keep it up,' she complained. 'Except I see little of anywhere else these days.'

'There's no reason why you shouldn't get out more,' the doctor said. 'You've a car and Gerda to drive you anywhere you want to go.'

Astrid put the bottle of pills down on the table beside her wheelchair. 'Only I can't leave the pain at home, can I?' she said bitterly.

Albrigtsen turned from the french windows. 'I saw Lars Nilsen last night at the club,' he said casually. 'He told me Catherine Durrell came to tea with you yesterday.'

Astrid stiffened. 'So?' she said defensively.

'What did you think of her?'

'I like her. I think she's got spirit,' Astrid said.

Albrigtsen nodded. 'Yes, I agree.' He smiled. 'She asked a lot of questions I imagine.'

'Wouldn't you?' Astrid challenged him. 'If a total stranger had left you a handsome legacy in his will.'

'What did you tell her?'

'That you're a fool.'

Albrigtsen laughed. 'Apart from that,' he said.

Astrid moved uncomfortably in the wheelchair. 'What could I tell her?' she snapped. 'I don't know why Hjalmar did what he did any more than you do, do I?'

'Did she ask about Freya?'

'Naturally.'

'You didn't run on about her too much I hope,' Albrigtsen said with a note of concern in his voice.

'Oh for heaven's sake, Arne!' Astrid burst out angrily. 'I was curious about her. As we all were, surely. So I invited her to tea. Where's the harm in that?'

'Just so long as you were very careful about what you said.'

'You see! I was right!' Astrid growled. 'You are a fool! Bearing in mind my position, it's not likely that I would even come close to telling her the truth about Freya, is it?'

Albrigtsen studied her and then, reassured, shook his head. 'No, of course not. I'm sorry. But if she visits you again . . .'

'I shall be pleased to see her,' Astrid interrupted. And then she added meaningfully, 'And I shall continue to guard my tongue. For both our sakes.'

Chapter Ten

Anders looked up from the painting he was holding. 'So what you're saying,' he re-capped, 'is that, sooner than risk it becoming widely known that his wife was out of her mind, Jordahl fixed it so that everyone believed she was dead. And then put her away in a private clinic somewhere.'

As soon as they got back to the farmhouse Catherine had fetched the six canvases from the cellar and had set them up prominently around the sitting room.

'Said like that it sounds absolutely crazy,' she admitted.

'It is,' Anders told her.

'It's no more way out than your theory that Jordahl was murdered.'

Anders put the painting down on the table. 'Oh come on now!' he said. 'This is really stretching your imagination. Why would he do such a thing?'

'You told me yourself that he was obsessed with keeping his private life very private,' Catherine said. 'And that fits with his having brought Freya out here to Jordahlsholmen.'

'That was only later. At first they lived in Alesund.'

'Precisely. There has to have been some personal trouble behind a move to somewhere as isolated at this. Some domestic crisis he didn't want people knowing about.'

'But he was happy enough to let people believe the story that she had killed herself,' Anders scoffed.

'Yes. He could handle that. Because he knew it wasn't true. And it was a fairly easy lie for Jordahl to live with,' Catherine argued. 'But having the truth come out though;

that his wife had gone mad and that, in some way, he'd perhaps contributed to her madness, well that would have been something else.'

'But to chance an even greater scandal if what he'd done was ever uncovered . . .' Anders shook his head. 'No. Besides to get away with something like that he'd have needed the co-operation of Astrid Linderman, the family doctor and a lot of other people. And a guarantee of their silence.'

'He was an extremely powerful man. And very rich.'

'Even so. You can't buy everything. And people aren't that easily intimidated into breaking the law.'

'It's easier to persuade them if they're dependent on you in one way or another,' Catherine countered. 'And as far as Dr Albrigtsen is concerned, well they'd been friends for years, and Astrid Linderman could have been just as anxious as Jordahl to cover up the truth about her niece.'

Despite his doubts and against his better judgement, Anders found himself strangely disturbed by Catherine's fantastic proposition. 'But what hard evidence is there that Freya Jordahl had a complete mental breakdown?' he asked.

'Well, for one thing Ingrid told me that Jordahl kept her and Anna Marie away from their mother when they were children. Why?'

Anders shrugged. 'Who knows? Assuming that's true of course,' he said.

'And yesterday,' Catherine went on, 'Astrid as good as admitted that Freya was a bit strange to say the least. "She'd been ill. For a long time." That's what she said. But however physically ill someone is, you don't shut them away on an island. And what was Astrid doing living out here on her own with her niece if it wasn't to keep an eye on her? Besides there are these paintings. I've seen pictures like this before. The agency I worked for once handled a mental health campaign for one of the big charities and I visited a hospital where they kept the criminally insane. And the Arts and Crafts room was filled with paintings just like these. When I found them I thought they might be some more of Ingrid's work.'

Anders gave her a startled look.

Catherine nodded. 'Yes. That worried me too. But she paints as well. And she obviously inherited much of her style from her mother. Along with a lot of her temperament I'd say. But when Astrid mentioned that Freya was an extremely talented artist and then got very cagey about that, well the penny dropped. And there can't be any question that these are the product of a disturbed mind. I mean, well just look at them. They have to be.' She pointed. 'This one and those three particularly. And there's more than just a hint of madness in the others too.'

Anders looked thoughtful. Then, relieved to have found at least one seemingly sustainable flaw in her theory, he smiled mischievous!y. 'Now, after all these years, Freya's escaped from the clinic Jordahl put her in, eh? And taken to travelling on the Hurtigruten.' He gave her an incredulous look.

'Her condition may have improved,' Catherine said stubbornly. 'Could be that she's let out from time to time.'

'To roam the countryside!' Anders said scathingly. 'And come back to the scene of her supposed tragic end!' He shook his head in disbelief.

'All right then,' Catherine said, resenting his obvious enjoyment and self-satisfaction. 'Perhaps she has escaped.'

'And pops over to the island at will to play with her dolls and then clean up after herself,' Anders teased. 'In between running you down in a boat that is. Why do you suppose she did that?'

Realising that she was rapidly losing ground, Catherine plucked an explanation out of the air. 'Perhaps because she knew that by now I must have recognised her from the portrait. And to protect herself.'

Anders regarded her sceptically. 'Now you don't really believe that, do you?' he said.

It was a bit far-fetched and Catherine saw that now. And yet . . . She walked over to the fireplace and stared up at the portrait. 'It was her,' she said doggedly. 'It was Freya I saw last night. And on the boat.'

Studying her Anders was suddenly seized by a telling realisation. 'That's the woman you saw?' he exclaimed triumphantly and moving to her side. 'Just as she is there?'

Surprised, Catherine looked at him. 'Yes of course,' she said irritably. 'I told you. And last night she was wearing that same dress.'

Delighted, Anders put his hands on her shoulders and turned her to face him. 'And this . . . this apparition,' he asked. 'How old would you say she was?'

'I don't know. I only saw her for a moment.'

'Roughly.'

'Somewhere in her early to mid twenties.'

'No older?'

'No.'

Anders laughed happily and Catherine gazed at him, confused. 'Don't you see?' he said. 'If you'd been right in any of this and if Freya Jordahl *was* alive today she'd be forty-four, approaching middle-age.'

As the truth of this dawned on her, Catherine saw what a fool she'd made of herself and at that moment she'd have gladly changed places with anyone.

'So there goes one very inventive proposition,' Anders said, only gently mocking her. 'And if you're still convinced that it was Freya you saw, well then it has to have been her ghost, doesn't it?'

'Only there aren't such things.'

Anders grinned. 'I was joking,' he said. 'I told you. It was some woman off a boat that had put in there.'

'And before? On the steamer?'

'Just a fellow passenger. Who happened to resemble young Freya Jordahl.'

'It was much more than a resemblance.'

'Well, we're all supposed to have a double somewhere, aren't we? But there's no way it can have been the lady herself. We've settled that, haven't we? Mrs Jordahl is dead and buried. Okay?'

112

Catherine nodded and then moved away from him. 'I feel such a fool,' she said angrily.

'If it helps I have to admit that you almost had me convinced for a while,' Anders said.

'Well, whatever else I got wrong I'm still positive that that illness of Freya's wasn't anything physical. These paintings prove that clearly enough.'

'Yes, that's true.' Anders picked up one of the canvases and studied it. 'Poor woman!'

'And what happened with the dinghy. That was just an accident?' Catherine said, still adjusting herself to the reality of it all.

'Of course. However it may have looked at the time.'

'That still leaves a lot of questions with no answers to them,' Catherine said. 'Like, for instance, how did those people on the island get into the house? And who straightened the place up?'

'They could have done.'

'No. I can't go along with that.'

'It has to have been them. We know it wasn't Mrs Tovan.'

'They weren't about to return to the island,' Catherine said adamantly. 'Not after having rammed another boat and drowned someone for all they knew.'

'If they'd all had too much to drink they might not have been aware of hitting you,' Anders reasoned. 'And then, later, when they'd sobered up a bit in a fit of conscience about the house they went back and put things straight.'

'And got in for a second time without leaving any trace of how they did it,' Catherine reminded him.

Disconcerted, Anders frowned. 'It has to have been through a window,' he said. 'Maybe they weren't all fastened properly.'

Catherine sighed. 'Yes, I suppose that's possible.' She looked at the clock. 'Are you hungry?' she asked.

'I really ought to get back to town,' Anders said regretfully. 'There are one or two things I must do on the boat before tomorrow. If our trip's still on that is.'

Catherine nodded. 'Of course. I'm looking forward to it.'

'Good. So am I,' Anders said. Then he went on, 'If you've nothing better to do around here why not come in with me?'

Catherine shook her head. 'No thanks. To tell the truth I wouldn't mind taking it fairly easy for the rest of the day.'

'Of course. And so you should.'

Catherine showed him out and then walked with him to the Fiat.

Anders got into the car and wound down his window. 'Are you sure you wouldn't rather move back into Alesund?' he said. 'Not to the Nilsens again if you don't want to. And it doesn't have to be a hotel. I'm sure I can find a flat for you somewhere.'

'Why? I'm okay here.'

'It's a bit out of the way.'

'I quite like that.'

'Just the same.'

'You're not worried about me, are you?' Catherine asked.

'No, of course not,' Anders said dismissively. 'It's just that . . .' He shrugged.

'You've convinced me. I was imagining things.' Catherine laughed hollowly. 'And that's for sure. It won't happen again I promise. And so long as I don't go swimming I'm not likely to come to any harm, am I?'

Anders studied her uncertainly. He smiled. 'Well, if that's what you want,' he said. 'See you in the morning then.'

Catherine nodded. 'Fine. And thanks for . . . well, everything today,' she said.

'My pleasure.' Anders grinned. 'And that's something else you were wrong about I'm happy to say.'

'What?'

'The first time we met. Remember? When you said ours wasn't going to be a lasting relationship. 'Bye.' And with that he drove off.

Smiling, Catherine watched until the Fiat was out of sight and then she went back into the house. Quickly she gathered up the canvases and took them down to the cellar again. When she returned to the sitting room, though, she saw that she had left one of them behind. 'Damn!' she said softly, looking at it. It was one of the least tormented paintings and, out of context, might even have passed as nothing more than rather macabre.

Promising herself that she would put it with the others later, Catherine propped it against the wall on top of the sideboard. Then, picking up the telephone directory which she had used earlier to find the *Sunnmorsposten* number, she went to replace it in the drawer in the roll-top desk where she'd found it.

It was then that she saw the key.

It was lying right at the back of the drawer and from its size and shape she felt sure that it had to be the one that fitted the locked door in Freya's house.

For a few seconds she stared at it, excited but hesitant. Then, taking it out, she hurried down to the jetty where Anders had moored the dory on their return from the island.

The clinker-built boat was much heavier than the dinghy had been and although there was hardly any current running now, bruised as she was and in need of more sleep, it took Catherine almost ten minutes and a lot of effort to cross the channel. And, despite the fact that it was less than four hours since she had last been there, as she walked up to the house she was nervous about what new surprises might be waiting for her.

She let herself in and to her relief saw that the sitting room at least held none; it was just as she and Anders had left it. Going upstairs she walked down to the door at the end of the corridor and put the key in the lock. It turned easily.

Steeling herself, she pushed open the door.

The room beyond it was about ten feet long by eight feet wide, and it was empty except for a thick fitted carpet.

115

Smiling sheepishly at her foolishness, Catherine stepped inside and looked around.

All four walls were bare, and set high up in the one opposite the doorway was a small window which was almost out of reach from the floor. As she turned to leave, Catherine saw that there was no handle on the inside of the door, merely a keyhole.

Out in the corridor once more she relocked the door and put the key with the others on the bunch which she took from her pocket. Well, at least that's one mystery solved beyond any doubt, she told herself as she rowed back to the mainland. It's just an empty room.

Back at the farmhouse about an hour later, she was on the point of going upstairs to lie down for a while when the front doorbell rang. Answering it, she found Anna Marie standing in the porch. She was looking agitated and appeared to be very relieved to find Catherine at home.

'Anna Marie!' Catherine exclaimed. 'What a pleasant surprise.'

'I telephoned you several times this morning but there was no reply,' Anna Marie said urgently as she was ushered into the sitting room. Then, turning to Catherine and studying her closely and anxiously, she asked, 'Are you all right?'

Catherine smiled. 'Yes of course,' she said. 'I'm fine.'

'Thank God for that,' Anna Marie breathed.

'What made you think I might not be?' Catherine asked with a frown.

Anna Marie shook her head in bewilderment. 'Well obviously someone's made a mistake. Or there's no truth in the story,' she said. 'But the mayor rang me and said that a man who does odd jobs for him from time to time had just told him some incredible tale about picking up a half-drowned Englishwoman in the early hours of the morning who had asked to be taken to Jordahlsholmen.' She gazed at Catherine. 'It wasn't you?'

Catherine hesitated. She nodded. 'Well, yes, as a matter of fact it was,' she said.

Anna Marie looked at her in amazement. 'But what on earth . . .'

'I had a run in with a motor cruiser out on the fjord,' Catherine explained playing the incident down as much as possible. 'It rammed me and overturned the dinghy.'

'But that's awful,' Anna Marie gasped, appalled. 'Didn't it stop?'

'No.'

'Then we must report this at once.' Anna Marie strode over to the telephone.

'There's no point,' Catherine told her before she could pick it up. 'I didn't see the name of the cruiser and I certainly couldn't identify it.'

Anna Marie frowned and tut-tutted. 'That's a pity,' she said. 'Because whoever's boat it was ought to be charged with negligence. It's lucky you weren't drowned. But why didn't you call me?' she asked.

'I didn't want to bother you,' Catherine said lamely. 'Besides there was nothing anyone could do about it. And I wasn't hurt.'

'Even so.' Again Anna Marie studied her searchingly. 'You're sure you're all right?'

'Yes, I'm quite sure.'

Anna Marie accepted her assurance reluctantly. 'Well, if you say so.' She frowned again and looked puzzled. 'But what on earth were you doing out on the fjord at that time?' she asked.

'I couldn't sleep,' Catherine lied casually. 'And it was a nice night so I thought I'd go out in the boat for a while. Silly of me I suppose.'

'Not at all. It was a good idea. Better than lying in bed staring up at the ceiling. And if it hadn't been for some idiot who ought to be . . .' Anna Marie shook her head angrily. 'You should have called me though,' she said.

Catherine smiled. 'Next time.'

'Oh no, please!' Anna Marie said, laughing and holding

up her hands in protest. 'We don't want any repeat performances.'

'Would you like a cup of coffee? Or some tea?,' enquired Catherine.

Anna Marie nodded. 'A cup of tea would be nice.'

'Right,' said Catherine. 'Won't be a second.' And she went into the kitchen and filled the kettle.

'Wherever did you get this from?' Anna Marie called from the other room.

'What?' Catherine shouted back, turning on the hot plate on the stove and setting the kettle down on it.

'This painting.'

Oh my God, thought Catherine realising that the canvas which she had meant to put down in the cellar with the others was still standing on the sideboard. She went quickly back into the sitting room to find Anna Marie holding the picture and examining it. 'Oh that,' she said nonchalantly. 'I found it in the cellar.'

Anna Marie turned to her. 'Really!' she exclaimed. Then looking at the picture again she smiled wryly. 'So Ingrid didn't destroy all her other pictures then,' she said, amused. 'And she swore she had.'

'Ingrid painted that?' Catherine said, stunned.

'Well it's her style, isn't it?' Anna Marie said. 'Anyway,' she nodded, 'yes I'm sure I remember it. And all this time she's had everyone believing . . .' She broke off and chuckled. 'Still I suppose it's possible she gave it to Jordahl ages ago and then forgot about it.' She put the canvas back down on the sideboard and appraised it. 'Are there any others?' she asked.

Again Catherine was forced to lie. 'No,' she said. 'That's the only one.'

'Well I won't tease her about it,' Anna Marie said, her eyes still on the painting. 'It would only embarrass her. And she'd probably insist on putting a match to it.' She shook her head uncomprehendingly. 'I just can't understand why anyone would react so violently against something they'd spent all those hours working on as Ingrid did with her pictures.' She looked across at Catherine. 'Can you?' she asked.

In her mind Catherine saw all six of the canvases again. And she remembered the look on Anders' face when she'd shown them to him. 'No. I can't imagine why she did such a thing,' she said.

Chapter Eleven

The next morning Catherine got up early. When she opened the bedroom curtains she saw that there was a handsome ketch moored alongside the jetty. With its gleaming, mahogany-planked hull and deckhousing and its twin masts, the carvel-built, sea-going sailing boat was a magnificent sight. Catherine estimated that it must have been built about thirty years ago. Smiling with pleasure and anticipation, she was about to turn from the window when she saw Anders come up on deck, take a crumpled sleeping bag from the top of the wheelhouse and roll it up.

She dressed quickly and went down to the jetty to invite him into the house for breakfast. As they ate, she told him about Anna Marie's visit and of how she had identified the painting as being Ingrid's.

'But if that's true,' Anders exclaimed, aghast, 'that means that it's her sister who's . . .' He trailed off, lost for the right word.

Catherine nodded. 'Very sick indeed. And in need of help.'

'Did she see all the paintings?'

'No. Just the one I left behind when I put the others away.'

'What was her reaction?' Anders asked.

'Amusement mostly. It certainly didn't appear to disturb her at all. But then, fortunately, it wasn't the worst of them by any means. And she had no reason to think that I'd found it anything other than a bit surreal anyway.'

'So what are you going to do?'

'I'm not sure,' Catherine said. 'It's none of my business really. And who knows, maybe the family's aware of how ill she is. Or was, perhaps. I mean it has to be that those pictures were all painted some time ago and since then Ingrid could have been having treatment. In any case my bringing a skeleton like that out of the cupboard would only cause distress all round, wouldn't it?'

'That's true,' Anders agreed. 'But what if they don't know?'

'Exactly.' Catherine sighed. 'I need to think about it. Maybe I'll have a quiet word with Dr Albrigtsen and see what he says.' She smiled. 'But that's tomorrow's problem,' she said cheerfully. 'Right now I'm going to try and forget about it for a while and just enjoy today.'

As soon as they had washed up the breakfast things they went down to the jetty and, approaching the boat, Catherine saw the name *Skibladner* painted on its stern.

'Why did you spend the night here? And sleep on deck?' she asked.

Anders frowned and gave her a questioning look.

'I saw you cleaning up from the bedroom window,' Catherine explained.

Anders shrugged dismissively. 'It seemed like a good idea to sail up last night,' he said. 'So we could get away in good time. And it was a warm night so I slept topside.'

'And not for any other reason?' Catherine said, watching him closely.

'Such as?'

'That you were worried about me for instance.'

'Of course not,' Anders said unconvincingly, busying himself with the forward mooring line. 'Why should I be worried about you?'

They cast off and Anders started the engine. Using the deck wheel, he steered the boat out into the fjord and around the back of the island. He pointed. 'That has to be where the boating party landed,' he said. 'Anyone could come ashore there without being seen from the other side.'

Catherine gazed out from the rail and saw that, screened

from the farmhouse by a thicket of trees, there was another wooden jetty and a somewhat dilapidated boathouse with a slatted outer door. 'I didn't know there was a second jetty,' she said. 'But then I've never been beyond the house.'

Turning from the rail, she looked admiringly along the length of the ketch and then up at the top of the tall mainmast. 'What a beautiful boat this is,' she said. 'I envy you.'

'You like boats?'

Catherine nodded enthusiastically. 'Back home a friend of mine has a thirty-foot sloop down at Chichester and we often go out sailing together.'

'Oh I see,' Anders said, slightly crestfallen. Then he enquired, 'He's very keen on it, is he?'

Catherine gave him an amused, reproving look. 'Chauvinist!' she charged. '*He* happens to be a she. And yes, she's very keen. We both are.'

This cheered Anders considerably. 'Take the wheel for a while then,' he said, throttling back the engine. Catherine did so willingly as, having first checked the direction of the wind, Anders moved forward and unlashed the mainsail and began to hoist it. As the sail ran up the mast, billowed and began to fill, Catherine watched, thrilled and delighted.

When main, jib and mizzen were all set Anders rejoined her at the wheel and she offered it to him. He smiled and shook his head. 'She's all yours,' he said and, exhilarated by the vessel responding to wind and rudder, Catherine wasn't about to argue. She smiled gratefully and with a knowledgeable eye studied the set of the sails.

And for the time being at least all else was forgotten.

'How long have you had her?' Catherine asked.

'Six years,' Anders replied. 'But only on the water for three. She was in a hell of a state when I bought her.'

'And did you christen her?'

Anders nodded. 'Yes. Well re-christened her anyway.'

'What does it mean, *Skib* . . .?' Catherine had difficulty with the pronunciation and Anders laughed.

'Ski-blad-ner,' he said, breaking it down into syllables. 'That was the name of the boat the dwarfs built for one of the great Norse gods. It was magic. Faster than any other vessel. And what's more all he had to do was set the sails and it made straight for wherever he wanted to go without his having to steer it.'

Catherine smiled wryly. 'But according to you, you don't know where you're going,' she teased. 'Or even what you'll be doing six months from now. So there's no advantage in your having a boat like that, is there?'

'Perhaps not. Up until now anyway,' Anders said. 'Only just recently I think I've found a destination worth making for.'

'Well that's a definite improvement,' Catherine told him. 'And *Skibladner* will get you there, will she?' She looked across at him.

Anders fixed his eyes on hers. 'I hope so,' he said quietly. 'Part of the way at least.'

Catherine held his gaze for a while and then, disconcerted by it, stared out over the side of the boat. 'What's happening over there?' she asked.

Reluctantly Anders took his eyes off her and looked across at the near shore.

On a beach in one of the many bays a group of adults and a dozen or so children were piling up wooden and cardboard boxes, pieces of driftwood and old broken furniture. 'They're building a bonfire for Misummer Eve,' he said.

'Already!'

'It's only two weeks away. And if you want a fire that's going to last for a long time you have to start gathering the fuel for it well in advance.'

'That's going to be quite a blaze,' Catherine said.

'There'll be much bigger ones than that burning on the night. All the way round the fjord.'

Catherine eased the wheel a little. 'Where are we going?' she asked.

'I want to show you my house,' replied Anders.

'But you live in Alesund, don't you?' Catherine said, surprised and looking at him again.

Anders nodded. 'Most of the time. This is my summer place I'm taking you to. It was an inn once. A long time ago though. The boatmen on the fjord used to tie up there for a drink. I hope you like it. It's nothing special but that's where I spend most of my weekends at this time of the year. And it's home as far as I'm concerned.'

'It sounds great,' Catherine told him.

'Here, you take the wheel,' she said. 'And I'll make some coffee. If you've got some that is.'

Anders laughed. 'Of course. There's a full tin in the galley.'

They had a following wind all the way up to the head of the fjord and so they made a fair speed. They rounded the tip of Alesund and, with Catherine's help, Anders brought the *Skibladner* onto a port tack and took her into the waters of another fjord on the other side of the mountains. Here, once clear of the town again, the scenery was even more impressive and spectacular and for much of the remainder of their journey they were surrounded by almost sheer walls of rock draped at intervals with cascading waterfalls. Later, though, these ramparts retreated a little and gave way to a broad strip of gentler, rolling countryside.

'We're here,' Anders announced at last and Catherine, who had been stretched out in the sun on the roof of the wheelhouse, sat up and looked ahead.

They were approaching a headland whose tip flattened and widened and where, standing in a hollow and surrounded by an orchard, a small house overlooked a sheltered bay. On the rising ground behind the house and amid banks of wild flowers there was a wooden barn and a collection of other outbuildings. The house and the sunlit arcadian setting took Catherine's breath away. 'That's it!' she exclaimed and she shot a look at Anders at the wheel.

He nodded.

Catherine gazed ahead again, enchanted. 'Nothing special you said!' she remonstrated. 'It's like something out of a fairy story.'

'Here,' said Anders, indicating the wheel. 'Hold her steady.' And once Catherine had the helm he lowered the sails. Then, taking the ketch into the bay under power, he brought it alongside a landing stage hewn out of a shelf of rock that jutted out from one end of a curving beach. Together they secured the boat and then walked up through patches of cranesbill and marguerites and past trees laden with swelling fruit towards the house.

'Can you get here by road?' Catherine asked.

'Only as far as Stordal,' Anders said, pointing. 'On the other side of the headland. Then you either get a lift in a boat or you walk it. And it's nearly two kilometres and over pretty rough ground.'

'I wouldn't think you get many visitors then.'

'No, thank heaven,' said Anders. And with a warning sign that she should watch her head, he opened the front door and led Catherine first into a narrow hall with a flight of stairs off it and then through into a low-ceilinged sitting room.

The country furniture was plain and sturdy and presided over by a friendly, pot-bellied, cast-iron wood stove. An overflowing bookcase took up almost all of one wall and there were four decorative oil lamps strategically placed around the room, one of them alongside a veteran Remington typewriter which stood on a table by the window.

The atmosphere was one of timelessness and comforting durability.

'The place is more or less as it was in the 1800s,' Anders said. 'Except this room was a bar then. You like it?' he asked anxiously.

'Very much,' Catherine said, entranced by it and moving around the room.

'It belonged to my grandfather and when he died he left

125

it to me.' Anders smiled. 'So you see, we've both inherited something.'

Catherine peered out of the window and wondered at the view. 'The only difference being you know why you were left this place,' she said ruefully. She turned and saw the typed manuscript that was stacked next to the old Remington on the table beside her. 'Are you writing a book?' she asked interestedly and glancing at the top sheet.

Anders nodded. 'On and off.'

'A novel?'

'Yes. My second.' Anders smiled ironically. 'As a memorial to the first.' Catherine gave him a quizzical look. 'It died three years ago, on publication,' he explained. 'From lack of interest.'

Catherine walked over to the bookcase. 'Is there a copy of it here?'

Anders crossed to her and took one of a group of six identical volumes from a shelf and handed it to her. 'And in English. It sold all of two hundred copies in translation,' he said wryly. 'And that's only slightly fewer than it did in the original Norwegian.'

'Just the same, I'm impressed,' Catherine said, opening the book and reading the title page. '*A Voice On The Wind* by Anders Bjornson. What's it about?'

'Me I suppose. They say all first novels are largely auto-biographical, don't they? Which is probably one of the reasons why it didn't sell.'

Catherine turned to the dedication. '*To Norway. To which I owe what I am. With my thanks and regrets.*' She looked up at Anders. 'May I borrow this?' she asked.

'If you're not just being polite.'

Catherine frowned. 'That's not my style,' she told him. 'And I'll return it, I promise.'

Their eyes met and Catherine knew that he wanted to kiss her and she half hoped that he would. But he clearly decided not to risk it and he smiled again, dispelling the moment. 'Do you like trout?' he asked.

126

'Very much,' Catherine said, regretting she hadn't taken the initiative.

'Well, we'll have some for lunch then, shall we?' he suggested. 'If we're lucky that is.' And, collecting up two rods and a box of tackle, he took her to a fast flowing, crystal-clear stream that ran through the trees a few hundred yards behind the property.

Despite his attempts to instruct her in the art of fly fishing, Catherine found that she was hopeless at it. So, after many attempts and a lot of laughter, she sat on the bank and watched him wading in the water and expertly casting his line. And, doing so, she felt more at peace with the world than she had ever felt before.

After quite a struggle with both of them, Anders finally landed two succulent looking trout, and they carried them back in triumph to the house where he put them in a bowl which he filled with water from the pump in the kitchen. 'How about a swim before we eat?' he said.

'I didn't bring my costume,' Catherine told him regretfully and she was surprised when he smiled and said, 'I can do something about that I think.'

He led her upstairs and into what Catherine realised had to be his bedroom. There was a stout chest of drawers, a large wardrobe and a traditional Norwegian double bed with carved wooden head and foot boards, covered by a colourful and painstakingly stitched patchwork quilt.

Anders crossed to the chest of drawers, opened the bottom one and took out a green and white striped bikini. 'I hope it fits,' he said, handing it to her. 'I think it'll be okay. And here . . .'

Going over to the wardrobe he produced a feminine beach wrap and laid it on the bed.

Catherine gazed at the bikini in bewilderment.

'See you downstairs,' Anders said in the doorway, clutching his swimming trunks which he'd removed from another drawer in the chest. He went out onto the landing and closed the door behind him.

Frowning, Catherine examined the bikini. It looked

about right for her. Then, curious and seeing that Anders had left the door of the wardrobe slightly ajar, she went over to it and pulled it open.

In among the jackets and trousers which were hanging inside it was a summer dress and, draped over the rail, a silk headscarf. She took out the dress and looked at it, her bewilderment now tinged with hurt and disappointment. As she was replacing it she saw a pair of woman's shoes neatly racked among the others on the floor.

Closing the wardrobe, she returned to the bed and picked up the bikini again. She knew so little about him of course and for some reason, up until then, she hadn't even considered the possibility that he might be emotionally involved with anyone; married even. For a moment she felt like forgoing the swim and cutting short her stay. But why the hell should I, she decided. He's a friend, nothing more. And I've no right to pry into his private life. With a shrug and a sigh she dropped the costume back down onto the quilt and began to undress.

When she came out of the house Anders was already in the water and some way off from the shore. Seeing her, he trod water and waved. Then he struck out powerfully for the beach.

'Okay?' he enquired, wading up to her.

Catherine removed the wrap and tossed it aside, revealing the near perfect fit of the bikini. Anders gazed at her admiringly. 'You look lovely,' he said and he took her hand. 'Come on.'

Catherine held back. 'Just remember,' she said, 'I've already proved that I'm not a very good swimmer.'

Anders laughed. 'Don't worry,' he assured her. 'I'll look after you.' And he ran with her into the water.

Later, when they had both dressed again and while Anders grilled the trout on a barbecue which he'd improvised out of large stones, Catherine picked some of the wild flowers that were growing among the fruit trees.

Anders repositioned the fish over the white-hot ash of the charcoal and looked across at her wistfully. She walked over to him and knelt down on the rug which he had spread out on the grass in front of the house. 'What a fantastic day it is,' she said. 'And this is such a beautiful place.'

'It's even better now,' Anders said, looking into her eyes.

Flustered, Catherine looked away from him and down at the posy she was holding. Anders leaned into her, savoured the scent of the flowers and nodded approvingly. Again their eyes met. 'I'll find a vase for them shall I?' Catherine said briskly and she stood up.

Re-entering the house she went into the kitchen and, taking a jug from a cupboard, pumped water into it and arranged the flowers. Carrying the jug through into the sitting room, she placed it in the centre of the table that stood in the middle of it.

She gazed around the room again and crossing to the typewriter lifted the paperweight from the pile of paper alongside it and scanned the typescript but, written in Norwegian, it meant nothing to her.

The only photograph in the room was a framed snapshot of Anders standing with his arms around the shoulders of a middle-aged couple and, looking at it, Catherine felt sure they had to be his parents. All three of them were smiling happily. She put the photograph back where she'd found it and went outside again.

Anders was pulling the cork of a bottle of white wine which he'd earlier placed in a rock pool to cool. Catherine sat on the rug and Anders poured them each a glass and handed one to her. '*Skol!*' he said.

'*Skol!*' Catherine took a sip. Anders smiled at her and this time she held his gaze. It was no good pretending any longer. She was only fooling herself. She had to know. 'Who's are they?' she asked quietly.

Anders frowned questioningly.

'The bikini,' she said. 'The dress and the shoes in the wardrobe.'

Anders didn't flinch and he smiled understandingly. 'That was a passing interest,' he told her. 'Some time ago.'

'No more than that?' Catherine said, searching his face.

Anders shook his head. 'She left those things behind last summer.'

'And where is she now?'

'I've no idea. We haven't kept in touch. She married a Dane and he took her back to Legoland.' He shot an anxious look across at the barbecue. 'The trout are about ready I think,' he said.

Catherine smiled broadly. 'Good,' she said enthusiastically. 'I'm starving!'

The sun was almost touching the horizon when they sailed back down the fjord towards Jordahlsholmen. There was very little wind now and they tacked lazily across the water. Both were subdued and they had hardly spoken since they had left Anders' house. 'Why do glorious days like this have to end?' Catherine sighed.

Anders looked across at her at the wheel and gave her a faint smile. 'I was wondering that,' he said. 'It has to be the spite of the gods. Or they're just making sure they don't spoil us perhaps.'

'Do you suppose that if I took my hands off the wheel *Skibladner* would take us safely the rest of the way to Jordahlsholmen?' she asked him.

'Only if that's where you really want to go,' he said, gazing back at her.

Catherine glanced out over the rail. 'That's the Nilsen house,' she said pointing. Anders, who had been leaning against the wheelhouse beside her, straightened up and moved to the side of the boat. The house was only fifteen or twenty yards off from them and the Nilsens' motor cruiser was tied up at the jetty. Catherine sighed again and even more deeply. 'Back to reality,' she said grimly. 'And what to do about poor Ingrid.'

Staring across at the house, Anders frowned. 'I see they have a Jordahl 29,' he said.

As they came near to Jordahlsholmen Anders lowered

and secured the sails, and they nudged in alongside the jetty under power.

'Would you like to come in for a while? For a drink or some coffee perhaps,' Catherine asked once Anders had loosely moored up.

'Yes I would,' he said. 'Very much. But I'm not going to.'

'You're very welcome,' she told him.

'Yes I know,' he said solemnly. 'But I think that might be a mistake. And I don't want to spoil the day.'

'It's been wonderful.' Catherine held up the book she was carrying. 'And thanks for lending me this.'

'Will you have dinner with me during the week?' Anders asked. 'Thursday maybe? There's a place in town called The Pepper Mill. They have music and you can dance.'

Catherine nodded. 'Great! Yes, I'd like that. Thursday then.'

'I'll pick you up.'

'No, please,' she protested. 'You don't want to have to come all the way out here and then back again. I'll meet you there. The Pepper Mill, right?' Anders nodded. 'I'll find it,' she said. 'What time?'

'Eight?'

'Fine. Well, goodnight then.' Catherine said. 'And thank you. I can't tell you ... Well what I mean is, it was a special day. Okay?' She kissed him on the cheek and then walked slowly away along the jetty.

'Catherine!' Anders called.

She stopped and turned and, coming up to her, he took her in his arms and kissed her gently on the lips. Then, holding her away from him, he looked into her face.

Catherine gazed back at him, pleased but confused by the emotions which the day and his kiss had stirred in her. Then with a smile but without a word she walked on.

Once she was in bed she picked up Anders' novel from the bedside table, opened it and began to read. And as she read it was his voice that she heard in her head.

I can still hear my grandfather calling me. And I see

him as he was then; a tall, sinewy man, with his face leatherlike and sculpted by more than sixty years of sun, rain and cold, his blue eyes gentle and forgiving but the best and most awesome of lie detectors, standing outside the door of the house at Osbygd and calling, his voice echoing back across the fjord. And, always I would hide from him; mostly out of devilment, sometimes from shame but either way certain and reassured that sooner or later he would find me.

Catherine looked up from the page and, deep in thought, stared across at the window.

With the *Skibladner* anchored well out of sight of the Nilsens' house, Anders launched the dinghy that was hung on davits over the stern and quietly and cautiously rowed back to the jetty where the motor cruiser was moored.

Climbing ashore and keeping low, he made his way along the length of the cruiser and, peering down at the bow, reacted with a start.

The possibility had come to his mind when they had passed the house earlier and he had seen the Jordahl 29 there. It had been nothing more though – just a possibility and a crazy one at that. But now he was faced with a frightening reality. It has to be a coincidence, he told himself. It must be.

But whether it was or not, from the dented prow and the deep scratches and streaks of paint running along the starboard side of it, it was obvious that the Nilsens' boat had been in a collision.

And recently.

Chapter Twelve

'I will give Mr Tunheim your message as soon as he returns,' the woman at the other end of the line said, and Catherine thanked her and hung up.

She had telephoned the boatyard to see if Tunheim could let her have a replacement for the dinghy. The dory was really too heavy for her to manage on her own and with a smaller boat not only would she be able to go out on the water whenever she felt like it but if, as she intended, she was going to explore the whole island before she left Jordahlsholmen for good, then future crossings would be much easier in a runabout of some kind. And since she was still the owner of the yard, laying out hard cash for one seemed stupid.

She stretched and yawned. It had been two o'clock in the morning before, reluctantly, she had laid aside *A Voice On The Wind* and settled down to sleep. I really will have an early night tonight, she promised herself. She had found the novel not only deeply moving but also a fascinating insight into Anders Bjornson, and she'd been loath to stop reading. From now on though she'd decided she would ration her enjoyment and hoard the remaining chapters, learning more and more about him with each of them.

Grabbing up her handbag, she left the house and walked over to the Ford Fiesta, reminding herself that she must extend the hire contract on it when she was in Alesund. About to get into the car, she hesitated as she heard another one approaching. It was a black Saab, driven by Dr Albrigtsen. He parked close by her and got out.

'Morning,' Catherine said with a smile, wondering what he was doing in the area.

Albrigtsen strolled over to her. 'Good morning.' Then realising that she was on her way out his expression changed. 'Oh I'm sorry,' he said. 'I'm holding you up I'm afraid.'

'No. That's all right. I'm in no hurry. Just going to do some shopping that's all.'

'Well I won't keep you long. How are you?'

'I'm fine.'

Albrigtsen looked at her questioningly. 'Really? Are you sure?' he asked. 'I've been hearing all sorts of stories about an accident you had.'

'Oh that,' Catherine said, wincing.

'It's all over town,' Albrigtsen told her.

Catherine sighed. 'So I gather. Well, as you can see, no bones broken.'

'You had a very nasty experience by all accounts.'

'I could have done without it. I think I swallowed half the fjord. But apart from that . . .' She shrugged. 'And all that exercise has to have been good for me, wouldn't you say?'

Albrigtsen smiled. 'I just thought I'd check,' he said.

'That's very nice of you.'

'And I'm disappointed,' Albrigtsen confessed. 'I was looking forward to demonstrating my bedside manner. And here you are, hale and hearty.' Catherine laughed. 'No aches and pains?' Albrigtsen went on. 'No bruises? No cold? No headaches? Nothing like that?'

'Well a few bruises but they're fading I'm happy to say. Nothing else though. Really, I'm okay.'

'Good. I'm delighted to hear it. Well, you want to get on. You must come and have a meal with us before you go back to England. My wife and I would like that.'

'So would I,' Catherine said. 'Thank you.'

'I'll have a word with Liv and see when would be best for her. And then I'll give you a call.'

'Fine.'

'Enjoy your shopping. Goodbye for now.' The doctor started back to his car.

Watching him move away Catherine found herself in a quandary. She still wasn't sure that she should discuss the matter with Albrigtsen, but if she was going to, then this was a good opportunity. She decided that she must. 'Dr Albrigtsen,' she called.

Alongside the Saab, Albrigtsen turned to her as she walked over to him. 'Have you got a moment?' she asked. 'There's something I want to show you.'

The doctor smiled. 'Of course,' he said. 'What is it?'

Catherine took him into the house and brought the canvases up from the cellar. Laying the pictures on the table, she explained how she had found them and, without associating Ingrid with them in any way, told him what her feelings were about them and asked for his opinion.

Albrigtsen reacted to the paintings with a look of disbelief and then with mounting distress as, one by one, he examined them. Then he looked at Catherine, sighed deeply and nodded. 'Yes, you're right,' he said. 'These are clear evidence of an increasingly advanced psychosis. And I am not surprised that you were shocked by them because strangely, even after all these years, they still shock me.'

Catherine gazed at him in astonishment. 'You've seen them before!' she exclaimed.

Albrigtsen shook his head despairingly. 'Yes. Hjalmar Jordahl showed them to me.' He sighed again. 'Here in this room. That one and that one first,' he went on, pointing. 'Then the others as the collection grew. And soon after Freya had finished each of them.'

'Freya!' Catherine gasped, now completely bewildered. 'But I was told . . .' She trailed off.

Albrigtsen stared at the canvas he was holding and again he shook his head. 'I cannot imagine why Hjalmar kept these,' he said quietly. 'I've always assumed that, after her death, he destroyed them.'

'Then I was right,' Catherine murmured.

Albrigtsen looked at her enquiringly. 'I'm sorry?'

'When I first saw them I suspected they'd been painted by Freya. Only then . . .'

'You couldn't believe it,' Albrigtsen said, misinterpreting her hesitation. 'I know.' He put the painting down on the table with the others and looked at the portrait of Freya. 'Such a tragedy,' he continued. 'So young, so beautiful, so talented. And yet, at the end, beyond all help.'

'And is that the reason why Jordahl brought her out here? Because of her mental state?' Catherine probed gently.

Albrigtsen nodded absently and, walking over to the window, he stared out onto the drive. 'Catherine, my dear,' he said at last. 'Your having found those pictures puts me in a very difficult position. Both as a doctor and as a close friend of the family.' He turned to her. 'Quite by chance you have intruded into a secret. And although, ethically, I shouldn't, I don't really have any alternative now but to share it with you.' He shrugged. 'Besides, since the paintings now belong to you, you are entitled to an explanation.'

'Actually I'd guessed some of it already,' Catherine informed him, hoping that in some way that would ease his dilemma.

'I'm very relieved it was me you raised this with and not Anna Marie or Ingrid,' Albrigtsen said with a worried frown. 'Even now this would come as a terrible blow to them I think.'

'They don't know about their mother!'

'Only that in her later years she was ill. Not the nature of the illness though,' Albrigtsen said. 'Hjalmar wanted it kept from everyone. He dreaded the thought of perhaps having to have her put away somewhere.'

Well I came close to getting it right, thought Catherine. Obviously Jordahl had considered committing his wife to a mental hospital or some kind of clinic.

'They probably suspected the truth or something close to it,' Albrigtsen went on. 'But they were young and thank God, at that age, the ugly reality of madness is outside

136

your experience or comprehension. Besides the lie would have been much more comforting for them anyway. So, as far as I know, they accepted it gratefully and didn't question it too closely. And they were never with Freya on the island. Only here, occasionally. During those times when she was more rational. Almost her old self even. But those days got to be fewer and fewer.'

'And Astrid looked after her.'

'Freya would accept no one else,' Albrigtsen said. 'Her derangement turned her against Hjalmar completely. So Astrid gave up her job as a teacher in Oslo and moved here to be with her. For seven years she hardly left her side. And never once during that time was she able to close her bedroom door at night in case Freya needed her. She coped magnificently and without her . . .' He made a helpless gesture. 'She's a remarkable woman.'

'Yes, she has to be,' Catherine acknowledged. 'And the dolls?'

Albrigtsen sighed. 'They were among the first signs of Freya's unbalanced mental state,' he said. 'And later she seemed to find great solace in them.' Crossing to the table, he picked up one of the paintings and studied it. 'I cannot tell you what terrible days those were,' he said. 'Not only for Freya but everyone close to her. And particularly for Hjalmar.'

'I can imagine.' Catherine looked at Freya's portrait. 'As you said, so young, so beautiful.' Remembering, she turned her head back to Albrigtsen. 'There's a room in the house on the island which was obviously kept locked,' she said. 'Was that . . ?'

Albrigtsen nodded sadly. 'More and more there were times when she became quite violent and had to be restrained. For her own safety.'

'Oh how awful!' Catherine exclaimed. 'And then, finally, she killed herself.'

Albrigtsen hesitated but only momentarily. He replaced the picture on the table and then looked up and held her gaze levelly. 'With an overdose of sleeping tablets which she stole from Astrid. So now you know everything.' He picked up another of the canvases and gazed at it. 'It's quite extraordinary, isn't it? Ingrid not only inherited her mother's artistic talent but also her style. This could almost have been painted by her.'

'Yes, I agree,' said Catherine. 'And for a while . . .' She didn't finish. No point in going into that she thought. And now that the truth was out, as tragic as it was, she felt greatly relieved. The belief that Ingrid had painted the pictures had weighed heavily on her. What's more she no longer had the problem of what to do about it. And she could meet Ingrid again without any embarrassment knowing that although she was certainly neurotic she was nothing more than that.

'You'll not repeat anything I've said about Freya to Ingrid, will you?' Albrigtsen urged. 'Nor to Anna Marie. I can rely on that I hope.'

'Of course,' Catherine assured him. 'And as far as these are concerned, well . . .' She gathered up the canvases and, followed by the doctor, she took them into the garden.

Piling them into a pyramid and borrowing Albrigtsen's cigarette lighter, she set fire to them. They burned fiercely and soon they were nothing but ashes.

Catherine walked with Albrigtsen to his car. 'Thank you,' he said quietly.

By the time Catherine reached Alesund she had put the sad story and everything that had led up to it behind her, and she shopped lightheartedly and indulgently.

Coming out of one of the boutiques in an ultra-modern arcade in the centre of town, she paused to look in the window of the shop next to it, debating whether or not a pair of shoes which had caught her eye would suit her. She was still undecided when Anna Marie, emerging from a nearby doorway saw her and, smiling, walked over to her. 'Hello,' she said.

Catherine started and turned from the window. 'Oh

hello Anna Marie,' she said, returning her smile. 'Are you shopping too?'

Anna Marie pulled a face. 'No unfortunately. I've just come from a board meeting of Jordahl Industries. It's a monthly chore I'm afraid. Lars and Ingrid will be out in a minute I think. How are you?'

'Fine, thanks. And you?'

'Busy. And I feel I'm neglecting you.'

'Nonsense!'

Anna Marie looked at her quizzically. 'No more frightening adventures I hope.'

Catherine laughed. 'No,' she said.

'Well this is a pleasant surprise!' exclaimed Lars Nilsen as, with Ingrid by his side, he advanced on them. 'Hello Catherine.'

Catherine acknowledged them with a nod and a smile. 'Hello Lars. Hello Ingrid.'

'Hello,' Ingrid said coolly. She looked pale and appeared even more than usually subdued.

'You're well, are you?' Catherine enquired.

Ingrid held her look almost defiantly. 'Yes, thank you,' she said.

'This is nice,' Lars enthused. 'Now we can all have lunch together.'

'Not me I'm afraid,' said Anna Marie. 'I must get back to the office. I've so much to do. But I'm sure Catherine will join you.'

Catherine was enjoying being on her own and she still had some more shopping to do. 'Well I really . . .' she stammered.

'Of course you must,' Lars interrupted. 'We haven't seen you for ages. And we miss you, don't we Ingrid?'

'Yes,' agreed Ingrid dully. And then, fixing Catherine with a hard look, she added softly, 'You should not have moved to Jordahlsholmen.'

'Have you heard anything from Olav Tunheim?' Lars enquired.

Catherine shook her head. 'No, not yet. But he did say it might be three weeks before he could get his offer in.'

'Well, whatever happens about that, you'll be staying on for Midsummer Eve now, won't you?' Lars said.

'Yes, I'm looking forward to that.'

'You'll enjoy it,' said Anna Marie. 'I'm only sorry I can't be with you all.'

'Oh really! Why is that?' asked Catherine.

'Sadly there's a trade fair in Bergen on that Saturday and I've to go to it.'

'That's a shame,' Catherine said, disappointed. 'When will you be back?'

'Sunday. On the Hurtigruten. The return flights are all full for some reason.'

Lars glanced at his watch. 'Well, if we're going to get a good table,' he said.

'Yes,' agreed Anna Marie. 'And I must go.' She kissed Catherine on the cheek. 'Bye Catherine. See you soon.'

'Bye.'

Anna Marie turned and walked briskly over to her car which was parked in the square in front of the shopping precinct.

Lunch was something of an ordeal as far as Catherine was concerned. Although Lars chatted away amiably enough Ingrid hardly said a word and when she did speak it was in monosyllables. The rest of the time she just picked uninterestedly at the food she had ordered.

On the following Thursday it took Catherine a long time to get ready for her dinner date with Anders. She just couldn't make up her mind what to wear. On her shopping expedition to Alesund she'd bought a dress specially for the occasion but now, holding it up against her and studying herself in the mirror, she had doubts about it. Maybe it's a little too chic she thought. I've no idea what this place we're going to eat at is like. And the neckline's a bit low too. But in the end she put it on anyway, and it wasn't until she was driving into town that she realised that her hesitation had been just another symptom of her general nervousness.

When at last she found The Pepper Mill it turned out to be a bistro-style restaurant in the basement of a building alongside the narrow canal which connected the fjords on either side of Alesund.

It was crowded, mostly with students in jeans and tee shirts and instantly Catherine regretted her choice of dress. But when the waiter intercepted her at the entrance and led her across to a candlelit table in an alcove on the far side of the room and she saw that Anders was wearing a summer suit she felt better.

'What would you like to drink?' he asked, ignoring her apology for being late. And then he added meaningfully, 'And remember, you're driving.'

Catherine grimaced. She had been warned more than once since her arrival about the strict drinking and driving laws in Norway. If you were stopped by the police and they found that you'd had no more than a small beer that was enough to land you in jail.

'Your choice,' Anders reminded her with a grin.

Catherine sighed philosophically and settled for an orange juice.

A group began to play and although they were good musicians and the song which the lead guitarist was singing was one of her favourites, Catherine was grateful that she and Anders were sitting far enough away from the small dance floor for it not to make conversation difficult.

'How have you been?' Anders asked looking across at her through the flame of the candle.

'Okay, thanks,' she said, surprised by the note of reserve in her voice. And then compensating for it with a smile, she added, 'And I'm much better informed now.' And she told him what she'd learned from Albrigtsen.

'Well, that's it then. Everything solved. And you were almost right after all,' Anders said when she finished. 'Except that there wasn't any conspiracy and Freya Jordahl

141

is dead. And it's good to know that whatever else Ingrid got from her mother it didn't include madness.'

'Yes that's a great relief. She's still a bit odd though. And very highly strung.'

Anders was tempted to reveal what he'd discovered about the Nilsens' boat but he decided against it. The more he'd thought about the possibility that theirs was the boat that had run Catherine down the less likely it had seemed. What possible motive could the Nilsens or, come to that, anyone in Alesund have for trying to kill her? It had been an accident. There was no doubt in his mind about that now. And the damage to the Nilsens' motor cruiser had no sinister significance whatever. It *was* just a remarkable coincidence.

'With her background that's not very surprising, is it?' he said. 'So, end of mystery.'

Catherine nodded. 'Yes, I suppose so. Except . . .' She frowned.

'Nothing else has happened, has it?' Anders asked, cutting in on her.

'No. But that woman I saw. I'm not entirely convinced that . . .' Catherine shrugged. 'And I'm still none the wiser about why I was in Hjalmar Jordahl's will.'

'Forget about it. Is knowing really that important to you?'

'Yes. I don't like question marks in my life. Any more than you do. Or you wouldn't be so keen to prove your theory that Jordahl was murdered.'

'That's just a matter of wanting to see justice done,' Anders said. 'And I'm not going to let it become an obsession. Anyway, it's only a hunch on my part. One day though something'll turn up with the proof in it. But don't let's talk about that, eh? Or about wills. Not tonight anyway.' He reached out across the table and took her hand. 'I'm glad you're here,' he said. 'I've missed you.'

Catherine studied him and then smiled but at the same time she gently removed her hand from his. 'Snap,' she said flippantly.

Disappointed by her mild rebuff, Anders regarded her questioningly. Then he smiled again, 'Would you like to dance?' he asked.

Catherine nodded.

They stayed on until The Pepper Mill closed and although Catherine did her best to enter into the spirit of the evening she was aware of a restraint in her which she couldn't altogether overcome.

'I enjoyed tonight,' she said as they strolled up the street to where she had parked her car.

'Did you?' Anders glanced at her. 'It seemed to me that . . .' He stopped walking and turned to her. 'Has something upset you?' he asked. 'Something I said or did?'

'No, of course not,' Catherine said uncomfortably.

'Are you sure?'

'Yes. Quite sure.'

They walked on and when they reached the car Anders said, 'I was wondering if you'd like to come out to my place again this weekend. I'm going to be there. I could sail round and collect you like I did before.'

Catherine lowered her head. 'Thanks. It's a nice idea but I don't think I can.'

Anders frowned and, tilting her chin up, looked into her face. 'There is something wrong, isn't there?' he said.

'No.'

'You've got something else planned?'

Catherine took a step back from him. 'No, it's just that . . . well, I'm not going to be here that long and . . .'

'You think I'm looking for an affair?' Anders said.

Catherine studied him. 'Aren't you?' she asked.

'Nothing casual.'

Catherine nodded. 'That makes it even more difficult. I've got plans,' she told him candidly. 'Things to do with my life. I'm not sure I want to get too involved. Not with anyone. And not here, a thousand miles from home.'

Anders put his hands on her shoulders. 'I didn't want to get involved either,' he said. 'But I have. And for the first time I'm thinking of the future.'

'So am I. And there's a lot of it. I'd need to be very sure.'

'And you're not?'

Catherine shook her head. 'Just confused,' she said.

And that was the truth. She wanted him, needed him even. What she felt wasn't just a physical attraction either. She knew that now and she knew too that that was what she'd been fighting since the day they had spent together at his house. But she wasn't looking for a holiday romance; for just another lover, however appealing the thought of being in his arms, of giving herself to him, might be. She'd had enough of a few months of temporary fulfilment. And this time probably only days. A week or so at most. And after that there would be a sea voyage or four hours flying time between them. And even if he was telling the truth about the way he felt, despite everything, was she really ready to make any kind of long-term commitment?

Anders tried to draw her into an embrace but she resisted. 'And that wouldn't help,' she said. 'Goodnight.'

She got into the car. Dejectedly, Anders watched her drive away.

It was Olav Tunheim who resolved the doubts in Catherine's mind. Or rather Tunheim and the last chapters of *A Voice On The Wind* together.

The following morning she went for a walk along the fjord and for the first time since she'd moved into the farmhouse she was conscious of being alone. And not just at Jordahlsholmen but everywhere and in everything. She had her friends, of course, and her plans for the future, but she'd never deluded herself that her friendships had any depth to them. The kind of life she had led and the circles she moved in in London — pressurised, highly competitive, amusing but brittle and regulated by expedience and largely governed by a fluctuating set of highly commercial values — were not conducive to anything other than surface relationships. And, close to attainment, even her ambitions for herself, that only two months ago had overriden everything else, now seemed somehow pointless and unsatisfying.

Things had changed so much since that morning when she'd received the letter from Lambert, Stoddard and Price. And she had changed too. She recognised that and she was only too well aware that, as things stood, nothing she had or could have in England would in any way fill the emptiness or appease the hunger that she felt as, disconsolately, she headed back along the path at the water's edge.

But a hunger for what? And what would fill the void she felt inside her? Anders Bjornson? Perhaps. But in believing him there were terrible risks. And the greatest risk of all was of being hurt and of having to crawl to familiar cover anyway, badly wounded. Time. That was the answer she decided. I need more time.

As she walked up from the fjord and past the jetty she saw the pick-up truck bucketing down the track that led to the road behind the farmhouse. Puzzled, she waited for it. It pulled up outside the front door and Catherine saw that there was a fibreglass dinghy and an outboard motor in the back of it.

Olav Tunheim got down out of the cab from beside the driver. He was smiling. 'I have brought you what you asked for, Miss Durrell,' he said grandly.

'That's very good of you.' Catherine felt slightly embarrassed. 'But you shouldn't have gone to all the trouble of delivering it personally.'

'Please! It is my pleasure,' Tunheim said. 'I hope it is all right.' Catherine walked over to the truck and inspected the boat. 'She is not a new one,' Tunheim went on. 'But it is in excellent condition. And the outboard has hardly been used.' He looked concerned. 'Did you want a new one?' he asked.

Catherine shook her head. 'No,' she said. 'That'll be fine. I just need something I can handle to potter around in. And only for the rest of the time I'm here.'

Gratified, Tunheim signalled to the driver and the man drove the pick-up down to the boathouse.

'I was sorry to hear of your misfortune with the other dinghy,' Tunheim said. 'But greatly relieved when I learned that you had not been injured.'

'Thank you.' Catherine gestured toward the house. 'Would you like some coffee?'

'Thank you, no,' Tunheim said. 'I must not be away too long. But I had to come. Not only for the pleasure of seeing you again but also to tell you that this morning I heard from my bank.' He paused for effect and then smiled. 'They have approved my application for a loan,' he said proudly.

'Oh that's very good news,' Catherine said, genuinely delighted. 'I'm happy for you.'

'Thank you.' Tunheim gave her a polite bow. 'You are very kind. And that means that I can now make you a formal offer for the boatyard. I have one or two further calculations to make but you shall have it in writing early next week.'

Catherine nodded her approval. 'Great. But perhaps you'd better send it direct to Bjarne Langva. He's advising me on the sale and handling all the negotiations. You know Mr Langva I think.'

'Of course. And if I may say so you have chosen a good man to represent you. Very well, I will do that. And when he receives it I think he will agree that the price I am offering is a fair one.'

'I'm sure it will be. Right, well I'll call him and tell him to expect it.'

'Yes, please do that.' Tunheim studied her quizzically. 'So if, hopefully, we can come to an agreement, I imagine that you will be going back to England soon,' he said.

Catherine frowned slightly. 'Yes, I suppose so,' she said.

And at that moment she saw that she had a lot less time than she thought she had. With the sale of the boatyard concluded and with Jordahlsholmen either on the market or sold to Ingrid she would have little or no excuse for staying on much longer.

That night she finished Anders' novel.

My mother looked at me and I could see that she had been crying. 'This makes no difference I suppose,' she said. 'You're still going back to Oslo, are you?' I wanted to tell her that she was wrong; to lie, to comfort her with the thought that I would never leave her again. But I couldn't. So I said nothing, knowing that I could not explain, could never make her understand why that was not possible. And as we walked back to the house I heard it again, that familiar, demanding and insistent voice on the wind.

Catherine closed the book and put it on the bedside table. Then, turning out the light, for a long time she lay gazing up at the ceiling deep in thought and a long way away.

Anders Bjornson, looking for anything to keep himself occupied, was repairing the side door of the barn when he heard the boat approaching.

Curious, he glanced up and saw it entering the bay. It was one of the small open fishing boats from Stordal and Catherine was sitting in the bow.

The man at the helm brought the boat alongside the jetty and helped Catherine ashore. Slinging the tote bag she was carrying onto her shoulder, she walked slowly along the causeway and then up through the trees toward the house.

Anders threw down the hammer he had been using and ran to meet her.

Face to face with him Catherine slipped the bag off her shoulder, took his book out of it and handed it to him. 'I've brought your book back,' she said softly. 'You were right. It is about you.'

Anders stepped in closer to her, his eyes locked on hers. 'How long can you stay?' he asked, hoping against all hope.

Catherine smiled up at him. 'It looks like it's going to be another lovely weekend, doesn't it?' she said. 'Even better than the last one.'

She dropped the bag as Anders took her into his arms

and they kissed, each responding to the longing and the urgent needs in the other.

It was four days later that Catherine received the telephone call from Bjarne Langva and on her way back to Jordahlsholmen after her meeting with him she stopped off at the Nilsen house. Ingrid opened the door to her.

Catherine smiled. 'Hi!' she said cheerfully.

'Hi!' Ingrid's response was guarded.

'Have I called at a bad moment?' Catherine asked.

Ingrid shook her head. 'No, not at all,' she said, warming a little. 'I'm glad you're here. I was going to call you later as a matter of fact. Come in please.'

Catherine followed her into the sitting room. 'I won't stop,' she said. 'I just thought I'd look in and say hello and tell you my news.'

'You have accepted Olav Tunheim's offer for the boat-yard,' Ingrid pre-empted.

Catherine frowned. 'Yes. But how on earth did you know that?' she asked. 'I've only just left Langva's office.'

'Bjarne told Lars at the club last night that he would be seeing you today. And also that he would be advising you that Tunheim's offer was a generous one,' Ingrid said.

'Yes it is.'

'And that only leaves Jordahlsholmen for you to dispose of, doesn't it?' Ingrid continued. 'Then you will be free to return to London. That is why I wanted to speak to you. To ask if you have decided how much you want for it. And we will not argue. Because, as I told you, whatever the price I will pay it.'

'Oh no, that wouldn't be right,' Catherine demurred. 'I couldn't accept more than it's worth.'

Ingrid's face took on an anxious expression. 'But you promised!' she said urgently.

'Not to take advantage of you I didn't.'

'Well, then, whatever you think is fair,' Ingrid said impatiently.

'I tell you what,' Catherine came back brightly. 'If and

when I do sell Jordahlsholmen it will be to you. And that *is* a promise. How about that?'

'If!' Ingrid gasped, stunned.

'Well yes. You see I'm not sure I want to get rid of it now. At least not immediately,' Catherine explained.

Ingrid gazed at her with a mixture of alarm and bewilderment. 'But you said the property was of no use to you.'

'Yes I know I did. But since then though . . .' Catherine shrugged. 'Well a lot's happened and I've changed my mind. I like it there. And I've settled in very nicely. So now I'm thinking of staying on. For a while anyway.'

'But you can't,' Ingrid cried desperately.

Taken aback, Catherine looked at her in astonishment and, with an effort, Ingrid regained control of herself. 'I mean,' she went on and giving her a weak smile, 'do you really think that's a wise decision?'

Catherine laughed. 'I hope so.'

'Personally,' Ingrid said quietly and no longer smiling, 'I think that it is one that you will regret.'

And when Catherine arrived back at the farmhouse she still hadn't been able to decide whether that was a threat or not.

She telephoned Anders to tell him that the boatyard was sold. He was delighted for her. 'I love you,' he whispered under the noise coming from the newsroom.

'And I love you,' Catherine said. And then she added, steeling herself against possible disappointment, 'Will I see you later?'

'Of course. I told you last night. I'll be there around seven. Bye darling.'

And it was as she put the telephone down that Catherine decided that, with little else to do until he arrived, this was as good a time as any for her to look over the rest of the island.

The dinghy that Tunheim had brought out for her proved to be not only easy to handle but, under power, much faster than the old wooden one. Grudgingly Catherine had to admit that, with its lightness, fibreglass did have its advantages.

She pulled the boat up onto the shore and, skirting the house, made for the jetty on the far side of the island. Gingerly testing it and finding that it was strong enough to take her weight, she walked to the end of it and gazed out over the fjord. Then, retracing her steps, she paused alongside the old boathouse and peered in through a crack in the woodwork. The landing stage inside, although probably still serviceable, was, like the rest of the structure, badly in need of repairs and renovation.

She explored the island thoroughly but found nothing of interest. Returning to the house, she let herself in. As she closed the front door behind her, she looked around the sitting room and was instantly seized by an icy feeling of dread so that she almost cried out.

Standing facing the far window was an artist's easel with a canvas resting on it. And sitting on a small table alongside it were two of the dolls from the room upstairs. Both of them were Victorian and dressed in baby clothes of the period.

Sick with apprehension, Catherine walked slowly over to the window and, stepping round in front of the easel, looked at the canvas.

Her face took on a look of horrified dismay and the room swam around her.

The painting was a grotesque, cruel and hate-filled head and shoulders portrait of herself.

Chapter Thirteen

'Charming!' growled Anders staring at the portrait on the easel, his face a study of angry disgust. He glanced at the dolls on the table. 'And apparently the artist likes an audience.'

Catherine shivered involuntarily. 'Yes. And that's weird enough on its own.'

Anders looked at her anxiously. When he'd arrived at the farmhouse Catherine had still not fully recovered from her experience. He had not seen her so upset before and he'd been very concerned.

'Out there today, for the first time I was afraid,' she'd told him. 'Not just scared, I mean, but really afraid. And I ran.'

'I'm not surprised,' he'd said and he had taken her in his arms and comforted her.

Now, though, she was much calmer and appeared almost back to normal.

Anders touched the portrait with a fingertip. 'It was done very recently,' he announced. 'The paint's not fully dry yet.'

'Recognise the style?' asked Catherine grimly. Anders studied the painting and shrugged noncommittally. 'Oh come on!' she chided. 'It's unmistakable. The technique, the intensity, the colour harmony, the brush work. They're exactly the same as in those paintings of Freya's I found. Only this one shows an even more advanced state of madness.'

'Freya Jordahl's dead,' Anders said firmly and fixing her with an uncompromising look.

'Is she?' Catherine said quietly.

'She took an overdose of sleeping tablets. Fourteen years ago.'

'According to Dr Albrigtsen.'

'That theory of yours doesn't hold water,' Anders said patiently. 'That's been proved, hasn't it?'

'Then who did this? And why?'

'Why?' Anders shrugged. 'But as to who? Well we know one person who paints very much like Freya did, don't we? Someone who inherited her style from her.'

'Ingrid!' Catherine exclaimed, aghast. 'But that's . . .'

'Have you been over this place thoroughly?' Anders asked without letting her finish.

'No.'

'Then let's do that. Now.' Anders walked over to a small bureau and, opening it, started going through the pigeonholes.

'What's the point?' protested Catherine.

'Look, someone's been here,' he said. 'And they've almost certainly been here before. Often perhaps. And not just recently. Remember what Mrs Tovan said about her feelings when she comes over here to clean? And about finding that things had been moved since her last visit? Well there's a good chance that whoever it was who did that left something behind. Something that might help identify them.'

'So what are we looking for?'

Anders shrugged. 'Anything that doesn't fit in this museum. I don't know exactly. But an old envelope maybe. A scrap of paper. A book or a magazine published after January 1970. A fresh box of oil paints. Anything that's even slightly out of key.' Pulling out the top drawer of the bureau, he searched through it.

Catherine crossed to a shelf and, taking down the books on it one by one, checked each of them; first the date of publication and then, holding them by the covers and shaking them, to see if anything had been interleaved between the pages. 'I'm not even sure I'd know what was significant if I saw it,' she said.

Having looked through all the rooms on the ground floor without finding anything, they went upstairs and Catherine unlocked the door at the end of the corridor. 'Not that there's anything in here,' she said, as, with Anders just behind her, she stepped inside.

'I thought you hadn't got a key for that door,' Anders said, looking around. Catherine told him about finding it in Hjalmar Jordahl's desk and of how Albrigtsen had said that this was the room in which Freya had been kept when she had become violent. Anders regarded her incredulously. Catherine nodded. 'It happened from time to time I gather,' she said.

They went back into the corridor and Catherine locked the door again. Outside the nursery Anders said, 'I'll look around in here. You take the other bedroom.'

'Okay,' said Catherine and she moved along the landing.

The wardrobe in Freya's room had nothing but clothes and shoes in it. And removing each of the hangers Catherine studied the suits and dresses on them with interest. Nearly all of them had labels showing that they had been designed by some of the top haute-couture houses.

Closing the wardrobe, Cathering gazed around the room. Then, crossing to the dressing table, she sat on the stool in front of it and opened the drawers and rummaged through them. The centre one contained nothing but lingerie and the first five drawers in the twin pedestals were filled with nightdresses, blouses and accessories of all sorts. But then, in the sixth and last drawer, under a pile of gloves and some neatly folded silk scarves, she found a book. She took it out and examined it.

Its red leather binding was tooled with an intricate design in gold and the covers were secured with a metal clasp which had a small keyhole in it. Catherine tried to open it but found that the clasp was locked. And, as she was searching for a key among the bric-à-brac on the top of the dressing table, Anders came into the room.

'No luck in there,' he said. 'Just dolls and dolls' clothes.' He strolled over to the dressing table and saw what she was holding. 'Oh, what have you found then?'

'Looks like a diary,' Catherine said. 'But it's locked.' She tried the small drawers on either side of the mirrors in her search for a key but without success. 'And there doesn't seem to be a key for it anywhere.'

Anders took the book from her and, picking up a nail file from a manicure set on the dressing table, prised open the clasp.

Shocked, Catherine gave him a disapproving look but Anders was intent on the book and it went unseen.

He flipped through the pages, scanning some of the entries and then nodded. 'Yes, you're right,' he said. 'It *is* a diary.' He looked up. 'Freya's,' he added.

Turning his attention back to the book, he skimmed through some more of the pages. 'She didn't keep it up regularly it would seem,' he went on. 'Just odd days.' He walked over to the bed and sat down on the edge of it. Intrigued, Catherine got up from the stool and moving across to him, sat down beside him.

As Anders slowly went through it, he saw that the pages of the diary were lined but that there were no printed headings on them. Some of the entries, which were written in ink and in a very distinctive hand, were short, some long, and each began with nothing more than a note of the day and the month on which it was made.

Selecting an entry about half way through the book, Anders read it aloud, translating it into English.

Sunday, 18th September. Anna Marie and Ingrid both had bad colds so I kept them in today and in the afternoon I read to them. They liked the story so much that when it was time for bed they begged me to finish it. And then they went to sleep quite contentedly.

He chose another entry at random and read that.

Friday, 17th February. Now that there are no more shadows it is wonderful to be alive. I have lost much but I still have so many blessings, my dearests, Anna Marie and Ingrid, the greatest of them. We are so happy the three of us when we are together here on my island.

Anders glanced at Catherine and shrugged. 'They're all pretty much like that as far as I can see,' he said.

He turned several pages at once to a later entry.

Thursday, 18th April. Spring is on its way and soon the island will be looking really beautiful again. Already the early flowers are beginning to show but, just the same, I am impatient for the summer to arrive. And so are the children because it is then that we have such fun together when we are here on our own.

He closed the book and looked up. 'Just everyday happenings and random thoughts,' he sighed. 'Not very interesting or revealing I'm afraid.' He frowned slightly. 'But for someone who was supposed to be mentally unbalanced very lucid, wouldn't you say?'

Catherine took the diary from him and, opening it again, riffled through it. The last dozen or so pages were blank she noticed.

'There were times when she was perfectly lucid, I understand,' she said. 'Almost normal. In the early days of her illness anyway.' She snapped the diary shut. 'I'll give this to Anna Marie the next time I see her. I'm sure she'd like to have it.' And then, with a meaningful look at Anders, she added, 'And I'll apologise for having broken the lock. And for prying.'

Catherine locked up the house again and they walked down to the beach.

'What about the painting?' Anders said, pulling up sharply.

Catherine shuddered. 'Leave it,' she said. 'I certainly don't want it.' Then she added resolutely. 'We'll put it on a bonfire on Midsummer Eve. How about that?' They walked on. 'Well that was pretty much a waste of time,' she said. 'No one has left any kind of mark on that house. Only Freya. And okay, maybe she is dead. But she still lives there, doesn't she?'

Back at the farmhouse Catherine prepared a meal for them.

'Obviously someone is trying to frighten you away,' Anders said as they ate.

'And you think it's Ingrid.'

'Well, that painting certainly points to her. And she's the one who's so desperate to buy this place from you.'

'But I promised that if I sell it, it'll be to her.'

'When will that be though? Maybe she's not willing to wait. Besides, getting hold of Jordahlsholmen might not be her only reason. Perhaps she resents you being here.'

'Why?'

'Jealousy? A suspicion of some kind.'

'As to how come I was mentioned in her father's will you mean?' Catherine said.

Anders nodded. 'Right.'

'Well if that's what she thinks she's certainly not alone and that's for sure. Even I'm beginning to think it might be true.' Catherine shook her head in wonderment. 'But to go to such lengths! And the painting by itself doesn't prove anything, does it? Anyone could have faked that.' She picked up her glass of wine, drank from it and then stared abstractedly into space. 'If it is a fake,' she said quietly.

She sighed irritably and set her glass down on the table again.

'What is it?' Anders asked.

'I don't know,' she said. 'But something's nagging me. It's there at the back of my mind and I've a feeling it's important. But I just can't pin it down.'

156

It wasn't until they were in bed that it came to her.

They had made love and, completely relaxed and at peace with everything, she was lying with her head on Anders' chest, moaning with pleasure as he gently massaged the nape of her neck.

'How do you feel about children?' he asked, deep in thought.

Catherine chuckled. 'You don't have to worry about that,' she said lazily. 'I promise.'

'I was thinking of the future,' Anders said.

'That's rushing things a bit, isn't it?' Catherine murmured, half asleep. 'Let's see how things go with us. And anyway, first things first. Like getting married if that's what we end up wanting to do. Then we can think about . . .' She snapped open her eyes and sat up abruptly. 'Children!' she exclaimed. 'Of course! That's it! That's what was bothering me. The children!' Anders gazed at her in surprise and bewilderment. 'In her diary Freya writes about her children,' she went on excitedly. 'About Anna Marie and Ingrid. About them being with her.'

'Well,' Anders said, nonplussed.

'Dr Albrigtsen told me they were never on the island. They visited her here, occasionally. But never on the island. She mentions being on her own with them over there though. And anyway she was never on her own.' She switched on the light and reached for the diary on the bedside table. 'Astrid Linderman was always around.'

Frowning, Anders eased himself up into a sitting position and, taking the diary from her, opened it and leafed through the pages again. 'There are dozens of references to Anna Marie and Ingrid,' he said.

'But they can't be true! Not if what Albrigtsen said is right. She has to have imagined it all.'

Anders read one of the entries to her. '*Monday, 15th August. Anna Marie has decided that when she grows up she's going to be a ballet dancer and she tells me . . .*' He trailed off and turned to a much later entry. '*Friday, 8th June,*' he read, '*Anna Marie and Ingrid had a party today*

157

and invited all their friends. I taught them a new song and we had a very happy time. But then it was all spoilt when she came and . . .' Anders frowned and read on silently, his frown deepening as he did so.

'Well?' Catherine prompted impatiently. He looked up at her, deeply disturbed. 'Go on,' she urged.

' *. . . But then it was all spoilt when she came. I hid from her and the children said nothing to her and she went away again. This can't go on. And afterwards I did my best to show her that she is not welcome.'* Anders glanced at the heading of the entry again. *Friday, 8th June.'* Confused and with a frightening suspicion forming in his mind, he looked at Catherine. 'Today's 20th June,' he said. 'When did you go over to the island and find all the dolls having a tea party?'

'The weekend before last. On the Friday night.'

Anders did a quick mental calculation and, with a grim expression on his face, he nodded. 'That was 8th June,' he told her. Hurriedly he turned back to the earlier entries. *'Tuesday, 14th February,'* he read. *'Jordahl is dead. I have told Ingrid what happened and she understands.'*

'What!' gasped Catherine.

Anders turned over the page and read on. *'Friday, 17th February. I learned today that Jordahl has left my island to a bastard of his. This is more than I can bear. He has done this as a final insult to me and Anna Marie and Ingrid.'*

Catherine stared at him, horrified. 'When did you arrive in Alesund?' he asked urgently.

'5th June.'

Scanning the entries for June, Anders found the one he was looking for and read it to her. *'Wednesday, 6th June. She is here. Here to claim what is not hers by any right. Here to shame and rob us all. I tried to stop her but I was not successful. The fault and the insult are Jordahl's but she is the one who must be punished for them.'* He looked up from the page. 'Oh my God!' he breathed.

Astrid Linderman drew back a corner of the lace curtain over the bay window and stared at Anders' car parked in the drive. 'Who is he?' she demanded.

'A friend,' Catherine told her. Anders had wanted to come in with her but she had persuaded him to let her handle the interview on her own.

Astrid spun her wheelchair and moved away from the window. The expression on Catherine's face and her unexpected visit so early in the morning worried her. 'Is he local?' she asked.

'Yes.'

'And how long have you known him?'

'It seems like a very long time,' Catherine said quietly.

Astrid fixed her with a knowing look. 'I see,' she muttered. 'But you didn't ask him in.'

'I wanted to speak to you alone.'

'What about?' Astrid studied her warily.

Catherine opened the diary and offered it to her. 'Do you recognise this handwriting?' she asked.

Astrid sighed and, taking the book from her, glanced at the writing. She frowned.

'Do you?' Catherine pressed.

'Of course,' Astrid said irritably. 'It's Freya's.' She looked up and saw the bewildered expression on Catherine's face. 'Where did you get this?'

Catherine ignored the question. 'Are you absolutely positive?' she demanded.

'My eyesight is as good as ever, thank God,' Astrid snapped. 'I know this writing well. I've seen it often enough. There can be no question. It's Freya's. But you haven't told me. Where did you find this?'

'In her bedroom. In the house on the island.'

'Then you had the answer to your question already, didn't you?' Astrid said, exasperated. She closed the diary and held it out to her.

Catherine shook her head. 'Only it's not possible. Because, apart from anything else, there are references in it to me.' She took the diary and turning to one of the entries which Anders had bookmarked with slips of paper handed it back to Astrid. 'As Hjalmar Jordahl's bastard!'

For a few seconds Astrid stared at her in startled disbelief. Then she read the entry and, as she did so, she put a hand up to her mouth as if to stifle a cry of alarm.

'And that's not the only mention I get,' Catherine said grimly.

Astrid turned frantically to the other marked entries.

'So you see Freya couldn't have written any of that,' Catherine went on, studying her closely. 'Not unless she didn't commit suicide back in 1970 and she's still alive, that is.'

Astrid stared up at her, her face contorted, her hands trembling. 'What are you saying?' she cried out. 'What are you saying?'

'You positively identified that as your niece's handwriting,' Catherine said unyieldingly. 'Well, if it is, what other explanation is there?'

The old woman stared at her, her eyes wide, her mouth twitching convulsively. She thrust the diary into Catherine's hands and then looked wildly about her as though seeking a way of escape. She spun her wheelchair away from her tormentor and wheeled herself over to the french windows. 'Go away!' she cried pitifully. 'Go away!'

Feeling sorry for her but nevertheless determined to get at the truth, Catherine followed her. 'Help me, please!' she pleaded. 'There has to be an answer and I must know what it is.'

Astrid began to sob hysterically. 'Go! Leave me alone! Get out of this house!' she shouted. 'I have nothing to say. What you're suggesting . . . It's . . . It's cruel.' She gasped for air. 'It's . . . It's . . . I have nothing to say. I can tell you nothing,' she moaned. 'Do you hear me? Nothing. Go away! Please! Please! Go away!'

Greatly concerned, Cathering tried to calm her. 'I'm sorry,' she said soothingly. 'I didn't mean to . . .'

Still sobbing, Astrid closed her eyes and, resting her head

against the back of the wheelchair, let out an anguished howl. 'Go away! Go away!'

The drawing-room door was thrown open and Gerda ran into the room.

Pushing Catherine aside, she took Astrid's right hand in hers and held onto it tightly. 'There! There!' she said in Norwegian. 'It's all right. I'm here.' She looked angrily at Catherine. 'What have you been saying to her?' she demanded. 'Why have you done this?'

Catherine tried to explain. 'You don't understand. I only wanted . . .'

But the housekeeper cut her short. 'Miss Linderman has asked you to leave,' she said formidably. 'Please do so.' Catherine shot a look at Astrid, still racked with sobs. 'At once!' Gerda told her, with an expression that brooked no further argument.

Disconsolately Catherine left the room.

Gerda leant in over the wheelchair and stroked Astrid's forehead. 'There, there,' she crooned in Norwegian. 'Don't upset yourself. She's gone. She's gone.'

Catherine got into the Fiat alongside Anders. She was pale and her hands were shaking.

'Are you all right?' he asked anxiously.

She nodded. Anders started the engine. 'Did she recognise the handwriting?'

Again Catherine nodded. 'According to her,' she said quietly. 'there's no doubt about it. It's Freya's.'

Anders frowned. 'Well either she's lying or . . .'

'Why should she lie, for God's sake?' Catherine appealed wearily.

Anders glanced at the house. 'Yes, exactly,' he said thoughtfully. 'Why should she?'

Chapter Fourteen

Anders swore and swerved to avoid a cyclist who had ridden heedlessly out onto the main road.

Staring out of her side window, Catherine was too preoccupied to notice how close they had been to having an accident.

'It's not as far fetched as it may sound,' Anders assured her. 'It can happen. Has happened. There are documented cases of it.'

Catherine looked at him incredulously. 'Where someone has taken on a completely different personality?'

Anders nodded. 'Sure.'

'So what you're saying is that Ingrid is not just insane but that in her madness she thinks she's Freya.'

'No, not just *thinks* she is. On occasions she actually becomes Freya. And when she's in that state she not only paints like her but takes on Freya's handwriting too. She's totally possessed by her, in other words.'

'And the dolls?'

'They've taken on a life of their own for her. My guess is that the two which were sitting alongside the easel are the Ingrid and the Anna Marie she writes about in the diary.'

'Oh, but how awful! To live part of your life in such a fantasy!'

'But it isn't a fantasy to her. When she's Freya, to her it's reality. And those dolls are living beings.'

'Then if you're right it's as her mother that she's doing all this to scare me away.'

Anders glanced across at her. 'I think she's tried to do

more than just scare you,' he said gravely. He turned his attention back to the road ahead. 'I didn't say anything before because, well it could have been just a very odd coincidence. But I don't believe it is. Not now.'

'What?'

'I had a look at the Nilsens' motor cruiser after I dropped you back at Jordahlsholmen the Sunday before last. The bow was dented and there were deep scratches along the side of it. And streaks of paint. It had obviously been in a collision with another boat. And not long ago.'

'It was Ingrid who ran me down!' gasped Catherine. 'And you think she was trying to kill me?'

'I wouldn't mind betting on it.'

'But why?'

'She's spelled that out clearly enough in the diary. Because in her Freya persona she thinks you're Hjalmar Jordahl's illegitimate daughter. And that you've come to rob her of what she sees as hers.'

Catherine frowned. 'But it wasn't Ingrid I saw on the island. Or on the coastal steamer,' she said.

'No. You saw Freya,' Anders admitted. 'I'll go along with that now. But think about it. With her build and features and with her hair done the same way, Ingrid could be quite easily mistaken for her mother, couldn't she? At a distance anyway.'

'My God!' Catherine exclaimed. 'You mean she dresses like her too!'

'Not like her,' Anders corrected. 'As her. When she's Freya she wears Freya's clothes and does her hair in exactly the same way as her mother did. That would come naturally to her.'

Again Catherine gazed out of her side window. What he was suggesting was preposterous surely. And yet, discounting as she did both his previous explanation and that the woman she had seen was a ghost, in a strange way it was beginning to make some kind of sense.

'But it can't have been Ingrid I saw on the coastal steamer,' she said. 'She and Lars met me when I arrived.'

'The ship stopped at Torvik, didn't it?'

'Yes.'

'Well that's only about sixty kilometres away. If she had slipped ashore there and driven the rest of the way she'd have got back in plenty of time to meet you.'

'But why bother putting in an appearance on the boat at all? I mean there's no way she was going to frighten me off as Freya then, was there? At that time I hadn't seen the portrait.'

Anders shrugged. 'Yes, I agree,' he said. 'That doesn't make any sense at all. But then we're not dealing with a rational mind. But if, as she wrote in her diary, she was planning on trying to stop you reaching Alesund, well it would have been as Freya that she'd have made the attempt, wouldn't it? It has to be that whatever she had in mind just didn't work out. Maybe because Albrigtsen was on board and that frightened her off.'

'So I was in danger on that trip!' Catherine shuddered at the thought of what could have happened. 'But if any of this is even close to the truth then why did Astrid get so upset when I showed her the diary?'

'Because she genuinely thinks it is Freya's handwriting. And she *knows* she's dead. Either that or because she also suspects the truth.'

Catherine sighed. 'So what do we do? I don't want the police involved in this.'

'No. I agree,' said Anders. 'Not if it can be avoided. That wouldn't do anyone any good. Besides we don't have any hard evidence. Just supposition. I might be able to pick up something more concrete if I read the diary carefully right the way through. Can I hold onto it for a while?'

Catherine took the diary from her lap. 'You can keep it as far as I'm concerned,' she said. And she tossed the book onto the back seat.

When they reached the farmhouse and as she was getting out of the car, Anders said, 'I'd really feel a lot happier if you did move into town.'

'There's no reason to. I mean we're not sure we're on the right track, are we?'

'Sure enough. At least I am.'

'All right. So I'll be on my guard from now on.'

'And on your own. Please?' Anders begged.

Catherine shook her head. 'No. No one, mad or otherwise, is going to drive me away from here,' she said adamantly. 'Not Ingrid playing sick games. Not anyone. I wouldn't give them the satisfaction.'

'That's just being stubborn. And rather stupid.'

'That's me,' Catherine told him stiffly. 'The stubborn bit anyway.'

They got out of the car and Anders walked with her to the front door. 'I've got to go to Molde this afternoon to cover a political rally they're holding there tonight,' he said. 'And I doubt if it'll be over much before midnight.'

Catherine reassured him. 'Don't worry. I'll be okay. Really I will.'

'If you don't mind me turning up in the early hours though.'

Catherine took his hand. 'It's a nice idea,' she said smiling. 'And I'd like you to. But it isn't necessary. Honestly. And you can't spend every night way out here. You've got work to do. Call me in the morning.'

Anders regarded her, uncertain. 'Well make sure you lock up,' he said. 'And don't do anything foolish. Right?'

'Like what?'

'Like going over to the island for example.'

'Not without good cause.'

'Not for any reason,' Anders said firmly. 'Not alone. Promise?'

Touched by his concern, Catherine kissed him lightly on the lips. 'I love you,' she said. 'And I'm also quite fond of me. So I'm not going to take any unnecessary risks, am I?'

Putting his arms around her, Anders looked into her eyes. 'You'd better not,' he said. 'Because you're the best thing that's ever happened to me.'

She studied his face closely and smiled. 'Probably,' she said.

Anders drew her close to him and kissed her properly. 'I'll ring you from Molde,' he said.

Catherine nodded. 'Okay. But don't worry if you can't. Talk to you tomorrow if not.'

She watched him drive away and she frowned, angry with herself for not having been honest with him about what she was planning on doing. But, faced with the prospect that he could be right in everything he had said, she had to be sure in her own mind, one way or the other.

And that meant that she had to talk to Ingrid, face to face.

Ingrid's Mini was parked in the drive but there was no response when Catherine rang the doorbell of the Nilsen house. She tried again. And then, stepping back, looked up at the bedroom windows but she could see no movement behind any of them.

For a while she stood gazing at the house, undecided. What, only and hour and a half ago, had seemed to her to be the right course of action now appeared not only futile but also foolish and ill considered. After all, with suspicions which were based on nothing more than conjecture, she was not in a position to accuse Ingrid of anything outright. And it was ridiculous to imagine that she would do or say anything to give herself away in the course of a casual conversation. She hadn't up until now and without a direct challenge she was unlikely to do so today.

So what the hell am I doing here, Catherine thought. Small talk isn't going to achieve anything and if I turn the conversation into an interrogation and she is guilty and becomes suspicious then, in her mental state, God knows how she might react.

Grateful that the bell hadn't been answered, she walked back to the car and she was about to get into it when Lars Nilsen drove up to the house.

'Hello, Catherine,' he said smiling, getting out of his Volvo. 'You just leaving?'

'No, I've just arrived,' she said. 'I rang the bell but Ingrid must be out somewhere.'

Lars glanced across at the Mini. 'Her car's there. So she can't be far away. She's probably in the garden. Why didn't you go round the back?'

'Oh yes, of course. How stupid of me. I didn't think,' Catherine said lamely.

'Well come on in and we'll see.' Lars took his keys from his pocket and opened the front door. Reluctantly, Catherine followed him into the house, through the sitting room and out onto the patio. 'You're right, she's not here,' Lars said, looking around the garden. Puzzled, he frowned. 'I can't imagine where she can be. Anything I can do for you?'

Catherine shook her head. 'No. I didn't come for any particular reason,' she lied. 'I was just passing and thought I'd drop in for a chat. How are you?'

Lars smiled ruefully. 'Becoming very forgetful. I've got a meeting this afternoon and when I came to look for them I realised that I'd left the papers I need for it in the study. I can't stop I'm afraid but if you want to wait for Ingrid make yourself at home please. This is open house as far as you're concerned, you know that.'

'Thanks just the same but I don't think I will. Some other time.'

'Well we'll be seeing you the day after tomorrow, won't we?' Catherine gave him a quizzical look. 'It's Midsummer Eve,' he reminded her. 'You are going to celebrate it with us I hope. We've got some friends coming up in their boats for a drink and then we're all going out on the fjord to have a picnic somewhere. You've met most of the people already and I'm sure you'll enjoy it.'

'Well,' Catherine said hesitantly, searching for a way out.

Lars' face fell. 'Oh you are going to join us, aren't you? We'd be very disappointed if you didn't.'

'I'd like to,' Catherine stammered. 'The only thing is that ... well, may I bring someone?' she asked. 'You

167

see he and I were planning on spending Midsummer Eve together.'

'Of course!' Lars studied her and smiled understandingly. 'Bring him along. He'll be very welcome. And it's a good idea because then we'll all be couples.'

At least with Anders around and in a crowd it shouldn't be too difficult to get through one evening with Ingrid, Catherine assured herself. 'Thanks,' she said. 'What time?'

'Whenever you like. Sevenish.'

'Fine.' Catherine looked down the garden and, with a start, saw that the Nilsens' motor cruiser was not alongside the jetty. 'Where's your boat now?' she enquired casually.

Lars frowned and followed her gaze. 'Ingrid must have gone out in it,' he said. 'In which case she's almost certainly gone into town. She claims that she can get there quicker by boat than she can by car.' He laughed. 'On the other hand she might have taken it in to be repaired. I noticed the other day that it had been slightly damaged and although she swore it wasn't her fault I think she felt a bit guilty about it.'

Catherine smiled politely but her mind was racing. 'Well, goodbye Lars,' she said. 'See you on Saturday.' And she hurried out of the house and got into her car.

Disregarding all the speed limits, she was back at the farmhouse in three quarters of an hour, and minutes later she was heading across the channel in the dinghy. On a course which would take her round to the rear of the island.

There was no boat tied up at the second jetty nor in the old boathouse. But the rainbow-coloured streaks of oil on the water alongside the mooring looked fresh to Catherine and she ran through the trees to the house.

The front door was still locked but once inside her suspicion was confirmed. The portrait and the easel had gone. And so had the two dolls. And when she went upstairs and into the nursery she found that they were back in their places on the bed again.

And lying beside the bed was a crumpled handkerchief.

Catherine picked it up. It was limp and damp between her fingers and straightening it out she saw the initial 'I' that was embroidered on one corner of it.

Now it was no longer merely speculation. Here was just about all the confirmation that was needed. And, suddenly overwhelmed by pity, Catherine sat down on the edge of the bed and wept.

Anders didn't telephone that night but then she hadn't really expected him to. He had said that the rally wouldn't finish until late and she doubted that he had had even a moment to spare.

She lay for hours going over everything in her mind and by the time she telephoned *Sunnmorsposten* the following morning, only to be told that Anders wasn't there, she had already decided what had to be done. And without delay.

The Jordahl furniture factory lay just off the main highway into Alesund and Catherine had no difficulty in finding it. To her dismay though, when she was shown into her office, Anna Marie was obviously preparing to leave and in a hurry to get away.

'I'm sorry about this,' she apologised, taking a bundle of files from her desk and slipping them into an already bulging briefcase. 'But I haven't got long to catch my plane.' Catherine looked at her nonplussed. 'The trade fair in Bergen,' Anna Marie explained. 'I told you, didn't I?'

'Oh yes, of course,' Catherine said. 'I'd forgotten.'

Anna Marie looked up at her and for the first time saw the tell-tale signs of lack of sleep on her face and her deeply concerned expression. She frowned. 'Is it important?' she asked.

'Yes it is. Very.'

'Tell you what then.' Anna Marie smiled encouragingly. 'You drive me to the airport in your car and we'll talk on the way.' She studied her. 'What is it? What's the problem?'

'Ingrid,' Catherine said. And by the time they were on

169

board the ferry that connected Alesund with the airport on the island of Vigra she had told her everything.

Leaving the car they went up onto the boat deck where, stunned and clutching the handkerchief that Catherine had found, Anna Marie gazed out over the water. 'Have you got the diary with you?' she asked.

'No.'

'Where is it?'

Catherine hesitated. 'It's quite safe,' she assured her.

Anna Marie stared at the handkerchief. 'I'm sorry, I know how you must be feeling,' Catherine said. 'Although, to be honest, you don't seem to be all that surprised.'

'I'm deeply shocked. And horrified.' Anna Marie shook her head. 'But no,' she went on, 'I have to admit it, I'm not altogether surprised.' She sighed deeply and looked at Catherine. 'The fact is I've been worried about Ingrid for quite a while now. We all have. And even more so over the past year or so. She's always been a nervous, withdrawn sort of person. Even as a child. But then around about the time she gave up painting and burned all her pictures, well she became even more distant and, in my opinion, very disturbed emotionally. And since then there have been several occasions when it's seemed to me that, for quite long periods, she's been almost entirely out of touch with reality.'

'And has Lars noticed this too?'

Anna Marie nodded. 'He's extremely worried about her.'

'But neither of you have done anything about it,' Catherine said quietly.

'What could we do!' exclaimed Anna Marie. 'She's a grown woman, not a child. Besides she's my sister and his wife, for God's sake! We just didn't want to believe ... And on those occasions when she seemed particularly depressed or far away from us and we both suggested that it would be a good idea if she were to see Dr Albrigtsen she wouldn't hear of it. She always insisted there was nothing wrong with her and we were imagining it all. She even accused us of . . .' She broke off again and then went on, 'Well, all sorts of things. Besides, those moods of hers never lasted very long and when they'd passed she seemed okay. Not altogether happy or at ease in her mind perhaps. Always slightly tense and on edge maybe. Very neurotic even, sure. But no more than that. It's obvious now though that she's steadily been getting worse and worse. And Lars and I can't pretend or protect her any longer. Something's got to be done about it. For her sake even more than yours.'

'I'll go away,' Catherine suggested. 'Give up my inheritance. Happily. If you think it might help.'

Anna Marie shook her head. 'I don't think it would. From what's been happening I think we have to accept that she's finally gone over the edge. Anyway you can't give up your inheritance. Besides, even if you could, why should you?' She gazed out to sea again. 'Being kept away from our mother during her illness as we were affected Ingrid very badly you know,' she said. 'She never forgave Jordahl for that. And after she committed suicide well, although she was only eight Ingrid blamed him for it. She was convinced that he'd treated her cruelly and that's why she killed herself; because she couldn't stand it any longer and because he was being unfaithful to her. I tried to reason with Ingrid but she wouldn't listen. From then on my sister hated her father. Sometimes it frightened me the way she hated him so much. That's why, when he died, I had this awful feeling that she might possibly have . . .'

She didn't finish but she had no need to. In her mind Catherine heard Anders' voice, 'I don't believe Hjalmar Jordahl's death was an accident. I think he was murdered.' And she stared at Anna Marie aghast.

'But that's unthinkable,' Anna Marie said quietly and almost to herself. 'Even now.'

In the airport departure lounge they sat at a secluded table, an untouched cup of coffee in front of each of them.

Anna Marie reached out and put a hand on Catherine's

arm. 'Dear Catherine. What a terrible time this has been for you,' she said.

'Oh don't worry about me,' Catherine told her. 'Now it's all out in the open I can cope with it. I just feel so desperately sorry for Ingrid.'

Anna Marie sighed deeply. 'Yes, so do I. But everyone will do what they can to help her. And who knows, with the right treatment . . .' She shrugged and stared down at her coffee. 'By the way, who translated the diary for you?' she asked.

'Anders Bjornson.'

Anna Marie looked up, alarmed. 'The journalist!' she exclaimed. 'He knows about this!'

'He was with me when I found it,' Catherine explained. 'And I'd already told him what had happened up to then. But don't worry,' she said reassuringly. 'He won't use any of it professionally.'

'How can you be sure of that?'

'Because he's part of my life now.'

Anna Marie studied her closely. 'Oh I see. It's like that between you, is it?'

Catherine smiled faintly. 'Yes. Very much so. And he won't betray the confidence. In any way.'

'I hope not,' Anna Marie said. 'Because if this got out it's not only Ingrid who'd be hurt. The local gossips would turn it into a major scandal. So, please,' she urged, 'until I get back on Sunday and we've talked some more and worked out how to handle it for the best, don't say anything to anyone else. Not even to Lars or Albrigtsen. Please?'

Catherine nodded. 'Of course.'

Anna Marie smiled gratefully. 'Thank you,' she said.

There was an announcement over the tannoy which prompted a flurry of activity in the lounge. Anna Marie gathered up her briefcase. 'That's my flight, I'm afraid,' she said.

They stood up and joined the tail of the queue that had formed at the departure gate. 'So what will you do about

Midsummer Eve?' Anna Marie asked. 'Are you still going to spend it with Lars and Ingrid and the others?'

'I don't see how I can get out of it really,' Catherine said. 'Not without a very good excuse and I can't think of one.'

'No, you're right. It would be difficult,' Anna Marie agreed. 'Anyway, it would be better if you did I think. Otherwise it might look odd you're not being there.' She sighed. 'I wish I didn't have to go to Bergen. But it's too late for me to drop out now. I'm expected. And by some very important customers of ours.'

'There's no reason why you shouldn't go,' Catherine told her. 'Two days isn't going to make much difference to anything, is it? And I'll be okay.'

'Are you sure?'

'Of course.'

'Oh my God!' Anna Marie said despairingly. 'What a dreadful business this is. I only hope we can work it out without too much pain for anyone.' At the gate she turned to Catherine and smiled weakly. 'Bye,' she said. 'See you on Sunday.' She kissed her on the cheek and then, surrendering her boarding card, walked out onto the tarmac of the dispersal apron.

Catherine watched her cross to the waiting Boeing 737. At the foot of the steps she looked back and waved and then, wearily, she boarded the aircraft.

Returning to her car, Catherine drove back across the causeway that linked Vigra to the ferry terminal on Valderoy. Although breaking the news to Anna Marie had been difficult for her and she regretted having caused her so much distress, she felt greatly relieved. With her fully in the picture now, all that remained was the problem of how to resolve the tragic situation in the best possible way for Ingrid.

The incoming ferry docked and began to discharge its load of vehicles and foot passengers. Glancing idly at the stream of cars coming ashore, Catherine recognised Anders Bjornson's Fiat among them. Surprised, she tapped her horn and waved but he didn't see her and the car sped past her up the incline and onto the road that led to the airport. For a few seconds Catherine debated whether or not she should go after him but she decided against it. He could be going anywhere, she thought. And almost certainly on business.

It wasn't until late that afternoon that he telephoned her and she was somewhat taken aback when he told her that he was calling from Oslo.

'I rang you before I left,' he said, 'but there was no reply. And I've been tied up since then. Are you all right?'

'Yes, I'm fine,' Catherine told him. 'But I was out most of the morning. That's why you couldn't get me. As a matter of fact I saw you on Valderoy.'

'Really?' said Anders, puzzled. 'What were you doing there?'

'Waiting for the ferry. I drove Anna Marie to the airport. She's gone to Bergen. There's a trade fair there this weekend.'

'You didn't say anything to her about the painting and the diary, did you?' Anders asked with a worried note in his voice.

'Yes,' Catherine said. 'I told her everything.'

'But you shouldn't have done!' he complained. 'We haven't any proof yet.'

'We have now. That's why I went to see her.' And she told him about the handkerchief.

'You promised you wouldn't go over to the island again on your own,' Anders said anxiously.

'I didn't promise anything,' Catherine reminded him. 'I said I wouldn't take any unnecessary risks. Besides, it's just as well I did, isn't it?'

'Except that on its own the handkerchief doesn't prove anything. And we need some hard evidence before we can take this business any further. That's why I came to Oslo.'

'And have you got some?'

'I'm not sure yet,' Anders replied mysteriously. 'I won't

know until tomorrow. I'll tell you when I get back. Anyway how did Anna Marie take it?'

Catherine gave him a resumé of everything that Anna Marie had said to her about her increasing concern for her sister. Then she asked, 'What time does your flight get in tomorrow?'

'I'm booked on the one that arrives just after six.'

'Good. Because I'm afraid I've let us in for spending some of the Midsummer festivities with the Nilsens and their lot.'

'Us?'

'Of course. I couldn't think of how to get out of Lars' invitation but there was no way I was going to go without you.'

'I'm glad to hear it,' Anders said. 'But going at all, is that a good idea? With things the way they are?'

'They weren't quite so definite when I said we would and it could be almost as awkward if we cried off. Coming up with some kind of explanation I mean. And I promised Anna Marie not to do or say anything more until she and I talked again. Besides, there'll be quite a lot of people there and we don't have to stop long.'

'Well, okay,' said Anders reluctantly. 'When are we expected?'

'Around seven.'

'Right. The only thing is it'll be close on seven by the time I get across from the airport. Tell you what, I'll meet you there shall I?'

'Okay.'

'And meantime, for God's sake don't do anything foolish! Ingrid's still around remember. So take great care. Bye, my love.'

Catherine slept well that night and she woke to another warm, sunny day. When she'd bathed and dressed she went downstairs and, unlocking the front door, she stepped out into the porch.

Instantly her cheerful expression turned to one of horror.

Impaled on a rusty nail protruding from one of the uprights of the porch was the doll that she'd found sitting on a stool in a corner of the nursery. And its face had been smashed in by a savage blow.

Sickened, Catherine removed the doll from the nail and stared at it. Then, moving out of the porch, she gazed across at the island.

The front door of Freya's house was wide open.

Catherine's first reaction was to call Anders but then she remembered that he was in Oslo. Run! Run! her instinct told her, and she glanced across at the car. The easiest and by far the best thing for her to do would be to get into it and drive away fast, and she knew it. But, as frightened as she was, she couldn't bring herself to. That's just what she wants, she told herself. And I'm not dancing to her tune. Not any more.

A cold anger welled up inside her, dulling the edge of her fear. It's time to put an end to all this nonsense, she decided. Here and now. Still clutching the doll, she ran down to the jetty and launched the dinghy.

When she reached the island she pulled the boat up onto the beach and, picking up the doll from the centre thwart, cautiously approached the house. As she did so she was greeted by the sound of the old waltz tune coming from the record player at full volume.

Outside the open front door she hesitated. 'Ingrid! Ingrid!' she shouted over the music. She waited but nothing happened.

When, warily, she entered it, there was no one in the sitting room and crossing quickly to the record player she switched it off. 'Ingrid!' she called. 'There's no point in hiding. I know you're here. I want to talk to you.'

There was no response.

Slowly Catherine climbed the stairs. At the head of them she pulled up with a start. While all the others were closed, the door at the far end of the corridor was half open and there was a key in the lock.

Now very afraid once more but determined to have a confrontation, Catherine made her way down the corridor. Tentatively she pushed the door fully open. The room was empty and, puzzled, she stepped inside.

The door swung back behind her and she spun round as the woman who had been concealed behind it took up a position barring her escape.

Catherine felt a scream rising in her throat.

Standing between her and the door, wearing the same white dress that she'd had her portrait painted in and studying her with a faintly malevolent smile on her lips was Freya Jordahl.

Chapter Fifteen

Catherine gazed at the apparition, her horror giving way first to astonishment and then to fearful curiosity.

And, as she studied the woman, she realised that although superficially the likeness, enhanced by the familiar dress, was remarkable and that she had the same style of make-up and that her hair was combed identically to match the portrait, nevertheless it wasn't Freya who stood before her.

Catherine had more or less prepared herself to come face to face with a sad impersonation that, in reality, was Ingrid in the guise of her mother. But, as the woman took a step forward out of the shadows around the door, it dawned on her with sickening and awesome clarity that she was confronted with something entirely unexpected and much more chilling.

It wasn't Ingrid who had taken on the identity of Freya Jordahl as she and Anders had suspected. It was Anna Marie.

'Anna Marie!' she gasped.

Anna Marie regarded her mockingly. 'Hjalmar didn't tell me about you, you know,' she said. And there was a timbre in her voice and a clipped quality to her manner of speaking which were both alien to her. She laughed hollowly. 'But then when a man has a bastard by another woman he's not likely to let his wife in on the secret, is he?'

Mesmerised, Catherine stared at her in disbelief. 'Anna Marie! What are you saying?'

'I can see a likeness,' Anna Marie continued as if she'd

not heard her. 'I did from the moment I first saw you. That night on the coastal steamer. But you're no match for the two girls I had by him,' she sneered. 'Anna Marie and Ingrid are much more beautiful than you are.'

'Oh my God!' Catherine groaned. 'Anna Marie, listen.' She made a move toward her.

With a teasing laugh, Anna Marie stepped back quickly, pulled open the door and swung round the edge of it out into the corridor. And before Catherine could get to it she slammed the door shut again and locked it. 'Anna Marie!' Catherine shouted, beating on the door with her fists. 'Don't be silly. Open the door. Anna Marie!'

But her pleading and cajoling had no effect and she heard Anna Marie, still laughing, move away and onto the landing.

Catherine looked around urgently for a way of escape but there wasn't one. The sill of the one window was only just in reach of her fully outstretched arm, and she now saw that it didn't open. And had she been able to reach it and smash the glass, the window frame looked far too narrow for her to squeeze through. What's more, even if she succeeded in doing so beyond it there was a sheer drop of thirty feet or more.

Dejectedly and facing the door, she sank down onto the carpet, her back against the wall.

She had been stupid to come across to the island in the first place. She saw that now. But then she had been anticipating that it was Ingrid she would have to contend with and, even allowing for the fact that she had to be mad, that was something she had felt she could handle. She had never for a moment suspected that it was not her but her friendly and helpful sister, who only the day before she'd seen board a flight to Bergen, who was responsible for all that had happened; that it was Anna Marie who was insane. And the revelation was a horrifying one. Had she not been out of her mind, a highly intelligent and ruthless Anna Marie would have been formidable enough and much more dangerous than Ingrid. And, deranged to the extent that she clearly was, she represented an even greater threat.

I trusted her, confided in her, Catherine berated herself. I even liked her and enjoyed her company! But then why not? I had no reason not to. Nothing she'd ever said or done had as much as hinted that she was unstable in any way. Far from it. She had always given the impression of being eminently sane. And yet, from the beginning she had planned all this. Everything. It had been her who had been at the wheel of the motor cruiser that night. And now?

She couldn't imagine what Anna Marie's next move might be but she realised that, given the opportunity, her only hope lay in humouring her until either she somehow managed to get off the island or, finding that she was not at the farmhouse, someone might just come looking for her.

It was five minutes to four when Anna Marie finally returned and by that time Catherine had been locked in the room for almost six hours.

Hearing the sound of the key turning in the lock, she looked up in trepidation. Slowly the door was pushed open and Anna Marie, standing just outside it, regarded her with a cunning smile on her lips.

Catherine eased herself up off the floor. 'Why did you do that?' she said as calmly as she could and as though addressing a mischievous child. 'Why did you lock me in here for all this time?'

Anna Marie pouted. 'You found my diary, didn't you?' she said defiantly.

'Yes,' Catherine admitted cautiously.

'And that man Bjornson read it to you, didn't he?'

'Yes.'

Anna Marie nodded. 'I know. Anna Marie told me,' she boasted. She frowned sulkily. 'Where is my diary?' she demanded.

'At the farmhouse,' Catherine said nonchalantly. 'Come over with me and I'll give it to you.'

Anna Marie gave her an amused look and then laughed. Turning, she walked away down the corridor and into Freya's room. Catherine waited for a few seconds and then followed her along the passage. Pausing in the open doorway, she looked in.

Anna Marie was sitting at the dressing table gazing into the mirror and brushing her hair. She was humming quietly to herself and Catherine recognised the tune as that of the waltz on the old record. Many of the clothes that had previously been hanging in the wardrobe were now laid out neatly across the bed. Seeing Catherine reflected in the mirror, Anna Marie smiled happily and went on brushing her hair. Sitting there she looked not only harmless but unworldly and vulnerable and, despite everything, Catherine found herself feeling sorry for her. I have to try to get through to her, she decided. 'I saw you get on the plane,' she said quietly. 'You came back, Anna Marie. Why? What are you doing here? What do you want from me?'

'Come in. Come in,' Anna Marie said gaily and without turning.

Catherine shook her head. 'I must go.' She sighed. It was no use. The woman was in a world where no one could reach her. But looking at her now she seemed more pathetic than dangerous.

'I don't want you to do that,' Anna Marie told her in a matter of fact tone, but pouting again.

'I have to, I'm afraid. It's late. If I don't get back soon Anders will come looking for me.'

Anna Marie studied herself in the mirror. 'Do you think I'm beautiful?'

'Yes. Very.'

'Jordahl thought I was beautiful,' Anna Marie said conversationally. 'That's why he married me. To have a beautiful wife to go with all his money. I was only nineteen when we got married, you know. He was old. Too old.' She frowned deeply. 'It was a mistake. A terrible mistake.'

Smiling again, she put down the hairbrush and, getting

up from the stool, walked over to the bed and pointed to the clothes lying on it. 'And these are beautiful too, aren't they?' she said. She picked up one of the dresses and stroked the material across her cheek. Then she held it out to Catherine. 'Here! Feel the material.' Catherine hesitated. 'Please!' Anna Marie pleaded. 'Feel it!'

Cautiously Catherine stepped out of the doorway and, crossing to her, felt the material.

'It's pure silk,' Anna Marie said proudly. She dropped the dress back down onto the bed and ran her hands over the bodice of the dress she was wearing. 'But this one's my favourite,' she went on. 'And it's Anna Marie's favourite too. Do you like it?'

Catherine nodded. 'It's very attractive.'

Anna Marie picked up another dress and offered it to her. 'Try this one on,' she suggested.

Catherine shook her head. 'No thanks.'

Anna Marie frowned angrily. 'Put it on!' she commanded sharply.

Her fear flooding back, Catherine nevertheless managed a pleasant smile. 'Another time,' she said. 'I've got to go home now.'

Anna Marie darted over to the door and slammed it shut. 'Put it on,' she snarled dangerously, holding out the dress and barring her way once more.

Again Catherine hesitated but then, anxious not to provoke her, she shrugged. 'All right,' she said.

She took the dress from her and laid it on the bed. Then, with Anna Marie watching her closely, she stripped down to her underwear.

'You have a nice body,' Anna Marie said admiringly. She crossed to her and put a hand on her shoulder and stroked it, savouring the texture of her skin.

Catherine froze. 'Thank you,' she said.

'Very nice,' Anna Marie murmured. 'So smooth. So silky.'

Catherine, her eyes fixed on hers, didn't flinch. Smiling, Anna Marie caressed her chin and her neck and then, with her fingers, delicately traced the ridge of her spine down to the top of her briefs. 'Do you like men touching you?' she asked huskily. 'I like being touched.' Her hand was inside Catherine's briefs now, exploring the crease between her buttocks. 'But not by Jordahl though. I didn't like that. Not at the beginning even. And then, later . . .' She shuddered and abruptly removed her hand. 'I couldn't bear it. But there were others he didn't know about of course,' she went on with a conspiratorial smile and stroking Catherine's shoulder again. 'Lots of them. And I like them touching me.' Her smile faded and was replaced by a look of bewilderment. 'Kiss me,' she said simply and like a child seeking reassurance. She turned her head and offered Catherine her cheek.

Realising that a refusal or hesitation even could well be the trigger for a manic outburst of some kind, Catherine leant in towards her.

As she did so Anna Marie swung her head round and, with a sudden and wild expression on her face, she seized her by the hair and twisted it in her hands. And, as Catherine's lips parted in response to the pain, she kissed her passionately on the mouth, her probing tongue thrusting deep inside it.

Catherine struggled and with a look of disgust broke free of her and stepped back out of reach.

Relishing her reaction and humiliation, Anna Marie laughed. She picked up the dress from the bed and tossed it over to her. 'If it fits and you like it you can have it,' she said pleasantly, as though nothing had happened.

Terrified, Catherine put on the dress and buttoned it up. Anna Marie studied her, appraising the effect. She nodded. 'It looks nice on you,' she said. But then, with another change of mood, she frowned. 'But you don't like it, do you?' she claimed sulkily and offended.

'Yes, of course I do,' Catherine assured her. 'It's very pretty.'

'Really?'

'Really.'

'I don't like it,' Anna Marie said. 'I never have. It reminds me of . . .' Her face crumpled as she tried to remember. 'I don't know what it reminds me of,' she cried desperately. 'Why can't I remember?' But then, in an instant, her desperation evaporated. 'It doesn't matter,' she said and she smiled good-naturedly again. 'You can have it.'

'Thank you.' Catherine unbuttoned the dress. 'But you must let me give you something in return,' she said. 'I tell you what! Why not come back with me now and you can choose anything you fancy out of my wardrobe. And I'll give you the diary.'

'I've written about you in my diary,' Anna Marie told her slyly.

'Yes, I know.'

Anna Marie's face took on an expression of great anger. 'You shouldn't have come here!' she said vehemently. 'You shouldn't! And it was wrong and wicked of Jordahl to put you in his will. What right have you to anything of his? Everything. It all belongs to Anna Marie and Ingrid. You shouldn't have been mentioned. And then it would have been all right. He did it to humiliate me. To humiliate them.'

Then, with yet another alarming change of mood, she calmed down and, cocking her head to one side, she studied Catherine interestedly. 'How long was your mother my husband's mistress?' she asked. 'Tell me. I have the right to know surely.'

Catherine regarded her pityingly. 'Anna Marie!' she beseeched. 'Listen to me.'

Anna Marie laughed. 'Do you like music?' she enquired gaily. 'I like music.' Turning, she ran over to the door and out of the room.

Catherine gazed after her sadly and when, a few minutes later and having put on her own dress again, she went downstairs, Anna Marie had turned the record player on once more and she was waltzing around the room, humming to herself and lost in the music.

At the foot of the stairs Catherine paused and looked across at her. She seemed oblivious of her presence but as she crossed to the open front door Anna Marie, still waltzing, glanced at her. 'This is my favourite,' she said. 'It's very old. When I was a child I remember . . .' Again she was confused and she stopped twirling. 'I think . . .' she stammered. She shook her head. 'Perhaps it wasn't me.' And then, smiling, she went on, 'It's lovely, isn't it?' She ran to Catherine and took her hands in hers. 'Dance with me,' she urged like an excited child.

Catherine tried to reason with her again. 'Anna Marie, please! You must stop this.'

Anna Marie's expression turned to one of alarm and concern. 'Quiet!' she said urgently. 'Listen!' She hurried over to the record player and hastily and clumsily lifted the pick-up arm off the record.

Catherine listened but there was nothing to be heard.

'The children!' exclaimed Anna Marie. 'They're crying. We've woken them up.' She ran back up to Catherine and seized her by the wrist. 'All this noise. We've woken them up.'

Catherine tried to wrest herself free but Anna Marie's grip was too strong. 'I'm coming, my darlings, I'm coming,' she called. And, pulling Catherine off balance, she dragged her back up the stairs and into the nursery.

Just inside the doorway she released her and, crossing quickly to the bed, she picked up the two Victorian dolls which were lying on it. 'Don't cry,' she said comfortingly. 'Mama's here. Mama's here.'

Cradling one of them in each arm, she sat down on the edge of the bed and, rocking back and forth, crooned soothingly, 'There! There!' She looked up at Catherine. 'Aren't I lucky to have such lovely children?' she said. 'And they're so good. Well, most of the time. Not always though. Anna Marie's quite naughty sometimes.' She looked down at one of the dolls and smiled indulgently. Then, looking at Catherine again, she said calmly, 'She killed her father, you know.'

Catherine reacted with a look of horror. So Anders had been right. And it was Anna Marie who had murdered Hjalmar Jordahl.

'That was very naughty of her, wasn't it?' Anna Marie continued. 'But then he deserved it really. He was a bad man. And he said wicked things to her. He threatened to have her shut away somewhere. He said she wasn't well. Told her she took after me and that I was mad. And that isn't true,' she said indignantly. 'It was never true. And of course Anna Marie was angry about that. And frightened. So she hit him with an oar. Then she took him out on the fjord in the storm and overturned the boat and everyone thought he'd been drowned.' She smiled winningly. 'That was extremely naughty, wasn't it? But very clever of her, don't you think?'

Appalled, and now for the first time realising the true extent of the danger she was in, Catherine turned and ran. And, engrossed in the dolls, Anna Marie made no attempt to stop her.

Bursting from the house, Catherine raced for the dinghy. At the top of the steps to the beach she looked back. There was no sign of Anna Marie. Stumbling over the shingle, she reached the boat and began pushing it down to the water, but then she saw that it was useless to her. Several large holes had been made in the hull along the length of the keel and the oars had been removed.

So that's what she was doing while I was locked away upstairs, thought Catherine. And what else, I wonder. She looked around wildly and then, spurred on by fear, ran for the trees behind the house. Blundering through them, she headed for the jetty at the rear of the island. Anna Marie has to have used a boat to get here, she told herself, and it must be moored somewhere.

It was tied up alongside the landing stage in the old boathouse; a sleek and powerful looking motorboat with an inboard engine. But when she jumped down into it, to her dismay, Catherine found that there was no key in the ignition switch. For a moment she was at a loss as to what to do but then it came to her that if she could manoeuvre the boat along the landing stage with her hands and push it out onto the fjord there was a good change it would drift into open water.

Clambering out of the boat she cast off the rear mooring line and then ran to the outer door. The chain hoist that opened it was securely padlocked. Desperately she threw her shoulder against the woodwork but, as badly weathered as it was, it wouldn't give.

Now near to panic, Catherine ran out of the boathouse. Fearfully she shot a look in the direction of the trees and the house beyond them but her tormentor was nowhere in sight.

Looking out across the fjord, her heart leapt. Some considerable way off the jetty, and well out of hearing distance, a motor cruiser was passing the island. If she could attract the attention of the people on board and get them to alter course and pick her up then she would be safe. She raced to the end of the jetty and waved urgently. 'Help me!' she shouted although she knew they couldn't possibly hear her. 'Help me!'

There were four people visible on the boat. Two women and a man were sunbathing on the roof of the cabin while a second man was at the wheel in the aft cockpit, steering and drinking from a bottle.

The party were obviously in a holiday mood and Catherine concluded that they were probably making for somewhere further along the fjord where they planned to celebrate the Midsummer festivities. Willing one of them to look in her direction, she shouted again and waved her arms frantically above her head. It was to no avail, though, and it began to look as thought the cruiser would pass without her being noticed. But then one of the women sat up and glanced idly across at the island. 'Oh thank God!' Catherine muttered and she continued waving.

The woman attracted the attention of the man at the wheel and pointed. He turned his head and gazed across at the island and, to Catherine's horror, he and the woman waved back cheerfully. And they went on waving intermittently as the boat pulled further and further away.

Sobbing, Catherine watched it go. Then she looked back down the fjord in the hope that there might be another craft heading in the same direction. But there was nothing else on the water.

There was only one way off the island open to her, she realised. But not from here, she told herself. Not from here. That would be impossible. Running back through the trees and skirting the house she returned to the beach opposite the farmhouse.

Still there was no sign of Anna Marie anywhere.

Catherine kicked off her shoes and, taking off her dress and letting it drop to the shingle, she waded into the water. Immediately she felt the pull of the current, and as she went out further she was nearly knocked off balance by it. She hesitated, unsure that she could make it but terrified of the consequences of failing. With no other choice but to try, she started forward again.

Now the water was up to her thighs and she was even more unsteady on her feet. Again she hesitated.

'That's it! Go on! Swim,' Anna Marie called and, with a start, Catherine looked back over her shoulder.

She was standing at the top of the steps watching her. She was holding the doll that Catherine had left lying on the floor in the empty room in one hand and agitatedly twisting and pulling at its hair with the other. She smiled. 'You can make it,' she urged flatly. 'Swim! It's the only way. Don't be afraid. Go on! Swim!'

Catherine looked across at the farmhouse and then down at the water surging around her and threatening to sweep her off her feet at any minute. She took another step forward.

'That's it,' Anna Marie encouraged her. 'Go on! You can do it.'

But now Catherine knew that she hadn't a hope of swimming the distance with the current running as strongly as it was. And she knows it too, she thought. That's why she wants me to make the attempt.

Resignedly she turned and slowly waded back to the beach. Anna Marie's disappointment showed on her face. 'No?' she said sadly. 'Oh, well!' She shrugged and then, with a cheerful smile, she went on brightly, 'Anyway it's time for tea.' She turned and walked back toward the house, throwing the doll down onto the grass as she did so.

Beaten and despairing, Catherine picked up her dress and put it on again. There was no escape. Anna Marie had made sure of that. And now she had only her wits to keep her alive until, with luck, Anders, worried because she wasn't at the Nilsens as they had arranged, drove out to Jordahlsholmen in search of her.

When she got back to the house the record was playing again and Anna Marie and the two Victorian dolls were seated around the coffee table which was laid with the child's tea service.

'That's right. Come along. Sit down,' Anna Marie said briskly and she indicated a chair that had been placed at the other end of the table from her. Catherine did as she was told.

Anna Marie poured an imaginary cup of tea from the small teapot she was holding and passed it to her. 'There you are,' she said. She looked at one of the dolls and frowned. 'No. You know you can't have a cup of tea Anna Marie,' she said firmly. 'It's not good for you. Only grown-ups have tea. Drink your milk, there's a good girl.' She turned to the other doll. 'What did you say, Ingrid? . . . Yes, you're right. It is rude of her to keep staring at you.' She glanced slyly at Catherine. 'But then she thinks you're crazy. That you painted that picture of her and that you want to hurt her.' Giggling, she nodded vigorously. 'Yes she does. She really does,' she chortled. She picked up an empty plate and offered it to Catherine. 'Cake?' she enquired politely.

Catherine mimed taking a piece and putting it on her plate. 'Thank you,' she said and then she added casually 'I must go soon I'm afraid. And without a boat I'm just wondering how I'm going to get home. Will you take me?'

Anna Marie looked at her solicitously. 'Of course I will,' she assured her. 'But it's early yet. And it's Midsummer Eve. We must build a bonfire.' She looked at each of the dolls in turn. 'You'd like that, wouldn't you? Eat up,' she told Catherine. 'We must get started on it. But we mustn't have it too near the house because that would be dangerous.'

Tea over they went out to the front of the house and having seated the dolls on a fallen tree trunk, Anna Marie instructed Catherine to gather up any driftwood or fallen branches she could find and, as she brought them to her, she set about building the foundations of the bonfire.

Stooping half-heartedly to pick up some small sticks from the beach, Catherine looked urgently across the channel but there was no one around or even approaching the farmhouse. She was aware of being very hungry, and realised she hadn't eaten all day.

She carried the token bundle of firewood back to Anna Marie who looked at it scathingly. 'Oh come on! Bigger pieces than that!' she exclaimed. She smiled at the dolls 'We want a good blaze, don't we children?'

By half past seven the bonfire was still no more than waist-high and, as she watched Anna Marie place another dead tree branch on it, Catherine was suddenly inspired. 'Why don't we forget about this,' she said.

Anna Marie frowned. 'Oh no!' she cried. 'The children would be so disappointed.'

'But this isn't going to be much of a show, is it?' Catherine argued. 'Why don't we take them to see one of the really big bonfires? They'd like that even better, wouldn't they?'

Anna Marie studied her thoughtfully. 'Do you think so?' she asked.

Catherine nodded. 'I'm sure of it.'

Biting her lip and undecided, Anna Marie looked across at the two dolls. Silently Catherine prayed that her ploy was going to work.

Her mind made up, Anna Marie smiled and nodded eagerly. 'Yes, I think you're right,' she said. 'Let's do that.'

'Right,' replied Catherine, her eyes fixed on her. 'Give me the key of the boathouse and the ignition key for your motorboat and, while you're getting Anna Marie and Ingrid ready, I'll bring it round to the other jetty. That way you won't have so far to go.'

Anna Marie smiled happily and again she nodded. 'Good idea!' She took the keys from her pocket and handed them to her.

'We must hurry,' Catherine said. 'We don't want them to miss any of the excitement, do we?'

'Oh no! That would be a shame,' Anna Marie agreed, crestfallen at the thought.

'Okay. Well you make sure they've got something warm to slip on in case it gets chilly later and I'll bring the boat round.'

'All right.'

Catherine swung round and started for the trees.

As she did so Anna Marie's smile faded and was replaced by a look of contempt. Calmly she picked up a stout length of timber from the top of the bonfire.

As Catherine heard her coming up behind her she began to turn, but it was too late.

Anna Marie struck her savagely on the head. With a cry, Catherine dropped the keys and pitched forward onto the ground, unconscious.

Anna Marie dragged her into the house, up the stairs and back into the empty room. Leaving her sprawled on the floor, she went out into the corridor and locked the door. Back downstairs again she walked into the kitchen and took a can of paraffin from one of the cupboards. Returning to the sitting room she piled most of the furniture together in a heap in the centre of the room. She unscrewed the top of the can and doused everything. Then, ripping down one of the curtains and soaking it with what remained of the fuel, she set light to it.

Crossing to the front door with the blazing curtain trailing behind her, she looked back and then, smiling, she tossed it onto the pile of furniture. The paraffin exploded into flames.

Outside, Anna Marie took a doll in each arm and settled herself down onto the fallen tree trunk. 'Now you just sit here quietly with Mama and watch the pretty bonfire,' she said. And she kissed them both.

Catherine struggled back to consciousness, immediately aware of a searing pain in her head. She was having difficulty in breathing as, with a great effort, and still only semi-conscious and coughing and retching, she pulled herself up into a sitting position. The room was rapidly filling with smoke and she could hear the crackling of the flames and feel the heat rising from the room below. Swaying and gasping for air, she put a hand to her head and when she looked at it she saw that it was covered in blood.

The smoke pouring in under the door was getting thicker by the second. In attempting to breathe she was sucking more and more of it into her lungs. Crawling over to the wall, Catherine clawed her way up it and onto her feet. Staggering to the locked door, she pounded on it feebly, too near to suffocation to even cry out.

Reeling back, she felt her knees buckling. Vomiting now, and no longer able to breathe, she collapsed onto the floor again.

For a moment, as she teetered on the edge of the dark pit that opened up to swallow her, it seemed to her that someone had their arms around her and that they were holding her back.

But then she slipped from their grasp and fell into he blackness of the bottomless void.

Chapter Sixteen

Anders had not been able to concentrate on anything that had been going on around him at the Molde rally. As speaker after speaker had droned on and on and as resolution after resolution had been proposed, amended and voted on, his mind had been elsewhere; on Catherine and on the diary.

First thing the following morning he did his best to cobble together a report of the proceedings but, as he dropped it into the editor's 'copy in' tray, he knew that it just wasn't good enough and that he'd probably be asked to account for it.

Returning to his office, he picked up the bound volume of back issues of the paper that he'd been using for reference and took it back to the library. A colleague was sitting at the long table in the middle of the room with several more of the back number files open in front of him. He looked up from his notebook and nodded. 'Hi,' he said.

'Hi.' Anders replaced the volume in its place on the shelves. As he was leaving, he paused alongside the table and idly scanned the headlines of the issues the other reporter was taking his notes from. He stiffened with interest as one in particular caught his eye.

It was on the front page of the edition dated Thursday, 18th April 1982 and it read, 'New International Banking Centre For Alesund.' Beneath it was a photograph with the caption, 'Hjalmar Jordahl with his daughters, Anna Marie and Ingrid, together with her husband Lars Nilsen, were among the distinguished guests at the official opening yesterday of the recently completed Sunnmorsbanken building.'

It was the picture that intrigued Anders. He turned the volume to him so that he could see it more clearly. It showed Jordahl, flanked by the two women and his son-in-law, seated at a table and signing the bank's visitors' book.

Anders looked up pensively and then, going back to his office, he unlocked the drawer where he'd put the diary after dropping Catherine back at Jordahlsholmen. Taking it out, he studied one of the entries. If Jordahl signed the visitors' book then it's almost certain they all did, he decided.

Replacing the diary and locking the drawer again, he hurried out of the office.

'I'm afraid Mr Follestad has someone with him at the moment,' the director's secretary told him. 'And he has several other appointments this morning. I'm not sure he'll be able to see you.' She shrugged. 'But if you care to wait.'

Follestad's office was on the sixth floor of the Sunnmorsbanken building and his secretary had her desk in a wide corridor outside it.

'Well, just in case he can give me a couple of minutes,' Anders said with a smile. Moving over to a leather armchair he sat down and, picking up a magazine from the low table in front of it, flipped through it.

Less than three yards away from him, on display on a small lectern which had no doubt been specially made for it, was the visitors' book.

The director's secretary went on with her typing. As the minutes ticked by Anders began to wonder whether this had been such a good idea after all. He had remembered seeing the visitors' book there on a previous visit and he was delighted to find that it hadn't been moved. But what now? With its guardian tapping away on her Olivetti he was stymied.

He threw down the magazine, stood up and glanced at

his watch. The secretary gave him a sympathetic smile and he shrugged resignedly. Wandering aimlessly over to the lectern he opened the handsome leather bound book and casually went through it.

On the first page, under a heading, 'Official Opening 17th April 1982', were, as he had hoped, not only Hjalmar Jordahl's signature but also those of Anna Marie, Ingrid and Lars Nilsen.

One of the telephones on the secretary's desk rang and she answered it. After a brief conversation she hung up and, to Anders' relief, taking a file from one of the cabinets behind her, she moved away down the corridor. Quickly he turned back to the first page and carefully cut it out of the book with his penknife. Folding it, he slipped it into his pocket.

At that moment the door of Follestad's office opened and the director ushered his visitors into the corridor. As he walked to the lifts with them he glanced at Anders and recognised him.

'What can I do for you, Mr Bjornson?' he said when he returned.

'Well, I know how busy you are, Mr Follestad,' Anders told him, 'and I won't keep you, but I'm thinking of doing a piece on American interest rates and how they might be affecting local industry. And, well naturally, I'd like your views on that.'

Follestad checked his watch. 'I can give you five minutes,' he said.

When Anders returned to the newspaper he checked the signatures on the page he'd stolen from the visitors' book against the handwriting in the diary and he saw that, although there was a family similarity in the way in which Ingrid and Anna Marie signed their names, none of the signatures in any way matched the writing in the journal.

Reaching for an Oslo telephone directory, he found the number he wanted and dialled it. 'I'd like to speak to Professor Solberg,' he said when his call was answered.

His conversation with Solberg was inconclusive but

hopeful and before he left the office again Anders tried ringing the Jordahlsholmen number but there was no reply. I'll call her from Oslo, he decided and minutes later, and taking the diary with him, he was on his way to Vigra.

The flight to Oslo took just over an hour and it was another thirty minutes by taxi to the university.

'Are you looking for a deliberately disguised hand-writing?' Solberg asked once Anders had elaborated on his telephone call.

The professor was a neatly dressed, rather fastidious man in his sixties with grey hair and a pair of horn-rimmed spectacles which, when he had no need for them, he either lifted onto his forehead or let hang from a silver chain around his neck.

Anders had met him before, both when he was a student in Oslo and on two occasions since then when he had gone to him for advice on articles he had been writing. 'No. Something more than that I think, Professor,' he said. Solberg looked at him interestedly. 'What I really want to know,' he went on, indicating the page from the visitors' book and the diary, both of which were lying on the desk between them, 'is whether that diary could have been written by anyone whose signature is on that page there.'

Solberg compared one against the other. 'On the face of it that's unlikely,' he said.

'But possible?'

Solberg nodded. 'Yes. But, if the signature is genuine and the diary is a forgery, extremely difficult to sustain.' He riffled through the journal. 'Almost impossible over this length of text.'

'The person I believe . . .' Anders started to say but Solberg raised a hand to silence him.

'I would prefer not to know that,' he told him. 'Given choices I dislike being prompted.' He removed his glasses and let them hang from their chain. 'As I've told you before, Bjornson,' he went on, 'graphology's not an exact

196

science. And it's not my field. Only an interest and, to my mind, a valuable adjunct to clinical psychology.'

'But just the same, you are an acknowledged expert on handwriting. The police would never have got a conviction in the Hauvik case for instance without your evidence.'

'It was Hauvik's personality as an international swindler on such a grand scale that interested me on that occasion,' Solberg said. 'And the opportunity to analyse those documents he forged provided me with a further insight into it. My role as a prosecution witness was entirely secondary as far as I was concerned. And the documents on their own could not have convicted him. The infamous Dr Crippen's signature indicated that he was an inhibited, shy man who bottled up his emotions whilst at the same time being headstrong, extremely aggressive and possessing an inclination toward total moral detachment. It would not have proved that he was a murderer. Merely that he was perhaps slightly more capable of it than others. So if you're looking for evidence as such . . .' he shrugged.

'No. Not evidence,' Anders assured him. 'Well, not in the legal sense anyway. I just need to know if what I suspect is true.'

Solberg studied him and then, putting on his glasses again, looked at the diary and the page from the visitors' book once more. 'And how urgent is this analysis?' he asked.

'Very, I'm afraid.'

Solberg sighed. 'Well it's not something that can be done in five minutes. I'll need photographic enlargements of all these specimens. Slides will have to be made. And only when that's done can I even begin to form any kind of opinion. And note the word carefully, "opinion". Not judgement. And Friday afternoon is not the most convenient time to launch even the preparatory work for tests of this kind,' he said somewhat tetchily.

'I appreciate that,' replied Anders. 'And if it wasn't so desperately important I wouldn't . . .'

Again Solberg silenced him with a gesture. 'And if I

didn't know, respect and believe you, Bjornson, I wouldn't consider it,' he said and then he looked at his watch. 'Well, even allowing for my being able to persuade my technicians to stay on for a while and my forgoing part of the weekend, it will not be possible for me to give you an answer before noon tomorrow. And that is only an estimate. It could take longer.'

This came as a blow to Anders. He had planned on returning to Alesund that night. Still, he was asking a lot of Solberg as it was and if that wasn't possible, he'd just have to stay on. 'If I could catch the sixteen-fifty flight back to Alesund that would be fine,' he said.

'And equally so if I were free to spend Midsummer Eve with my family,' Solberg retorted. He smiled thinly. 'So we'll aspire to both those aims, shall we?'

Anders took a room in a small hotel not far from the campus and then he telephoned Catherine. Her news about finding the handkerchief and her report of her conversation with Anna Marie worried him. 'You promised you wouldn't go over to the island again on your own,' he said anxiously.

'I didn't promise anything,' Catherine reminded him. 'I said that I wouldn't take any unnecessary risks. Besides, it's just as well I did, isn't it?'

'Except that on its own the handkerchief doesn't prove anything,' he told her. 'We need some hard evidence before we can take this business any further. That's why I came to Oslo.'

'And have you got some?'

Anders' reply was vague and when she went on to tell him about having accepted the invitation for them to spend Midsummer Eve with Lars and Ingrid and their friends he was very uneasy about it. But her arguments against backing out were sound enough and he agreed to meet her at the Nilsen house as soon as possible after he got back.

That night, though, he lay awake for a long time regretting that he hadn't tried harder to persuade her that it wasn't a good idea.

He was back at Solberg's room at the university promptly at midday.

After telling him that he had completed his analysis and outlining some of his findings, the professor took him along to a laboratory where a slide projector and a screen had been set up.

Lowering the blinds, Solberg switched on the projector and, putting a slide in the carrier, slid it behind the lens. Two images appeared on the screen. Using a pointer, Solberg explained what they were. 'The lower case "n" on the right,' he said, warming to his subject, 'is the magnification of one in the diary. And the lower case "n" on the left is from one of the signatures on that sheet of paper you gave me. And notice that, despite the consistent flow of linkage in the rest of the writing, in each case the "n" is not connected to the next letter. And it's the same throughout. That's the most obvious proof. That and the general pattern of pressure and the structure of the arcades. Particularly in the earlier diary entries.'

'I was right then,' Anders said, pleased with himself.

Solberg picked up the diary from beside the projector where he had placed it before drawing the curtains. 'That this diary and one of those signatures was written by the same hand?' He nodded. 'In my opinion, yes. But there's more to it than that. Something quite extraordinary. Something very disturbing.'

'What do you mean?' Anders asked, frowning.

'In no way is this diary a calculated forgery. At the time the writer made these entries she was, at that moment, an entirely different person. She had taken on another identity. Become someone else. It's very clear evidence of advanced schizophrenia.'

'Which is just as I suspected.'

Solberg frowned. 'Really! It's a very rare condition. To that degree at least.'

'But not unprecedented.'

'By no means. There are a number of well-authenticated instances of total personality transference.'

'And you're positive about this, are you, Professor?' Anders asked.

'Like their fingerprints, a person's handwriting is unique,' Solberg said. 'No matter how you are taught to write as a child by the time you're an adult the *way* you write is exclusive to you, reflecting your character, personality and, to some extent, your potential. And, at any given time, it is also an invaluable indicator of your mental state. Of course anyone can copy another person's handwriting with varying degrees of success. But it's extremely difficult to maintain a forgery over several pages of text. Sooner or later your own style will intrude in ways which, however apparently insignificant, will betray the deception and incriminate you. And that is what has happened here. Despite the fact that, under the influence of this other personality, the diary is written in an altogether different hand and although, in this instance, that style has not been assumed but imposed on the writer and is very consistent, nevertheless there are, within the text, elements of her own style which are peculiar to her alone and from which it would be impossible for her to detach herself. And this, as one would expect, is most likely to occur when she writes her own name.'

He removed the slide from the projector, picked up another one and inserted it into the carrier. 'And, merely from this evidence, there is one other thing I am in no doubt about whatever,' he went on. 'This woman needs psychiatric help and care. And quickly. Because hers is a very sick mind indeed.'

'You mean she's insane.'

Solberg frowned. 'Insanity's not a word which appears in the psychiatric lexicon, my dear Bjornson. And it is certainly not a clinical diagnosis. But within the layman's understanding of the various aspects of psychosis, yes. Perhaps even dangerously so. And not only to herself.' He pushed the carrier into the projector and Anna Marie's signature appeared on the screen. 'You see it there?' he continued and indicating with the pointer. 'The break between the second "n" and the "a"?'

Totally unprepared for the shock, Anders stared at the screen, stunned and aghast.

Immediately he left Solberg he telephoned Catherine again but she didn't answer. She must have gone into town, he decided. And anyway, with Anna Marie in Bergen for the weekend, she's in no immediate danger.

Nevertheless the flight back to Alesund was an agony for him and when he arrived at Vigra the first thing he did was to ring Catherine again. Still there was no reply. Slightly alarmed, he checked his watch and then sighed with relief. Of course, he told himself. Even if she's been back to the house she'll be well on her way to the Nilsens by now and that's no longer a worry. She'll be okay with them until I get there.

But, as he had realised on the aircraft, in order to tell her the whole truth there was someone else he had to speak to first.

'And what are these?' Astrid demanded, examining the bottle of capsules which Albrigtsen had given her.

'They're to help you sleep,' he told her. 'This business has upset you. And you don't get enough rest as it is.' He put out a hand to take the bottle from her. 'I'll give them to Gerda,' he said.

'I'm not a child,' Astrid snapped and she slipped it into her pocket. 'Did you speak to Catherine?' she asked anxiously.

Albrigtsen frowned and shook his head. 'No,' he said. 'After what you told me yesterday about the diary I went straight out to Jordahlsholmen but she wasn't there. I'm seeing her tonight though. If I get the chance I'll talk to her about it then.'

Astrid stared dolefully into space. 'It's all over, Arne,'

she sighed. 'It's all going to come out now. I know it. It has to.'

'Nonsense,' Albrigtsen said sharply. 'There's absolutely no reason why it should. You mustn't think like that.'

A car pulled up outside, startling Astrid out of her reverie. She wheeled herself over to the window. 'Who's this?' she muttered. 'I'm not expecting anyone.' She peered out into the drive and frowned. 'I know that car!' she exclaimed and, agitated, she swung her wheelchair round to face Albrigtsen again.

He regarded her questioningly but before he could say anything the doorbell rang. After a short and increasingly angry exchange of words in the hall with Gerda, Anders Bjornson strode into the room followed by the housekeeper.

'I'm sorry to intrude like this, Miss Linderman, but I have to talk to you,' he said.

'He just pushed past me,' Gerda complained, outraged. 'I told him you had someone with you.'

Astrid studied him. 'You're the young man who drove Catherine Durrell here the other day, aren't you?' she said accusingly.

'Yes.' Anders glanced at Albrigtsen. 'Good evening, Dr Albrigtsen.'

'Good evening,' Albrigtsen said.

'You know him?' Astrid asked, surprised.

Albrigtsen nodded. 'Yes. Mr Bjornson works for the *Sunnmorsposten*.'

Appalled, Astrid looked at Anders again. 'You're a journalist!' she cried.

'Yes,' Anders confirmed. 'But I'm not here on behalf of the paper.'

'What do you want?'

Anders shot a look at Gerda. 'It's a private matter,' he said.

Astrid frowned and hesitated but then she waved Gerda away. Giving Anders an indignant glare, the woman left the room, closing the door behind her.

'Well, in that case,' Albrigtsen said and making a move as if to follow her. He looked at Astrid. 'Unless you want me to stay?'

'No, don't go, Doctor,' Anders said. 'This concerns you too.'

Scowling, Astrid wheeled herself over to him. 'Well?' she demanded. 'What is it?'

Anders took the diary from his jacket pocket and, seeing it, Astrid reacted with a start and backed away. 'Catherine brought this diary to you and you identified the writing as Freya Jordahl's,' he said.

Concerned for his patient, Albrigtsen moved to her side.

'I've nothing more to say about that,' Astrid blustered. 'Not to anyone.' She put out a hand. 'Please give me that book and go away,' she said imperiously.

'May I?' Albrigtsen asked quietly and also putting out his hand. Anders handed it to him. 'Thank you.' He opened the journal and examined one of the entries.

'I don't think you realise what's been happening to Catherine since she arrived in Alesund,' Anders said, holding Astrid's withering gaze. 'Almost from the first day she's been persistently harassed. And an attempt was made to kill her.'

Shocked and surprised, Albrigtsen looked up from the diary.

'What are you saying?' Astrid gasped.

'Twice now she's seen a woman who she thought was your dead niece.'

'She said nothing to me about this,' exclaimed Albrigtsen.

'No. Nor to me,' Astrid said scornfully.

Anders nodded. 'I know,' he said. 'And at the outset I didn't believe it either. But it happened. I'm quite certain about that now. And that same woman tried to murder her. Well, we all know that it can't have been Freya Jordahl. Just as we know that that isn't Freya's diary.' He took the diary from Albrigtsen. 'At first all the evidence pointed to Ingrid,' he went on. 'And that being so she quite clearly had to be out of her mind. But just to make sure,' he held up the diary, 'I took this to Oslo and showed it to the leading clinical psychologist in Norway. A man who also happens to have a special interest in graphology. And, after comparing those entries with some signatures I gave him, he's convinced that it wasn't Ingrid who wrote all that in her mother's handwriting. It was her sister. And, according to him, Anna Marie's a dangerous schizophrenic.'

'Oh dear God! Dear God!,' Astrid cried, her face a study in abject horror. She covered her mouth with her hands.

'But this is outrageous!' Albrigtsen said angrily. 'You burst in here with some wild story about . . .' With an effort he contained his anger. 'You surely don't expect us or anyone else to give any credence to . . .'

'Professor Solberg is prepared to testify to it if necessary,' Anders said, breaking in on him.

Astrid reached out and clutched Albrigtsen's hand. 'I knew it!' she moaned pitifully. 'I knew it! It's happening all over again.'

'What is?' Anders asked. 'What's happening all over again?'

'Nothing,' Albrigtsen said dismissively. 'Miss Linderman has been under considerable stress for some time now. And a shock like this, well it doesn't help. She's confused.'

'She meant that Anna Marie's suffering from the same kind of mental breakdown her mother had, didn't she?' Anders retorted.

'You know about that!' the doctor exclaimed.

'Yes.'

Albrigtsen sighed. 'Of course,' he said resignedly and realising where he'd got the information from. 'Catherine told you, didn't she?'

'In the strictest confidence.'

'Look,' Albrigtsen suggested. 'Can't we discuss this somewhere else? And at some other time perhaps.'

'No, I'm afraid we can't. There's something I have to

know. It's very important. And I think it's just possible that Miss Linderman might have the answer.'

Astrid shook her head despairingly. 'What is it?' she asked dully. 'What do you want to know?'

'It's clear from the diary,' Anders told her, 'that Anna Marie's hatred for Catherine stems from the fact that she genuinely believes that she's Hjalmar Jordahl's illigitimate child.' He moved in closer to Astrid and looked down at her. 'Is she?' he asked gently.

Astrid spun the wheelchair away from him, wheeled herself back over to the window and stared out onto the drive once more.

'How could Miss Linderman possibly be expected to know that?' Albrigtsen argued.

'She's more likely to know the truth than anyone else I can think of,' Anders said. 'She and Jordahl were very close. For seven years they lived through the tragedy of his wife's illness together. If he confided in anyone it has to be her.'

'But does it really matter?'

'Yes. Because Catherine has to know, one way or the other. And I want to be the one to tell her when I see her tonight. And if it isn't true, and somehow Anna Marie can be made to accept that fact, well perhaps that might be the beginning of a successful course of treatment for her.' He walked over to the window. 'Well, Miss Linderman. *Is* it true?'

Astrid did not reply immediately. Then her shoulders drooped and she heaved a sigh of relief as if finally accepting the inevitable. Still staring out of the window she shook her head. 'No, it isn't,' she told him wearily. 'Catherine Durrell is not Hjalmar Jordahl's bastard.'

She turned the wheelchair to face Anders. 'She's Freya's child,' she said.

Chapter Seventeen

Lost in memories, Astrid sipped the whisky which Albrigtsen had poured for her.

The doctor put the bottle back on the table next to Anders. 'Did you know this?' Anders asked him.

Albrigtsen shook his head. 'No,' he said quietly, his eyes on his patient. 'Nor did I even suspect it.'

Astrid dragged her thoughts back to the present. 'I wanted to tell Catherine the truth the first time she came to see me,' she said pensively. 'But I couldn't. For Freya's sake I thought. For Jordahl's sake. To protect everyone.'

Albrigtsen moved to her side again. 'You don't have to say any more you know,' he told her gently. 'Not if it distresses you.'

'Oh, but I do,' she said, looking up at him. 'Because of what's happening now. I no longer have any choice. And you don't understand. I have to. I need to.' She took another sip of whisky and went on, 'According to Hjalmar he fell in love with Freya the moment he saw her. In the National Gallery in Oslo. She was doing some research for her studies and he was idling away time between meetings. He persuaded her to have dinner with him and it was when he brought her home that night that I first met him.'

Putting down her glass, she wheeled herself over to the french windows and gazed into the garden. 'He was supposed to return to Alesund the next day but he stayed on, just to see her again. He said nothing about the way he felt, though, and finally he went home and tried to forget her. But that didn't work. So, a year later when he was in Oslo again, he called at my house to see her. But

Freya wasn't there. She was in hospital. She'd tried to kill herself.'

'But she can't have been more than ...' Albrigtsen protested, shocked.

'She was eighteen,' Astrid said dully.

'She attempted suicide!' Anders exclaimed. 'At that age! Why?'

'The student she'd been having an affair with deserted her. She was four months pregnant.' Remembering, Astrid shook her head in admiration. 'Hjalmar was wonderful to her. He visited her every day. And when she was released from hospital he made a great fuss of her and they became very close. And, well, eventually he asked her to marry him. And by this time Freya had become very fond of him. And she was grateful to him too I think. Anyway she agreed. But he made one condition. He wasn't prepared to take on the responsibility for a child who wasn't his. So, if they were to marry, he insisted that the baby she was carrying had to be adopted.'

She returned to her glass and, picking it up, drank from it once more.

'And she was quite happy about that?' Albrigtsen asked.

Astrid nodded. 'She was all for it.' Putting her glass down again, she wheeled herself over to the bookshelves and took down one of the photograph albums. 'And, as it happened, one of my ex-pupils, a girl called Kirsten Enger, was planning on adoption at that time.'

Turning the pages she found the photograph she was looking for and handed the album to Anders. He recognised the picture as a duplicate of one of the photographs in the diptych that Catherine had on her bedside table. He passed the album on to Albrigtsen.

'She had been married for more than three years and was still childless,' Astrid continued. 'Both she and her husband desperately wanted a baby but Kirsten had recently been told that she couldn't have any.' Restlessly she took herself over to the french windows again. 'When I told Hjalmar about the Durrells he asked me to approach them. To him the idea of their taking the child had two great advantages. The baby would be going to a mother I knew and could vouch for and the adoption could be done without going through official channels. That meant that no one outside the three of us would ever know that Freya had had a child before her marriage to Jordahl.'

Albrigtsen put the photogrpah album down on the table. Astrid sighed. 'So Freya had the baby and, almost immediately, it was handed over to Kirsten,' she said. 'The Durrells registered the girl as their own with the British Embassy and six months later, when Richard Durrell's contract in Norway expired, he took his wife and family home with him to England.'

'And they never returned to this country?' queried Anders.

'No. They had no reason to. In any case I think they were afraid that if they did . . .' The old woman shrugged. She wheeled herself away from the french windows and picked up her glass.

'Did Freya know who her baby had gone to then?' Albrigtsen asked.

Astrid shook her head. 'No. So any fears they had were quite unjustified. And the Durrells didn't know who it's real mother was either. Just that she was a girl of a good family who didn't want to keep it. And that was the end of the matter as far as Hjalmar and I were concerned.' She took another sip of whisky and then stared down into the glass. 'I stayed in touch with Kirsten though. We exchanged letters regularly. And, right from the start, Hjalmar was very anxious that I kept him informed about the baby. And I went on doing that. For years. Up until long after Catherine had left school. He wanted to know everything that happened to her.'

'Which has to be why she was in the will,' Albrigtsen said. He looked at Anders. 'She was on his conscience. Hjalmar obviously felt that he'd robbed her of something which, if he hadn't insisted on her being adopted, would have been hers by right. And he wanted to make amends.'

'Yes,' Astrid agreed. 'That is the only explanation.' She finished her drink and, trundling herself over to the whisky bottle, poured herself another one.

'Did Freya show the same kind of interest in the baby?' Anders enquired.

'No. Not at the beginning,' Astrid told him. 'Not even a casual interest. For two or three years after they got married she and Jordahl seemed very happy together. Jordahl became even more successful in business and, as far as one could tell, Freya had settled into her new life in Alesund without any problems. But shortly after Ingrid was born she changed completely. She became very introverted and obsessed with her first child. She began to question Hjalmar about her, endlessly, demanding to know what had become of her.'

'And what did he tell her?' asked Anders.

'Only that she was well and happy. He assured her of that. And he begged her to put the child out of her mind and forget what had happened in the past. But she wouldn't. Or couldn't. And then, as she became increasingly disturbed, she started accusing him of robbing her of the baby; claiming that he had forced her to give it up against her will.'

Anders regarded her questioningly. 'Is that when she started collecting dolls?'

'Yes. And Hjalmar bought her more and more of them. Although I don't think he realised then what the collection really was to her.'

'A search for her lost child,' Anders said thoughtfully. He looked at Albrigtsen. 'And eventually she became totally deranged?'

The doctor nodded. 'I did what I could for her. But of course I knew nothing about any of this. If I had . . .' He sighed deeply and then shrugged. 'I doubt if it would have made much difference though. And Hjalmar refused to have her hospitalised.'

'Instead he bought Jordahlsholmen and installed her in the house on the island,' Astrid went on. 'And I gave up my job to look after her. Because, by then, she couldn't bear to be near Hjalmar. Or to have his children round her. Except occasionally in those brief periods when, unbelievably, she seemed almost her old self. Only they got fewer and fewer. And then, at the end . . .' She broke off and stared into her glass once more.

'She finally succeeded in committing suicide,' Anders prompted.

Slowly Astrid lifted her head and looked at him, grim faced. 'No,' she said.

Puzzled, Anders frowned.

'Astrid!' Albrigtsen exclaimed, alarmed. 'No more! That's enough!'

Astrid turned to him and shook her head. 'I can't carry the burden any longer, Arne,' she said plaintively. 'It's too heavy. I want to be free of it.' She looked at Anders again. 'From time to time Hjalmar would come across to the island late at night,' she elaborated. 'That way I was able to tell him how Freya was getting along. We both thought she didn't know about his visits but one night, when he was returning to his boat, she was waiting in hiding for him. And she tried to kill him with an axe. Fortunately he managed to disarm her and he wasn't hurt, thank God. But we both knew then that there was no longer any alternative. She was homicidal. She had to be put away.' She was weeping now, the tears coursing down her parchment cheeks. 'The thought of her being shut away for the rest of her life with a lot of other mad people was more than I could bear, though. She was only a baby when her parents were killed. And, after all those years of bringing her up and looking after her, to me she was everything. Almost my own child.' She shook her head despairingly. 'I couldn't, I just couldn't let that happen to her. So, when Hjalmar had left, I gave her an overdose of the phenobarbitone Arne had prescribed for her.'

She gave a great shuddering sigh and then looked at Anders and, through the tears, held his gaze levelly. 'So you see,' she said, 'Freya didn't take her own life. I killed her.'

Anders and Albrigtsen left the house together. Outside the front door Anders paused and looked at the doctor. 'You guessed what she'd done of course,' he said.

Albrigtsen shook his head. 'She told me she'd given Freya an overdose. And why. She saw it as a mercy killing.'

'And that's true I suppose,' Anders said thoughtfully.

'Yes. The way things were. It was a kindness anyway. That's why I didn't report it and covered up for her.'

Anders studied him and then nodded understandingly. 'Will she be all right?'

'Gerda will look after her. And I'll call back later and make sure.' Anders made a move toward his car. 'Where are you going now?' Albrigtsen asked.

'To the Nilsens. I'm meeting Catherine there. And they have to know about all this too.' He glanced at the house and sighed. 'Well, most of it anyway.'

'I'll come with you,' Albrigtsen said.

And it was he who broke the news to Lars and Ingrid. Sitting side by side on the settee and holding hands, they listened to him in silence while, outside on the lawn, those friends of theirs who had already arrived and moored their boats at the jetty chatted and laughed and enjoyed their drinks.

The only thing Albrigtsen didn't tell them was that Astrid had administered the fatal overdose.

When he'd finished Ingrid, who toward the end had begun to cry and whose only outward show of surprise had been at the revelation about Catherine, slowly raised her head. To Anders' surprise, she confessed, tearfully, 'I've known about Anna Marie for a long time. But it was only recently that I realised just how ill she is.'

Lars gazed at her in astonishment and squeezed her hand to comfort her.

'I found out ages ago that she was going across to the island,' she went on abjectly. 'And pretty regularly. I followed her once and saw her playing with the dolls; dressed in mother's clothes.'

'Oh Ingrid, my dear,' Albrigtsen sighed. 'Why didn't you tell me about this at the time?'

'How could I?' she cried. 'How could I tell anyone a thing like that? That my sister was going out of her mind. And if I had, what would you have done about it?'

'Made sure that she received treatment,' Albrigtsen told her.

'Had her committed you mean.'

'Yes, if necessary,' he admitted.

'Exactly,' Ingrid retorted defensively. 'And I couldn't do that to her. Besides, then there didn't seem to be any great harm in what she was doing. And most of the time she appeared quite normal.'

'So you kept quiet,' Anders interjected. 'And whenever she went to the house you tidied up after her.'

Ingrid nodded. 'I had to keep checking. Just in case she'd been over again. I couldn't risk the cleaning woman discovering anything out of place and talking about it. And I was happy enough to do that. Anyway I had to. To protect Anna Marie. And, like I said, this aberration of hers wasn't hurting anyone. It was just rather pathetic. And if it made her happy.' She got up from the settee and moved aimlessly around the room. 'When Catherine turned up though and moved into Jordahlsholmen, well that worried me,' she explained. 'So I tried to buy the place from her.'

'Yes, Catherine told me,' Anders said. He looked at his watch and frowned. It was twenty past seven and she still hadn't arrived.

'Were you aware of what was going on?' Albrigtsen asked Lars.

Nilsen shook his head. 'No,' he said gravely, his eyes on his wife. 'Only that Ingrid was very distressed and bottling something up inside her. I tried to get her to talk to me about it but she wouldn't.'

Ingrid turned to him. 'I wanted to, Lars!' she cried

desperately. 'Oh how I wanted to! But I couldn't share a secret like that. Not even with you. And, after that business with the motor cruiser when Catherine nearly drowned and you found those marks on our boat, I realised that it had to be Anna Marie who'd tried to kill her. And if I'd said anything to you then you might have gone to the police.'

Anders went over to her. 'Has it occurred to you that by taking your boat that night she was deliberately trying to implicate you?' he said. 'She's been using you to cover her tracks all along, Mrs Nilsen. And very successfully. Up until this morning she had me convinced that it was you who was psychotic. Not her. She even painted a grotesque portrait of Catherine in your style and left it for her to find.'

'Yes, I know. It was there when I went over to the house the last time.' She gasped. 'Did she see it?' Anders nodded. 'Oh God!' Ingrid moaned. 'I hoped she hadn't. That's why I took it away.' Moving across to the painting hanging above the woodstove, she stared up at it. 'We both inherited some artistic talent from our mother,' she said distantly. 'Catherine too probably.' She looked at Albrigtsen. 'We're bound to have a lot in common, aren't we? The three of us.' And then, gazing at the painting again, she went on. 'But Anna Marie's a far better painter than I could ever hope to be. And there was something in my pictures that frightened me. But it wasn't until I discovered what was happening with Anna Marie that I knew what it was. A hint of madness. So I stopped and burned everything I'd done except this one.' She turned to Anders. 'And when I saw the hate in that portrait, well I knew then that I couldn't keep it all to myself any longer. So I drove out to Jordahlsholmen this afternoon to warn Catherine and tell her everything. She wasn't at home though.'

Again Anders checked his watch. 'And where is she now, for God's sake?' he said anxiously. He glanced at Lars. 'I think I'll give her a call and see what's holding her up.'

Lars got to his feet. 'Of course,' he said. 'Use the phone in the study.' And crossing to the study door, he opened it for him.

'Thanks,' Anders said, hurrying past him.

Lars closed the door again and then went over to his wife. 'Are you okay?' he enquired solicitously.

Still staring at the painting, Ingrid nodded. Moving to the drinks cabinet, Lars poured her a drink and took it to her. Then, crossing to Albrigtsen, he asked, 'So what will happen about Anna Marie?'

Albrigtsen shook his head sadly. 'There's no question,' he said. 'She has to be confined somewhere. And properly looked after.'

'Can she be cured?'

Albrigtsen shrugged. 'Who knows?' he sighed. 'Hopefully.'

Anders came back into the room looking worried. 'Catherine's not there,' he said.

Ingrid frowned. 'She can't still be on the island surely.'

'On the island!' Anders exclaimed, shooting a look at her.

'Well that's where she was when I drove out to talk to her,' she said. 'I saw her boat on the beach.'

With an expression of alarm, Anders started toward the front door. 'I'm going out there,' he announced.

'And pass her on the way probably,' Albrigtsen reasoned.

'Yes,' Lars said. 'Why not give her another half hour or so? She can't have come to any harm. And Anna Marie's in Bergen.'

At the top of the steps up to the hall, Anders turned and looked at him. 'But is she?' he said urgently. 'Or is that what she wants everyone to think?'

Seizing on the frightening implications in this possibility, Lars was immediately infected by his concern. 'It'll be quicker by boat,' he said briskly and heading for the patio.

As the Jordahl 29 cut through the water at full power with

Lars at the wheel, Anders stood alongside him, his stomach tightly knotted with anxiety. Behind them in the stern Ingrid sat, pale and erect, clasping Albrigtsen's hand for support.

They saw the column of smoke when they were still some distance off from the island and then, as they got nearer, the glow of the flames behind the trees.

'Oh my God!' gasped Anders and when Lars brought the cruiser in toward the old boathouse he was already crouching in the bow. There were still three or four feet between the boat and the jetty when he leapt ashore and sprinted for the house.

Exploding out of the trees, he pulled up sharply, horrified. The house was well alight and the ground floor was already an inferno. And a woman who could have been Freya Jordahl but who had to be Anna Marie was sitting on a fallen tree tunk calmly watching it burn, a doll in each arm.

Anders raced over to her. 'What have you done?' he shouted. 'And where's Catherine?'

Anna Marie looked up at him and smiled. Anders grabbed her by the shoulders and savagely pulled her to her feet. She dropped the dolls. 'Where's Catherine?' he roared, shaking her violently.

Lars, Ingrid and Albrigtsen ran up to them and all three stared at Anna Marie in stunned disbelief. She giggled and looked across at the house.

Anders let out a cry of anguish. 'Oh no! You murderous bitch!' He threw Anna Marie down onto the grass and ran toward the burning building.

The sitting room was a mass of flames but, standing in the doorway and shielding his face against the glare and the heat with his arm, he saw that the stairs were still intact. Hurling himself forward and with the fire closing in around him, he gingerly edged his way up them. 'Catherine!' he called. 'Catherine!'

Ingrid looked down at her sister. 'Oh, Anna Marie! What have you done?' she sobbed.

With a wild, uncomprehending look on her face, Anna Marie dragged and pushed herself away from her, feverishly looking around for an avenue of escape. Seeing the doll with the smashed face lying nearby she grabbed it and held it up in triumph. 'You see,' she whimpered. 'She came here to cause trouble. His bastard. She's not wanted. She's not wanted. I had to do it to protect Anna Marie and Ingrid. To protect us all.'

Ingrid gazed at her with a mixture of disgust and pity. 'But she's not Hjalmar Jordahl's child,' she moaned through her tears. 'She's not related to him in any way. She's our mother's child. Born before she married Jordahl.'

As this registered, Anna Marie stared up at her in amazement. Confused, she shot a searching, incredulous look at Albrigtsen. He nodded. 'Yes. She's Freya's child,' he said.

Anna Marie, even more bewildered and confused now, glanced at Nilsen. 'It's true,' he told her.

'No! No! You're trying to trick me,' Anna Marie cried, shaking her head. 'She can't be.' She looked at the doll she was holding. 'She's mine?' she whispered, trying to get it straight in her mind. 'Mine?'

'No,' Ingrid said. 'You're not Freya. You're Anna Marie Jordahl.'

Lars picked Anna Marie up and set her on her feet. 'Freya was your mother,' he said gently. 'And Catherine's mother too.'

A twisted truth registered in Anna Marie's mind. 'She's my baby!' she screamed. 'She's my baby!'

Before anyone could stop her and still clutching the doll, she raced for the house calling, 'Catherine! Catherine!'

'Anna Marie!' Ingrid shouted. 'Come back.'

Anders had his shoulder to the locked door when Anna Marie, her hair scorched and her clothes smouldering, staggered down the smoke-filled corridor, the doll in one hand and the key in the other.

He snatched it from her and, unlocking the door, eased it open against Catherine's prone body. Gathering her up in his arms he carried her out into the corridor. Distraught,

Anna Marie put out a hand to touch her but Anders pushed past and stumbled away onto the landing.

Anna Marie looked down at the doll and her face crumpled. 'You're my baby. What have I done?' she wailed. 'You're my baby. Oh, I'm sorry. I'm sorry.' She hugged the doll to her breast. 'But don't worry. It'll be all right,' she said. 'I promise. It'll be all right.'

Coughing and gasping for air, Anders staggered out of the house with his burden and Lars and Albrigtsen ran to help him. They laid Catherine down on the grass and Albrigtsen tried to revive her, first giving her artificial respiration to pump some of the smoke out of her lungs and then the kiss of life.

Lars stared at the house in horror. There were flames behind all the upstairs windows now. Ingrid came up beside him. 'Anna Marie!' he exclaimed. And although it was hopeless, and he knew it, nevertheless he still had to make an attempt. But as he started forward Ingrid put a hand on his arm and restrained him. He looked at her in bewilderment. 'But your sister,' he said. 'She's still in there. She'll be killed.'

'But think,' Ingrid said quietly, her eyes fixed on his. 'After this what real hope is there for her? What kind of a life would she have? I won't inflict that on her. All along that's what I've been trying to save her from.'

Lars stared at her, anguished and undecided, but then, seeing the truth in what she'd said, he swept her into his arms and they held on to one another tightly.

Nursing the doll, Anna Marie knelt on the floor in the centre of the nursery. She was almost encircled by flames and above her the rafters were on fire. All around her, the other dolls burned, their bodies and their hair smouldering and igniting, their faces melting grotesquely in the heat.

Looking across the room Anna Marie saw her mother standing by the window, smiling at her. She gazed at her in wonderment and then glanced down at the doll cradled

217

in her arms. And at that moment and for an instant she was sane again.

Dropping the doll, she stretched out her arms to Freya. 'Mama! Mama! Help me!' she cried, very afraid. She started to get up off her knees and, as she did so, she looked up at the ceiling. Her face became a mask of horror and she opened her mouth to scream but before she could the blazing beam crashed down onto her.

Albrigtsen was back at the farmhouse very early the next morning and Anders waited in the sitting room while he examined Catherine.

He was standing in front of the fireplace gazing up at the portrait of Freya, looking tired and drawn, when the doctor came downstairs again. 'How is she?' he asked, turning.

'She'll be fine,' Albrigtsen told him. 'You sat up through the night with her?'

Anders nodded. 'Yes. She slept all right.'

'I'm not surprised. That was a very strong sedative I gave her. You should rest.'

'Later.'

'What will you tell her?'

'The truth,' replied Anders. 'And hope that she can take it.'

'She's always struck me as being very well adjusted.'

Anders glanced at the portrait again. 'Not easy for anyone though,' he said, 'suddenly discovering your mother died insane. And that she passed that insanity on to your half-sister.'

'Only a particular vulnerability perhaps,' Albrigtsen corrected. 'There's no evidence of direct biological transmission of mental disorders.'

'Just the same.'

'And a child's upbringing and home environment, that has a great deal to do with it. She has that on her side.'

'May I see her?' Anders asked.

Albrigtsen nodded. 'She's asked for you.' And then as

Anders crossed to the door he went on, 'Astrid Linderman's dead.' In the doorway Anders paused and looked back at him, shocked. 'Sleeping tablets,' Albrigtsen said.

Anders shook his head sadly. 'Poor woman,' he said. And slowly he climbed the stairs.

Epilogue

At the gateway to the churchyard and as the rest of the mourners filed silently past them, Ingrid turned to Catherine. 'Thank you,' she said.

'For what?'

'For saying nothing. For letting it all be just a tragic accident.'

'Well, in a way it was, wasn't it?' Catherine said. 'An accident of birth.'

The two women embraced and kissed one another and then Lars took Ingrid's arm and they walked over to their car with its black cross mounted on the roof and got into it.

As they drove off, Albrigtsen detached himself from the couple he and his wife had been talking to and walked over to Catherine and Anders. 'How are you feeling?' he asked Catherine.

'Okay,' Catherine said.

'I imagine you'll be going back to England soon.'

Catherine shook her head. 'No. I'm staying.'

Albrigtsen looked surprised and slightly troubled.

'I'm all right,' she assured him. 'And I'm not afraid. My name is Catherine Durrell. My mother was Kirsten Enger. To me Freya Jordahl is just a portrait. I've no past here, Doctor Albrigtsen.'

She looked up at Anders and took his hand. 'Only a future,' she said.

And later, as *Skibladner*, under full sail, ran with the wind down an empty fjord and toward Anders' house at Stordal, Catherine stood at the helm, happy and confident.

She lashed the wheel and moved to the aft cabin hatchway just as Anders emerged from it. Catherine smiled and, putting her arms round him, kissed him.

Quizzically Anders looked across at the wheel.

'It's all right,' she told him. '*Skibladner* knows where we want to go.'

Anders laughed.